INTRUSION

INTRUSION

REECE HIRSCH

THOMAS & MERCER

Published by Thomas & Mercer, Seattle
www.apub.com

Amazon, the Amazon logo, and Thomas & Mercer are trademarks of Amazon.com Inc. or its affiliates.

ISBN-13: 9781477827239
ISBN-10: 1477827234

Cover design by Marc Cohen

Library of Congress Control Number: 2014944829

Printed in the United States of America

For Jean and Ernestine,
my enablers, in the best sense of the word

"What's going on here? These are some of the best companies in our nation. Why are they being hacked? Let me explain. They're the ones that know they're being hacked. Our experience is, when the FBI and others look into it, for every one that knows it's being hacked there are more than 100 companies that don't know they've been hacked. That's significant. In fact, in my opinion, it is the greatest transfer of wealth in history."

General Keith B. Alexander,
Director, National Security Agency

"I wish to note that intellectual property theft by a government represents the very essence of organized crime."

US Representative Howard Berman

1

The phone woke Chris Bruen at 3:00 a.m. from an unsettled sleep. The floor-to-ceiling windows of his loft apartment looked out on the Bay Bridge, which was now illuminated by thousands of glimmering LED lights. The light sculpture, as it was called, was a public art project that cast a series of random, repeating patterns across the bridge's spires. He had promised himself to buy curtains to cover the upper portion of the windows, because the shape-shifting images, which could be read as electric clouds, schooling fish, and raindrops, had begun to infect his dreams.

Chris grabbed the phone off the nightstand. "What?" he said dully, his voice cracking.

"Bruen?"

"Who's this?"

"It's Dez Teal."

No response.

"From Zapper," Teal added, clearly uncertain whether Chris was awake yet. Desmond Teal was the executive vice president of Zapper, the world's most popular Internet search engine, and one of Chris's biggest clients.

"Dez." Chris said it slowly, like he was working out a problem. "What's up? You know it's 3:00 a.m. here."

The sheets undulated as Zoey Doucet, his sometimes/maybe girlfriend, rolled over, trying to cling to sleep.

"We've been hacked," Teal said.

"How bad?"

"Bad enough that I'm calling you at three in the morning, and that's all that I'm going to say over an open line."

"I can be at your offices first thing in the morning."

"No, he wants you here tonight. He wants you here *now*."

"He" was Paul Saperstein, Zapper's twenty-eight-year-old CEO and, as a result of a recent IPO, a newly minted billionaire. Chris drew a deep breath and gave up any hopes of finishing his night's sleep, troubled as it had been. Chris was a privacy and security law specialist who helped his clients combat hackers and cybercriminals, and this was not the first time he'd been woken up in the middle of the night to respond to a hack.

"Okay, I'll be there."

"Thank you. This is circle-the-wagons time. See you soon." Teal hung up the phone, no doubt moving on to spoil someone else's slumbers.

If the team at Zapper was circling the wagons, Chris wondered who the Indians were. But he already had a pretty good guess.

Chris rolled out of bed and began dressing. After slipping into black pants and a gray wool pullover, he stretched his long arms and ran his hands through his unruly black hair, wild from sleep.

Zoey finally roused herself, pulling her T-shirt down around her and giving him a look of disbelief. "Who could possibly need you at this hour? Aside from me."

"It's Zapper. They've been hacked."

"Must have been pretty bad if they want you there tonight. Like, tank-the-stock-price bad." Zoey was the director of the computer forensic lab at Reynolds, Fincher & McComb, the San Francisco law firm where Chris was a partner.

"Apparently so, but I don't have any details yet."

Zoey gulped some water from a glass on the nightstand. She was probably a little hungover from the night before. Chris certainly was. She put both hands on her cheeks, then ran them around her head, pulling her brown hair back and away from her face. "So should I leave with you or . . . ?"

"No, no," Chris said, realizing how unready he was for this conversation. "Here's an extra key I had made. I was going to give it to you anyway."

"Okay," Zoey said, nodding. She took the key, only noting the significance of the moment with a cocked eyebrow and the ghost of a smile. "Why don't you at least have a cup of coffee before you go?"

Chris shook his head as he pulled on his shoes. "I'd better get down there."

"If you spend too much time over there at Zapper, you're going to start wearing hoodies. Don't be that guy, okay?"

"My life is a hoodie-free zone," Chris promised, and gave her a kiss good-bye.

"Say hi to the boy king for me," Zoey said, pulling up the covers and seeming to fall back asleep the instant she rolled over.

*   *   *

Traffic was nearly nonexistent on the 101 heading south down the Peninsula to Menlo Park. Dawn wasn't close to breaking, but the sky had begun to soften from black to indigo. As Chris pulled off the freeway onto Hamilton Avenue, Zapper's stylized lightning-bolt logo glowed electric blue from atop a tower.

Menlo Park initially seems like a town with a split personality, its shaded, tree-lined residential streets around the Stanford campus contrasting with the sleek concrete-and-glass office parks of Sand Hill Road. But it was all part of the carefully balanced ecosystem of Silicon Valley. The intellectual resources of Stanford fed the tech companies, and being at the heart of tech-sector innovation bolstered Stanford's academic cachet.

Zapper's corporate campus embodied that symbiotic relationship. It truly did resemble a campus, with meticulously weathered redbrick buildings that looked like they had been expensively imported from a place that actually had a history. Paul Saperstein was one of those latter-day pharaohs of Silicon Valley who felt the need to create a sense of permanence and inevitability about his company's ascendance. Perhaps it was a way of denying the fact that Zapper had been built on the shifting sands of ever-evolving technology.

There was an unusual number of cars in the parking lot for the hour, most of them high-end and foreign, and more were converging on the lot as Chris arrived. Lights shone from several windows of the main building where the executive offices were housed. Chris found the doors to the building unlocked but no receptionist on duty at the front desk. Instead, EVP Dez Teal was playing the role, ushering people in as they arrived.

"Chris, thanks again for doing this." Teal greeted another entering behind him. "Ah, Sergei. How was the flight in from Berlin?"

Sergei Timoshev glared. "Oh, it was delightful. I feel refreshed. Like new man."

With a traffic-cop wave, Teal said to both of them, "Right through to the Edison conference room."

As Chris and Timoshev began the walk, Chris asked, "You know what this is about?"

"No, but it is catastrophe. Clearly." Timoshev, the president of Stryker Security in Berlin, was a top authority on malware. He wore his black hair cropped close to the skull and looked more like a middle-grade crook than an executive, an impression he cultivated with his glossy black leather jacket and Cyrillic-lettered neck tattoo.

They heard the gathering before they reached the so-called Edison room. Zapper's conference rooms were named after pioneers of American technology, from Thomas Edison and Henry Ford to Steve Jobs—a not-so-subtle attempt to place Paul Saperstein in that firmament. When Chris pushed open the frosted glass doors, he and Timoshev were greeted by a rare scene. Arranged around a table at four in the morning sat nearly a dozen of the country's most respected data-security experts. There was freelance white-hat hacker Doug Reeves, British expat Carina Blount of Blunt Object Consulting, and SoNar, a notorious black hat who appeared to have discovered that the dark side wasn't always the most lucrative. The rest of the luminaries around the table brought similarly impeccable pedigrees. As a fellow data security geek, Chris recognized this as an assemblage of A-list talent akin to Marvel's Avengers or the 1992 US men's Olympic basketball team.

The tired faces turned to Chris with a few nods that seemed to acknowledge they weren't surprised that he had also been called in.

"This is quite a lineup," Chris said loud enough for everyone to hear. "I'm not even going to try to calculate the collective hourly billing rate."

"Oh, we are all off the clock, Chris," Timoshev said.

A handful of nods and murmurs seemed to confirm Timoshev's statement.

"Since when did you all become so altruistic?" Chris asked.

Doug Reeves, in his early twenties, with the washed-out blond hair of a surfer, spoke up. "We didn't. We're off the clock because we're all on Zapper's payroll now."

Chris gave a low whistle. The magnitude of the crisis must have seriously shaken Zapper. If the company felt the need to hire all of these security experts on such short notice, then they had really opened up their considerable checkbook—and must be in serious trouble.

"Is someone going to tell me what's going on here?" Chris asked when no one else spoke up.

Shrugs all around.

The group waited for another half hour as several more top-tier data security experts arrived, all of them guzzling coffee to ward off jet lag and/or sleep deprivation.

Finally, Teal entered the conference room and closed the doors behind him. "I've been waiting to brief you all together. Since we've made preemptive offers of employment to everyone, with the exception of our lawyer, you understand already that this is a serious event. We've experienced an intrusion, one so massive that it potentially jeopardizes the entire company."

"Someone has stolen the algorithms. Clearly," Timoshev said.

Teal held up a hand. "Please, save your questions and comments for the end. But yes, it's the algorithms. They've been compromised."

Zapper's status as one of the most successful companies on the planet was based in large part on its proprietary algorithms, a complex skein of mathematical instructions that enabled Zapper to cull the Internet's vast sea of data and produce results that were more accurate than any other search engine's. In fact, they were so far ahead of the marketplace that their company name had become synonymous with Internet searches.

"We discovered the intrusion at 2:25 p.m. yesterday, but now we can see that the adversary had been present on our servers for quite some time, probably months. Our security team noticed an unusually high volume of email traffic last night. Upon closer examination, it became clear that huge files with terabytes of data were being exfiltrated from the system."

Given the timing of the intrusion and the arrival of international experts like Timoshev, Chris realized that he'd likely been the last person called to this meeting. Clearly he had catching up to do, so he didn't hesitate to interrupt Teal again. "Can you tell us where they were being exported to?"

"Before we hit a dead-end IP address, we were able to trace the activity to a district of Shanghai."

"Hacked by Chinese," said SoNar, who looked freshly arrived from the Old Testament—or a Phish concert. He was tall, thin, and hirsute, with a neatly trimmed beard, moustache, and shoulder-length brown hair.

"Yes, I'm afraid so," Teal said.

"How'd they gain access?" Reeves asked.

"It appears to have been a fairly straightforward phishing exploit," Teal said. "Fifteen employees received an email on February 20 from someone posing as Sid Harris, one of our board members. A meeting invitation. At least one of the employees clicked the invitation, and that was all it took to introduce the malware."

"Do you think it's government backed, or are we talking private actors?" Chris asked.

"We can't tell yet," Teal said. "As you know, it can be a hard line to draw in these cases."

It had been openly speculated for years that the People's Republic of China was either sponsoring or tacitly abetting a systematic series of hacking attacks focused on the theft of intellectual property and trade secrets from major US corporations. The Chinese government was believed to be involved because the attacks were so sophisticated and it was hard to imagine such a massive and coordinated offensive occurring without the state's knowledge or cooperation, particularly in a country as tightly controlled as China. The attacks seemed to be a natural extension of China's drive to become an economic superpower. It had the burgeoning population and the natural resources— all it lacked were the cutting-edge inventions that US entrepreneurs seemed to produce so effortlessly. There weren't many things in life that couldn't be bought, but one of them was the spark of innovation. That had to be stolen.

One security consultant had been widely quoted as saying that, for Fortune 500 companies, it was not a matter of whether Chinese hackers had stolen their intellectual property but rather whether they *knew* it yet. In fact, China's plundering of US corporate intellectual property was one of the greatest transfers of wealth in human history. It made Cortez's looting of the Aztec gold and the Nazi seizure of the art treasures of Western Europe look like dime-store theft.

"Isn't it a little late to be upgrading security?" asked Carina Blount, who wore an elegant brown suit that contrasted with her spiky and unabashedly dyed blond hair. "The cows are out of the proverbial barn at this point, aren't they?"

"Frankly, we don't know the extent of the damage. We can tell that a large volume of data was extracted, and we've identified areas of the system that could have been accessed, including some that contained our most sensitive IP, but the rest is a mystery. We're hoping that those of you with forensic expertise can help us figure that out."

"You'll know how much they've taken when a Chinese start-up company appears out of nowhere and starts stealing your market share," Blount said.

Teal introduced a bleary-looking young man in jeans and a black T-shirt with a laptop in hand. "I'm going to let Jonathan continue your briefing, walk you through the details of the forensics that we have so far."

Chris followed Teal out into hallway. "Hey, Dez, I must admit that you're hurting my feelings a bit here."

"What do you mean? Did you expect us to make an offer of employment to you too? We thought you were too independent to go in-house, and besides, some matters are best handled by outside counsel."

"No, it's not that. I just don't think I belong as part of the scrum in there. And why didn't you call me in on this earlier today?"

"Everyone's a bit shell-shocked around here right now. And we knew you were just down the 101 from us, so we concentrated on bringing in the international experts first."

"I don't think this is the best use of my skills."

"What are you asking, Chris?"

"I'm asking where Paul is. I'd like to speak to him directly."

"Oh, you don't want to speak to him right now. Trust me."

Chris strode off down the hallway in the direction in which Teal had been heading.

"What are you doing?" called Teal from behind him. "You don't have access to that area."

Chris ignored Teal's entreaties, striding down a long corridor past a break room, a daycare center, and a Pilates studio. Zapper was famous for its employee perks. Everything was brightly colored and oversized, sort of like a preschool for adults. Most of the Silicon Valley tech giants had long ago given up the extravagant perks of the first Internet boom, abandoning the notion that the workplace was primarily about play and creativity. By virtue of its astounding success, Zapper had been able to hang on to that illusion.

At the end of the hallway, Chris pushed through double doors into a cavernous gym. At the far end of the facility was a full basketball court with a lone figure in a green hoodie shooting baskets from the foul line—Paul Saperstein. He must have heard them coming, but he didn't look their way.

A jump shot caromed off the rim, and he darted to retrieve the ball.

Teal hurried across the court to catch up with Chris. "Paul, I told him that you couldn't see him now, but he wouldn't listen."

Saperstein finally turned to face them. He was still youthful, but there were lines around his eyes and mouth that hadn't been there a few years ago when Zapper had moved out of his Stanford dorm room and into proper offices. Saperstein's curly brown hair was scruffy, he needed a haircut, and his jeans looked lived in. Chris was reminded of a child star trying to play the role that made him famous a little longer than was believable. Saperstein was many things, but a prodigy was no longer one of them.

Still, Saperstein was entitled to a few quirks. After all, he had accomplished something that not so long ago would have seemed unthinkable—he had perfected a new utility, the Internet search engine, which was now nearly as essential as electricity or water. And based upon the power of Zapper's proprietary algorithms, which were constantly being refined by an army of programmers, Zapper had a virtual monopoly on that utility.

Saperstein reached out and shook Chris's hand. "Thanks for coming out at this hour, man," he said. Then, to Teal, "I'd like a few minutes with Chris."

"Sure," Teal said, quickly retreating across the blond, parquet hardwood floor.

After Teal was gone, Saperstein pulled back and hurled the basketball as hard as he could, hitting the backboard with a resounding metallic smack. "Those thieving bastards!" he shouted, his voice echoing to the rafters. When the ball came back to him, he drop-kicked it across the gym.

Saperstein seemed slightly calmer after the outburst. "Sorry, but this company is my life's work. I put everything into it. They do not just get to steal it away." He retrieved the ball and shoveled a bounce pass at Chris. "You play? You've got the height for it."

"Used to. A little," Chris said, tossing up a short jump shot that bounced around the rim and fell in. "You think it's really that bad?"

"Hard to tell at this point, but probably," Saperstein said. "This isn't like when a laptop is stolen out of the backseat of a car. Nine times out of ten that's going to be someone who just needs a laptop.

But whoever was behind this breach was very sophisticated. They went to a lot of trouble to get behind our firewall, and they had to have known what they were after."

Saperstein dribbled the ball once and looked off into the middle distance. "Sometimes I walk around this campus, with all these employees, and I think this is going to be here for a while. But it's all based on information . . . and being just a nanosecond faster than our competitors. It's so easy to lose that edge. IBM lost it, Netscape lost it, and so did AOL and Yahoo."

"And the algorithms are that edge."

"They are. Which is why this theft cannot be allowed to stand. I am not going to just let some team of hackers—or even the Chinese government—tear my company down."

"Have you tried contacting the State Department? If China is really involved, then this is a matter of international relations."

"One of the first calls I made was to the White House. They answered too. I gave 'em enough money last campaign."

"And?"

"They're not going to do anything. Sure, the president has talked tough on this issue. And the Justice Department did file an indictment against some Chinese military hackers as a sort of shot across the bow. But it's not like the White House is going to intervene on behalf of my company."

"But aren't there national interests at stake if China produces a search engine that can compete with Zapper?"

"There are, and I wish the administration fully appreciated that," Saperstein said. "Hoodu, the second-largest search engine in the world, is based in China, and they're planning to enter the US market later this year. If they arrive with better search results and billions of dollars in the bank, it's not inconceivable that they could replace Zapper as the dominant search engine. Not in one year or two, but you know how fast these pivots can occur in the tech sector. What those myopic politicians don't get is that if Hoodu becomes the top search engine, the Chinese could take their economic espionage to a whole new level."

"It would be like handing them the keys to the front door and the security alarm pass code," Chris said.

"Exactly. And a Chinese company would also be a lot less inclined to play ball with the NSA in their domestic surveillance programs."

Saperstein dribbled the ball, practicing a feint to the basket, then pulling back for a jumper that bounced off the front of the rim. "So why did you want to see me?"

"I think I can help."

"I agree. That's why I brought you in."

"But I think I can help in a different way than the other members of the security team. I want you to send me to China."

"Really. To do what exactly?"

"I'd like to take a shot at tracking down the people who stole your property."

"Look, Chris, I realize that you have certain, well, situational skills that can be very valuable, but we're probably talking about the Chinese government here. This isn't like a knock-and-talk where you convince some pimply-faced hacker to return stolen IP."

"I appreciate that. But I've been pursuing APT1 for years now." The series of corporate hacks widely attributed to the People's Republic of China (PRC) were commonly referred to as Advanced Persistent Threat 1. "I've been watching them rob my clients blind time and again with impunity, and I'm starting to believe that the only way to make real headway on this is to have boots on the ground there. My boots."

"But what exactly would you do?"

"I won't know until I get there. But if I hit a brick wall, then I'll just pack it in and come home."

"What would the objective be? I realize that we're never going to retrieve those algorithms, especially if they're in the hands of government-affiliated hackers."

"Granted," said Chris. "But if this is what we think it is, then maybe I can gather hard evidence that the PRC engineered the intrusion."

Saperstein nodded. "Well, if we had that, we'd have some leverage with the State Department."

"Right," said Chris. "One would hope. And if they still didn't help, and we took that evidence to the press, then they'd have to take action against Beijing. What do you say?"

Saperstein lined up his feet on the free throw line and stared at Chris for a long moment. "Well, this is a bit of a Hail Mary, but you know what they say about desperate times. Yeah, go to China."

"Thanks. After we've gathered more of the forensics, I should have a better idea of where to start."

"You'll have all the resources that you need for this. But you understand, of course, that this is off the books," Saperstein said. "You are not acting on behalf of the company when you're over there. We can't be seen to be taking actions that are adverse to a foreign government—even if that government is acting like a bunch of thieves."

"Understood."

Saperstein palmed the basketball. "You know, running a global company like Zapper is a little like running a country."

"You have your own foreign policy, don't you?"

"Yeah, we have to. And sometimes we have to go to war."

Chris nodded. International corporations were much like nation-states. And when the comparison broke down, it often favored the corporation. After all, which was more of an actor on the world stage—ExxonMobil or Luxembourg?

"Well," Chris said. "I'm something less than an army."

Saperstein shot the ball, made the basket. "That's all right. I'll settle for anything you can win us in single combat."

Single combat . . . It was an apt metaphor for Chris's work defending corporations from cybercriminals and hackers. Whether the adversary was a black-hat hacker or a hostile corporation, the battle often felt like something out of antiquity: two champions struggling to the death in the no-man's-land between the assembled forces.

It was 4:00 a.m. and Chris was still a little groggy, but his head was clearing as he began to contemplate his trip to China. If Saperstein's single-combat analogy proved apt, then Chris wondered who on earth he'd be facing, and on what terrain the battle would be joined.

2

Tao Zhang did not like Tokyo. Everything was too bright, too fast, too new, and, most especially, too vertical. Many cities were filled with sky-high office towers, but Tokyo truly embraced that verticality, stacking businesses one on top of another. Tao passed a grocery store and, glancing upward, noted a restaurant one floor above, a nightclub above that, and a men's clothing store above that. He couldn't discern what came next as the low sun glinted off the mirrored tower.

There was plenty of new construction at home too, but the PRC had a way of making even brand-new structures seem dusty and tired as soon as they were up. Visiting Tokyo was like looking into the future—a future Tao hoped would never arrive.

He strode quickly through the swarming streets of the Shinjuku district, past the sky-high LCD ads as tall as buildings themselves, past the image of a giant, grinning cartoon cat, past the enormous faces of American celebrities hawking bourbon and luxury cars. It was late afternoon on a cloudy spring day, and as the day darkened the LCD screens seemed to glow brighter. But Tao was no gawking tourist. His attention was focused on Ryuichi Naruse, the man he was following.

Naruse was ten yards ahead of him and seemingly unworried about being spotted in the crowded streets of Tokyo. He had been following Naruse for three days, from an investor conference in Osaka to an electronics show in Tokyo to business meetings at the Ritz-Carlton. The night before a woman who was clearly not Naruse's wife had spent the night in his room. Tao didn't think that she was a prostitute but more likely a mistress, judging by the ease they displayed in public together. Whoever she was, Tao was glad that she had parted ways with Naruse that morning. He wanted to avoid a situation where he might have to kill her too.

Tao preferred to have a better sense of a target's habits when planning a hit, but there had been no inside source to provide that sort of information. Naruse's movements were difficult to predict because he was on a business trip and outside his routine. It made Tao's job more challenging because it required improvisation. He had to remain vigilant, and when the right moment presented itself, he had to be ready.

To further complicate the job, there was a deadline. One way or another, Naruse had to be dead by noon the next day.

Tao heard a wail and saw that in his rush he had plowed into a young boy, no more than six years old, breaking his mother's grip on his hand and knocking him to the sidewalk. His mother—a small woman with a tired, fine-boned face—stared ninja stars at him as she tried to create a human barrier to keep the crowd from trampling the boy.

As the pedestrians coursed around them to avoid the mother, Tao reached down and lifted the boy to his feet. The boy, who wore a bright-blue windbreaker, seemed grateful but not particularly rattled. He was too young to realize just how fragile he was and how quickly he could be injured.

The mother said something stern to Tao. He didn't speak Japanese, but no translation was needed. She was grateful that he had stopped to help but was not letting him off the hook for causing the incident.

Tao gave what he hoped was a gentlemanly bow of apology and then hurried on, certain that he had now lost his target.

He ducked and weaved through the gaps in the crowd, nearly dancing, trying to make up the lost ground. If his man turned off onto a side street, he would never find him that day. Tao didn't want to have to return to his hotel and spend another night in Tokyo.

After a few minutes, just when he was ready to give up, he spotted Naruse turning off the boulevard and strolling down a side street. Tao dropped back farther and farther as the pedestrian traffic grew sparse, watching as Naruse stepped through an arched gateway into Shinjuku Gyoen National Garden. It was strange to find a place as peaceful as the garden so close to the Times Square–like tumult of Shinjuku. There were people admiring the cherry blossoms, but closing time was nearing, and the crowds were thinning out. The setting wasn't perfect, but it was probably the best opportunity he was going to get. The Ritz-Carlton was full of security cameras, and the city streets were too crowded no matter the hour. That was the problem with Tokyo as the setting for a hit—there were too many damned people.

Tao grabbed a brochure as he entered to look more like a tourist. As he followed Naruse from a distance, he made a point of stopping frequently to scrutinize the brochure. The park had once been imperial gardens reserved for royalty, but they had been destroyed toward the end of World War II. After the war, the grounds had reopened as a public park.

Naruse walked slowly across a grassy expanse blanketed in fallen cherry blossoms, or *sakura*. From Tao's viewpoint, his target seemed to have entered a pink-and-white snow globe. A breeze began to blow, causing the blossoms to rustle on the ground. It was a lovely sight, and Tao hoped that Naruse appreciated it. It would be a shame if he were simply lost in thought, dwelling on whatever misstep had brought him to this pass. Life was too short—especially Naruse's life—to ignore moments of beauty like this.

Of course, Tao had no idea what was running through Naruse's head. Nor did he know what his target had done or not done to cause Tao's client to want him dead. There was no need for Tao to know those sorts of details, and it was safer if he didn't. He did know that Naruse was a senior vice president of a Japanese consumer electronics company.

The target never once looked back to see if he was being followed. He stopped for a moment at a koi pond and gazed down at the muscular, orange fish that churned the green water, twisting to the surface, hoping to be fed. Tao could have walked up behind Naruse there, but the spot was too open. Someone might see him from across the meadow.

If Naruse had turned then and walked back across the open field, he probably would have lived another day. Although Tao was anxious to return home, he wouldn't have minded that much. He did not feel eager to kill this man. He was a hit man, but he wasn't doing it for the money. He had no choice.

But instead of returning, Naruse checked his watch and looked back toward the park's gate, probably gauging how close it was to closing time. Then he stepped gingerly over the red, arched wooden bridge before him. He probably wanted to enjoy the gardens just a bit longer.

At the crest of the bridge, Naruse stopped again to observe the pond's water lilies and scattering of floating cherry blossoms. The sun fell below the clouds, and for one brief moment before sunset the garden was bathed in a soft, bright light. It was the kind of light that was the embodiment of nostalgia, like a reprise of morning before the coda of evening.

On the other side of the bridge, a narrow brick path led up a hillside among cherry trees and Himalayan cedars. When Naruse descended the other side of the bridge, taking careful steps on the steep incline, Tao began his approach.

Naruse's head rose slightly from the path when he heard the quick footsteps on the wooden bridge behind him. He didn't turn, probably because that might be perceived as rude. But he was listening.

By the time Naruse turned around, perhaps expecting an attendant warning him that the park was closing, Tao already had his knife drawn and was only five yards away. He would have preferred to use an automatic pistol and a silencer, but that would have looked too much like a professional hit. He couldn't even use a common handgun, because there was no such thing in Japan. Nearly all forms of gun ownership were forbidden in the country, and the annual number of gun-related homicides was in the single digits. If he had used a gun to kill Naruse, the incident would have grabbed headlines for weeks in the Japanese press.

The knife was nothing special, just a sharp kitchen blade. This needed to look like a routine robbery gone wrong. Tao took the last long strides closing the distance to the target, the knife in his hand glinting in the sun. Pollen and blossoms drifted lazily in the air, heightening the sensation that time was slowing down.

Naruse saw the knife and gave a jolt of recognition. He looked in Tao's face, his eyes registering confusion. If he knew his attacker, he might at least understand what was happening, but he did not. Naruse spun around and attempted to scramble up the stone path through the trees, but it was too steep, and he pitched forward onto his knees.

Tao plunged the knife into Naruse's lower back near the kidney. It required some force to drive the blade in deep. Then he slid it into the side of the man's neck, which was much easier, and blood began to spurt onto the brick path. He would be dead in minutes.

As adrenaline coursed through his body, Tao quickly checked Naruse for weapons and valuables. Nothing notable in the man's pants pockets. In order to make this look like a robbery, he would need the wallet, so he turned Naruse over to face him. He lifted open the sport coat and extracted a brown leather wallet from the inside pocket. Tao made a point of not looking in Naruse's eyes.

The victim's hand reached up and clutched Tao's wrist, the one holding the wallet. Now Tao could not help but look at the man. Surprisingly, Naruse still seemed alert, but the light in his eyes was fading as fast as that brief flash of sunlight a moment before. Tao gazed into the target's eyes and studied his face in a moment of thrilling intimacy.

Something seemed to bloom deep inside Tao's chest, like a small, dark flower—the sort that might secrete a toxin. He knew instantly that this was a scene he would be returning to later, whether he wanted to or not. Finally, the man's grip loosened, and his hand fell limply to his side.

Tao removed all of the money from the wallet, wiped it down for fingerprints, and tossed it in a bush. He knew he couldn't walk out through the main gate, so he would need to find another exit. After checking to make sure that Naruse was gone, Tao stood and walked on up the hill.

He strode quickly along the narrow stone path, studying the black iron fence that bounded the park, looking for a way out. Tao heard voices shouting in the distance. Naruse's body had been discovered more quickly than he had expected, probably by park security looking for closing-time stragglers.

He quickened his pace but kept it short of a run. At last he spotted a cherry tree near the fence. Tao pulled himself up on the lower branches and climbed over onto the fence, then jumped down on the other side.

Five minutes later Tao was once more moving through the densely crowded streets of Shinjuku. He stepped into a crosswalk that seemed to be about a hundred yards wide. When the light turned, Tao was swept along like a petal on a river, feeling pleasingly anonymous.

He was safe now.

Another job successfully completed. One step closer to his salvation.

The trick to being a competent hit man wasn't in the killing but in how you felt about it afterward. This was his third hit, so he felt qualified to generalize. Tao had received some basic training in weapons and hand-to-hand combat from a People's Liberation Army instructor, but he was not particularly well practiced in the lethal arts. The characteristic that had distinguished him thus far in his brief career was the ability to remain focused on the task at hand, both before and after the killing. It had always helped Tao to know why he did what he did, and whom he did it for.

But this time felt a little different from the others. Tao wished fervently that Naruse hadn't grabbed his wrist and forced him to look into his eyes. Something had changed in that moment. His attitude toward his work would be different from this point forward, but he wasn't sure yet if that would make it easier or more difficult.

3

It was 7:00 a.m., and Chris was waiting to cross Market Street as the Pirate Ship passed in the pale morning light. The Pirate Ship. That was how he always thought of the massive shoeshine stand on wheels as it rolled to its place of business for the day. It was like a decrepit, vaguely ominous parade float, consisting of black-painted, jerry-rigged plywood that elevated three chairs for the customers to sit high above the Financial District as their expensive footwear was buffed.

The proprietor, a heavyset black man with close-cropped gray hair and an improbable top hat, was pushing the stand into place, along with his two employees. As the stand slid into its patch of turf next to the taxi stand of the Grand Hyatt, the proprietor stepped back and let his colleagues finish the job.

The man turned to Chris, who was advancing toward him through the crosswalk, and looked him over bottom to top, starting with the shoes.

Apparently, Chris's black slip-ons were not as well maintained as they might have been, because the man delivered his signature line in a stentorian voice: "Where is your pride?"

After leaving his girlfriend in bed to satisfy the whims of his billionaire client, Chris could only mutter to himself, "Excellent question as always."

Chris swiped his security pass, wiped his shoes on the antistatic mat, and entered the law firm's computer forensic lab on the thirty-eighth floor of Four Embarcadero Center at 7:30 a.m. Zoey was already there, and it looked like she had been there a while. The second large cup of coffee stood next to her bank of three monitors, and a greasy breakfast sandwich wrapper was crumpled beside them.

She was leaning over and adjusting something strapped around her ankle.

"What's that?" he asked.

"It's a HealthBot," she said, tightening a Velcro fastener that held a small device with a display face that looked a bit like a digital watch.

"And what is a HealthBot?"

"It's a new product from our client FrostByte Technologies. They were handing out free samples to the staff to celebrate their IPO."

"So what does it do?"

"Well, it's a pedometer, but it also monitors your heart rate, calories burned, and temperature. Stores everything in the cloud. Since I find working out at the gym to be mind numbing, I figured it was worth a shot. Maybe I'll move around more and burn more calories if I'm monitoring it."

"Good idea," Chris said. "After all, you were the one who was just arguing that playing *BioShock Infinite* was exercise."

"I put a lot of body English into the gaming console," she said. "It works all the muscle groups."

"Maybe the HealthBot will help you realize that you shouldn't be eating those things," Chris said, pointing at a bag of chili-cheese jalapeño barbecue chips on her desk.

"You don't understand," Zoey said. "Those are flavor blasted, Chris. Literally *blasted* with flavor. See, it says so right there on the bag."

Chris was booked on a flight to Shanghai out of SFO later that morning, but he wanted to spend some time in the lab first, gathering all of the information available on the Zapper intrusion. The forensic lab was an invaluable resource in Chris's practice, from solving thefts of confidential data by rogue employees to tracking down hackers.

Since taking over as head of the lab, Zoey had given it her own personal touch. The windowless room was ringed with computer monitors, and an image bounced from screen to screen as if it were circling the room. It was a photo of the Clash's Joe Strummer with the caption in bold red type, "I Fought the Law—And the Law Won." Zoey wore an antistatic band secured by Velcro around her wrist with a wire that ran to a grounding point under the desk. Static was the enemy in a computer forensic lab, as it could instantly destroy valuable evidence.

She cast an appraising look his way. "You didn't go back to bed, did you? You look like you could use some coffee."

Chris picked up the paper cup next to the monitor and took a big sip. "You're right," he said. "Thanks. So how's your day going?"

"So stressful that I'm pretty sure someday I'll be acting it out with puppets," Zoey said. "I hate working with that new security team at Zapper. Talk about a bag of cats. Everyone over there thinks they're running their own independent investigation." Chris had updated Zoey on the Zapper assignment by phone earlier that morning, and she had already been fully briefed by Dez Teal.

Zoey was every bit as egocentric and skilled as any member of Zapper's new all-star security team. Before Chris had hired her to run his computer forensics lab, Zoey had been a hacker, but more of a hacktivist and prankster than a black hat. Bringing her into the staid law-firm environment had been a bit of an experiment. So far the experiment seemed to be working, but some days were better than others.

"I think Saperstein buys into the 'team of rivals' approach," Chris said.

"More like *Lord of the Flies* if you ask me," Zoey said. "But I did manage to get some information out of them, and I also uncovered several new clues. It's not like this is the first major intrusion based out of China. It seems to be the same crew that we've been chasing for a while now."

Over the past few months, Chris and Zoey had helped several clients respond to APT1 hacks, but they had never gotten close to identifying their source.

Chris sat at the monitors next to Zoey. "What have you got?"

"Well, we've got a dead-end IP address that originates from the Pudong New Area of Shanghai. And guess who has a headquarters in that district?"

"I've got a pretty good guess, but why don't you tell me?"

"People's Liberation Army, General Staff Department, Third Department, Second Bureau."

"So you think we've found the ones behind APT1?"

Zoey pulled up a photo of a modern, generic eight-story office building that stood alone behind an imposing security fence. "This appears to be the unit's new headquarters building on Datong Road in Gaoqiaozhen, which is in the Pudong New Area."

"What do they do there?"

"Well, I dug up some public but extremely obscure PRC records that provide clues. For example, here's correspondence with China Telecom where they're agreeing to provide state-of-the-art fiber-optic communications infrastructure for the building. The installation is being offered at a discount because it's for national defense."

"What makes us think that it isn't just standard defense work?"

"Well, while we don't know what's going on inside that building, we do know the type of people they're hiring. And it suggests that they're playing offense, not defense."

Zoey pulled up job listings translated into English, and Chris leaned in to see.

"Looks like they're staffing an IT department, looking for people with computer security and network operations experience."

"Right," said Zoey, scrolling down through page after page of job listings. "But look at how many of those people they're hiring. Hundreds of them. They're assembling an army of network security geeks."

Chris looked at the listings again and added, "And everyone has to be able to speak English. Almost all of APT1's targets have been in English-speaking countries."

"Exactly."

"What else have you got?"

"Well, it's hard to tell what a particular unit of the PLA is up to because they disguise their units' identities using MUCDs."

"Which stands for?"

"Military Unit Cover Designators. A five-digit number. But there's a Unit 61398 that I think must be the Third Department, Second Bureau. I tried Internet searches and found absolutely no results that linked the two. Don't you think that's odd?"

"Not if they really aren't connected."

"But I've scoured Chinese academic journals and municipal records and found some references to the areas of expertise found in Unit 61398. See, here's a member of the Heibei Chamber of Commerce who says in minutes of a meeting that he learned English at the unit. And here are academic articles that list Unit 61398 as a source of technical information on topics like covert communications, operating system internals, digital signal processing, and network security."

"The Heibei Chamber of Commerce? You're digging deep here, aren't you?"

"Nothing escapes the all-seeing eye of Zoey."

"Does the Zapper team have all of this?"

"Some, but a lot of it is my work."

"This is good. You'll be very popular with the new security team over there."

Zoey grinned. "They could have just hired me and saved themselves a lot of money."

"But you're already getting the big bucks here, aren't you?"

"If you say so."

"Seriously," he said, "this is great work. Let me know right away if you find anything else."

Zoey and Chris had set up a secure website separate from the law firm's IT system that they could use to chat securely and exchange video and documents from anywhere in the world.

"I will," she said. "But what do you intend to do once you get to Shanghai? They aren't going to just let you stroll through the front doors of that building on Datong Road."

"I haven't figured that part out yet."

"Be careful. The PLA will probably be watching for someone like you."

"Are you worried about me?"

"I'm worried that you're going to try to handle this the way you handle all those other solo script kiddies that you've tracked down in the past. What you're dealing with here is basically the Chinese army. Don't underestimate them, superspy."

"If I'm a spy, then I guess that would make you my handler, right? I've always wanted one of those."

"You're hopeless," Zoey said. "Just go and get on the plane. And I hope you've already seen the in-flight movie."

4

On the twelve-hour flight to Shanghai, Chris had plenty of time to contemplate just how sketchy his plan was. For the moment, it consisted of little more than going to the Pudong New Area of Shanghai and staking out the building that appeared to house APT1. He was going to need a more subtle approach than that, or he would soon be enjoying the hospitality of the People's Liberation Army.

If the Zapper intrusion was state backed, then the government might even be expecting this sort of response. And the adversary, whoever it was, had gained access to Zapper's systems for an extended period, so there was no telling how much they knew about the company and Chris's relationship to it. Chris tried to dismiss these musings as low-grade paranoia. Paranoia was a good default position in his line of work, but there was a point at which it became counterproductive.

He reviewed the few tools he had at his disposal: a laptop loaded with EnCase forensic-imaging and analysis software, software for running dictionary and brute force attacks to crack passwords, a write blocker, a set of small screwdrivers, and some plastic baggies. All of the software was disguised on his laptop to look like home videos. It wasn't much of an arsenal, but Chris found that the most valuable information he obtained was usually through what hackers referred to as social engineering.

Of course, even a routine business trip to China had to be treated like a mission behind enemy lines. It had to be assumed that the Chinese government was prepared to use military-grade technical resources to gain an advantage for the home-team companies. Chris always observed secure protocols when doing business in the PRC. He did not make sensitive calls over Chinese telecom lines. He never brought his personal laptop or phone into the country, instead using loaners that could be wiped clean when he was done. During negotiation sessions, he turned off his phone and removed the battery to ensure that no one could remotely activate its microphone. To foil key-logging software, he carried his Internet passwords on a flash drive so that he could copy and paste them rather than keying them in.

Chris was fairly confident that his cover story for the trip would withstand any questioning he might be subjected to at the customs desk. He was scheduled to meet with a Chinese consumer electronics company headquartered in Shanghai. He had represented the company for many years and had even learned to speak passable Mandarin for their benefit. The company no longer needed his services, because they had failed to gain traction in the US market. Nonetheless, the company had agreed to a meeting, ostensibly to permit Chris to make a last-ditch attempt to rekindle the business relationship. The general counsel, whom he had worked with for many years, had been too polite to refuse his insistent request.

The interminable flight also gave him plenty of time to think about his relationship with Zoey. Since his wife Tana's death seven years ago from cancer, Chris hadn't really had a serious relationship—well, with one exception, which had ended badly, to put it mildly. Even though he had not led much of a life since Tana's death, the loner habits that he had acquired were tenacious. It wasn't that he missed his former life. That wasn't it at all. It was more like certain muscles had atrophied over the years, and he was stretching and testing them again for the first time in a great while. He wasn't used to talking so much for one thing.

When Chris first met Zoey, he could not have imagined that they would end up together. She was quirky, opinionated, and loud—his exact opposite in many respects. To Chris's surprise, that appeared to be what he had been looking for.

Chris inventoried some of the things that he had learned about Zoey since they had begun seeing each other. Although this should have been blindingly obvious, she was not Tana. Unlike the calm, sunny Tana, Zoey was a bit of a cynic, at least outwardly. Zoey was messy, where Tana had been meticulous. Sometimes Zoey stayed up all night drinking coffee and chatting online with her hacker friends. She said the late-night sessions were research for work, but Chris worried that she might still be engaging in hacktivism or, worse still, some hack that might cross over into illegality. In short, living with Zoey was in no way a return to the old patterns of his life with Tana. A new blueprint was required.

Now that he had given her a key to his apartment, it was only a matter of time before his colleagues at the law firm found out about it. He was already bracing for the conversation that he would have one day soon with Don Rubinowski, the firm's managing partner, about sleeping with the director of his forensic lab. He had no idea where his relationship with Zoey was headed, but he wasn't about to bring it to a halt just because it was improbable or inconvenient.

The plane's wing dipped as it circled for landing, and he was able to get a look at Shanghai spread out before the delta of the Yangtze River, which was glinting under steely afternoon skies. Observing the city endlessly sprawling beneath him, he had a visceral recognition of the scale of modern China. He knew that Shanghai was the world's largest city proper by population, but seeing it from this vantage point was another thing.

Chris was equipped with a stack of tourist guides, determined to look as much like a common sightseer as possible. He'd actually spent much of the flight absorbing an array of touristy factoids. For example, the derivation of the city's name: *shàng* meant "above," and *hăi* meant "sea." Upon-the-sea.

Shanghai was the symbol of twenty-first-century China, and the airport announced that fact with its manta ray–like roof design. As he strode quickly through the terminal, the effect lingered. He felt like he was in the belly of some great sea beast as he passed through a cavernous atrium suspended by skeletal-looking struts.

Chris picked up his bags and waited in the customs line. It was probably his imagination, but the customs agent seemed to examine his passport for an inordinately long time. Chris wondered once again whether he might be on some watch list, but he was allowed to pass.

He boarded the green-and-orange-striped Maglev Train, which ran downtown. The Maglev was the fastest passenger vehicle in the world that was not a plane. The German-built train traveled the eighteen miles from Pudong Airport to Shanghai in less than eight minutes while "magnetically levitated."

As the train accelerated and he felt the g-force in the pit of his stomach, a digital counter displayed the speed in miles and kilometers per hour. A few minutes into the brief trip, the counter hit a peak of 267 miles per hour. No sooner had the train reached that velocity than it was decelerating into the terminus. Chris wondered whether it made sense to run such a fast train over such a short distance, but he sensed that a larger point was being made, something about China's modernity and new leadership on the world stage.

As he rode in a taxi from the bullet train terminus to the hotel, rain began to fall, and the roads and shop windows took on a lurid sheen under the streetlights. Chris realized that he recognized this place. This was the Shanghai in which William Gibson had grounded his cyberpunk novels. It was also the urban landscape of *Blade Runner*.

Chris arrived at the Park Hyatt and checked into his room, which was so tiny and black lacquered that it reminded him of a jewel box. The international flight had left him tired but jittery, so he decided to have a drink in the bar to help him sleep. He was going to need to have his wits about him tomorrow.

The hotel bar was on the ninety-first floor and displayed a dizzying panorama of nighttime Shanghai. Below, he saw the futuristic towers of the Pudong district and the Huangpu River. All the tables at the windows were taken, so he grabbed a seat at the long bar and ordered a Maker's Mark. He gazed up at the high ceiling, which rose through the ninety-third floor. It was a grand room, but all he really wanted at the moment was a drink to take the edge off.

Two seats down from him sat a Chinese man in a sport coat and slacks with the tired, open-faced look of a salesman, nursing a beer and half watching a soundless soccer game on the bar's television.

After Chris's drink arrived, the man turned and said, "*Wăn shàng hăo*—Good evening. American?"

"Yes," said Chris. "Is it that obvious? No one ever guesses Canadian."

"More Americans doing business over here. The odds were with me."

Chris returned to his drink, but the man wanted to talk.

"May I?" he asked, motioning to the stool between them.

Chris paused. "Sure," he said, already looking for the bartender to see how quickly he could settle his tab.

The man lifted his glass and said, "*Gān bēi!*" "Dry the cup!"—a traditional Shanghai toast.

Chris lifted his drink and took a swallow. "Your English is good. Wish I could say the same about my Mandarin."

"You speak Mandarin?"

"I represented a US tech company doing business in China for many years and decided I needed to learn the language. But let's stick to English. I'm a little out of practice."

"Certainly. My name's Jingguo Lok."

"Chris Bruen."

"What brings you to Shanghai, Chris?"

"Business. I'm an attorney." It was a relief to have a cover story that was largely true.

"What sort of attorney?"

"Corporate." If he said he was a privacy attorney, it would be too much of a red flag.

"Here to take part in the great economic renaissance?"

"Something like that."

"What part of the United States are you from, Chris?"

"San Francisco. California."

"I've never been there, but it sounds beautiful. Golden Gate Bridge. Transamerica Pyramid. Tony Bennett."

"It is beautiful. Sometimes we forget that."

"Do you have a business card?"

Chris made a show of fishing in his pockets. "No, I don't seem to have one with me."

"It's no problem, since it's just me, but Chinese businessmen consider that to be poor form. You should always have your card with you. Here's mine."

Lok slid a business card along the bar.

"I'll remember that." Chris was beginning to wonder who this fellow was. "So what line of work are you in, Jingguo?"

"Import/export."

"That's pretty broad."

"Well, the details are not very interesting. I'm a distributor selling plastic bathroom items to Walmart—soap dishes, soap dispensers, toothbrush cups."

Chris laughed. "You're right. That's not very interesting. But I could say the same about my job. Have you ever been to Bentonville?"

Lok stared back at him with a blank look.

"Bentonville, Arkansas," Chris repeated, "Walmart's corporate headquarters."

"Oh, of course. No, never been there."

A suspicion began to bloom in the back of his mind that the man might be affiliated with the government or the PLA. Even if he had never visited Bentonville, Chris thought that anyone whose livelihood was dependent upon Walmart would know where they were based.

"So what kind of work are you doing on this trip?" asked Lok, apparently anxious to change the subject.

"Well, I do mergers and acquisitions, but I can't really say much more. Attorney-client privilege and all that."

"I understand completely. Your clients rely upon your discretion. You can't just share information like that with a salesman that you meet in a hotel bar. Especially one who's had a few too many." His voice rose a few decibels, as if he might be taking offense.

"If you've had too many, you don't show it."

"A salesman who can't hold his liquor isn't going to make many sales." He paused. "It's funny, though. I deal with quite a few lawyers in my work, and you don't strike me as one of those slick deal lawyers." Lok paused. "I see you as more of a regulatory guy."

The conversation had started to make Chris uneasy. He had a strong sense now that the man knew who he was and why he was there. "Nope. M&A."

"I guess my radar is off."

"I'm afraid so." Chris conspicuously checked his watch. "You know, I just got off an international flight, and it's finally hitting me. I'm going to have to get some sleep."

"You sure you won't have one more? I'm buying."

"Thank you, but I think that's it for me."

Chris settled his tab and slid off the barstool. "It was a pleasure meeting you, Jingguo."

Lok took another sip of his beer and nodded. "Good luck with your deal, Chris. But can I give you one last bit of advice about doing business in China?"

"Sure."

"Local custom is important here. It's very easy to make a mistake that you don't even understand is a mistake. And here in China, there is always someone watching."

"Who's watching?"

Jingguo stopped smiling. "That depends on what you're doing. But someone will be watching. Count on it."

"I'll try to remember that."

Chris felt Lok's eyes on him as he crossed the bar, past the rain-streaked windows smearing the lights of the towers of Pudong. When Chris glanced back to confirm his suspicion, Lok caught his gaze and raised his glass.

Back in his room, Chris stretched out on the bed, eyes wide open. He no longer felt like he would be able to sleep.

5

Chris had the taxi drop him two blocks away, then walked down Datong Road toward the presumed headquarters of Unit 61398. The rain had stopped falling, but the pavement was wet and the sky overcast. He wondered how much his drinking companion from the night before, Jingguo Lok, actually knew about him and his assignment. He wondered if his arrival at Datong Road was expected.

It was 10:00 a.m., and there was no foot traffic in the area, a street of modern office buildings behind iron gates and concrete walls. Chris felt exposed walking toward the white office tower. He crossed to the opposite sidewalk and quickened his pace, trying to look like someone with someplace to be.

This was going to be even more difficult than he had expected. There was no easy vantage point that he could use to stake out the building, no coffee shops, no stores. As he approached the building at Datong Road 208, he saw that there were two soldiers posted at a guard station by the gate. They would probably take notice of him if he loitered on the street for long. The fact that he was the only Westerner in sight didn't help.

Chris walked a block past the building to a bus stop with a bench. He sat as if waiting for a bus and studied the eight-story building.

It was estimated to house two thousand workers. There were pipes visible at the rear of the structure that might be generator exhausts. Making a show of examining his smartphone, Chris surreptitiously snapped several photos of the building and its surroundings.

He didn't see a large parking structure, so it was likely that a decent number of the employees took public transportation home. That would offer his best opportunity to learn more about the workings of the unit.

Chris thought he noticed one of the soldiers at the gate glance his way. He could not stay there much longer. If they decided to come over and question him, his mission would be over before it had begun.

Fortunately, at that moment a bus rumbled down the road toward him, stopping with a hiss and squeal of pneumatic brakes. Chris climbed on board and rode to the next stop. He walked in the direction of the Pudong commercial district, breathing easier the farther he got from Datong Road. He had already formulated his plan, but he had a few hours to kill before he could put it into play.

Chris walked until he reached the Bund waterfront, Shanghai's most famous landmark, centered around Zhongshan East No. 1 Road. Zhongshan was a broad street flanked on one side by the Huangpu River and on the other by a series of grandiose hotels and former bank buildings that dated to the colonial era. Across the river were the futuristic, Lego-like spheres and towers of Pudong's skyline.

Chris strolled the broad promenade along the river side of the Bund, looking down from the embankment at a procession of barges and the smooth, slate-green waters of the Huangpu. When the rain returned, he moved indoors, spending the next few hours exploring the imposing colonial-era buildings, drinking coffee, and watching pedestrians milling on the Bund.

By late afternoon Chris had exhausted the sightseeing possibilities, so he wandered into the Shanghai Club Building, now the

Waldorf Astoria hotel, for a drink. The columned, baroque building had once been the principal men's club for British residents of
Shanghai. There was a time when gaining admission had required
membership in a certain social strata and a certain race.

In the early 1800s, Western merchants seeking to correct a trade
imbalance with China were looking for something that the Chinese
craved the way Londoners craved tea—and they found it in opium.
The British traders began smuggling opium into China, developing
what became an avid market. The British argued that the Chinese
ruling dynasty, the Qing, were stifling free trade by barring Western
commerce. The Qing countered that the British were unscrupulously
getting their citizens hooked on a dangerous narcotic. The so-called
Opium War broke out when tensions finally boiled over into a battle that the British won. The Treaty of Nanjing gave the British a
self-governing settlement in Shanghai, and this room at the former
Shanghai Club had been the epicenter of the colonial outpost. Chris
knew that the trade war between China and the West had never
really ended, but now it was being fought with hackers and malware
rather than muskets and gunboats.

Chris grabbed a seat at the famous Long Bar, an L-shaped bar
of unpolished mahogany that stretched endlessly across a room that
seemed to extend the length of the hotel, with ceiling fans revolving
languidly overhead. Noël Coward was said to have laid his cheek on
the bar and noted that he could see the curvature of the earth. Chris
sipped a Tsingtao beer, read the *New York Times*, and waited as the
afternoon evaporated as slowly as the beads of sweat on his glass.

* * *

At a quarter to five, Chris boarded the sputtering bus back to Datong
Road, arriving at the bus stop at 4:55. According to Zoey's research, a
large segment of Unit 61398's workforce maintained banker's hours,

leaving the building at 5:00 p.m. sharp. He took a seat and once again made a show of concentrating on his smartphone while he snapped more photos of the facility. He was going to see what this hacker army looked like.

At five on the nose, the gates opened, and cars began to emerge, along with a sea of people headed purposefully for his bus stop. Everyone wanted to get there first so that they could be on the first bus home. Chris snapped as many photos as he could of the license plates of the passing cars and the employees power walking toward him. Then the bus stop was engulfed by a swarm of young Chinese men and women, most in their mid- to late twenties and dressed in business casual. If Zapper had a slightly more conservative dress code, this group could have been the young coders getting off work at Paul Saperstein's Menlo Park campus.

As Chris boarded the crowded bus, he faced a decision. He had to figure out who was the most important member of the unit on the bus. He had no doubt that the more senior managers had cars and would not be riding public transportation. Nevertheless, he had to work with what he had.

You could tell a lot about a workplace by the demeanor of its employees. If the Datong Road operation was run by the People's Liberation Army, Chris expected that it would be a grim and authoritarian place, but if that was the case you wouldn't know it by the chattering, laughing young hackers who filled the bus. As far as he could tell, their jobs seemed to make them happy.

There was one young man in a black North Face jacket who cracked a lot of jokes. More importantly, he was getting polite laughs, which meant that he had some influence. Genuine laughs meant that he actually had a good sense of humor. Obligatory chuckles indicated respect for whatever degree of power he possessed. Not enough to drive a luxury car to work certainly, but sufficient to command attention here. An up-and-comer. Chris decided that he had found his high-value target.

The bus chugged out of the commercial district and into a residential area full of shoddy, student-quality apartment buildings. The young man in the black jacket rose and exited the bus. Chris got out after him.

Chris followed the hacker at a discreet distance through a backstreet that seemed to have been largely cobbled together from sheets of fiberglass and cinder blocks. At close range, China's growth was messy and improvisational. The apartment buildings, leaning precariously over the street, looked as if they could collapse on top of him at any moment. Chris suspected that if he returned to this street a month later, it would look radically different.

He passed a stall with live ducks and chickens, a small electronics store, and a stand selling freshly made pancakes and fried bread. Vines groped out of a vacant lot, trying in vain to reclaim the street. The buildings were a patchwork of colors, none of them attractive—cream, brown, and gray, with many of the windows in the newer buildings tinted a deep blue.

Chris's target stopped at some sort of convenience store and emerged with a plastic bag, then continued on. He never looked back once and didn't seem to suspect that he was being followed.

Farther into this neighborhood, the street remained paved, but the sidewalks were a work in progress, some blocks of concrete cracked and others missing entirely. The neighborhood smelled of wet sawdust, trash, and cooking. Chris felt nearly as conspicuous on this crowded backstreet as he had in the empty business district of Datong Road. He found no other Westerners in sight.

The man in the black jacket walked up the steps of a three-story apartment building that appeared marginally nicer than those around it. A moment later he pulled back the curtains of a third-floor window. Chris snapped a couple of photos.

It wasn't much, but now he had something—the identity, or at least the face and address, of someone who appeared to occupy a position of some responsibility in Unit 61398. Lacking a better strategy, Chris decided to observe the man for a while and see what happened.

Chris found a food stall within sight of the apartment building and took a seat at a tiny table with uneven legs. He and the proprietor, a small, gnarled man, reached a tacit accommodation. Chris was allowed to remain there as long as he kept buying Cokes and orders of fried bread. When he couldn't eat any more, he began feeding his portions to a couple of mangy dogs that prowled the street. They were suspicious of him at first but soon seemed to reach the conclusion that he was the best thing ever, this fried bread–dispensing *yang guǐzi* ("foreign devil").

Night fell, and the street life took on a different rhythm. Blue-collar workers headed to work the night shifts at factories. Small groups of young men staggered drunkenly over the uneven pavement. More scraggly dogs arrived to eat his fried bread.

Chris sat there long enough for the incongruousness of his situation to fully sink in. He was a successful, respected partner in a major American law firm, and yet here he was essentially playing private detective on a backstreet in Shanghai, risking imprisonment by the Chinese government. It was not lost on Chris that he was pursuing supremely techno-savvy criminals using investigatory techniques that could have been employed by Sam Spade.

And what was he doing it for? To help Paul Saperstein and Zapper maintain their stock price and market share? Chris wasn't one to walk away from a challenge or let down a client, but he realized that he would probably be facing a decision point soon, and he wanted to know in advance what he would do when he reached it. He could already tell that there would come a time when pursuing this assignment would put either his life or his freedom in jeopardy.

He decided in that moment that, no matter how well Zapper paid him, he wasn't going to risk everything for them. No matter what the Supreme Court said, corporations were not people, and he wouldn't put his life on the line for one. After all, if he was locked away in a Chinese prison, he knew that Zapper would probably deny he was working for them. To do otherwise would create an international incident.

Less than a year before, Chris had gotten the news that his thyroid cancer was in full remission. The aftershock of that event was still rippling through his life, altering everything, but in ways that were subtle and hard to pinpoint. It was like the air that he was breathing now had more oxygen to it. Somehow nearly dying had both made him value life more and made him willing to risk more.

And while he was engaging in this moment of self-assessment, Chris had to consider the next logical question. Why did he embark on these sorts of missions at all? He could just stay in his office in San Francisco, enjoying his view of the Bay and advising on privacy and security regulatory matters. You don't find many regulatory attorneys rotting away in Chinese prisons.

Chris knew the answer—this was what he was good at. Whatever *this* was.

Chris stared at the third-floor window of the apartment building for a couple of hours. Finally, he decided to take a calculated gamble. He stood up, left a generous tip for the owner of the stand, and walked over to the building. The proprietor watched him go.

What sounded like a frenetic Chinese game show blasted from a television set on the first floor. Chris examined the names on the mailboxes. The name of the third-floor resident was Bai Hsu.

Chris climbed the narrow stairs to the third floor and paused, contemplating his exit strategy if things went south. He rapped on the door.

The hacker opened the door and seemed surprised to see an unfamiliar face.

"*Láo jià, nín huì jiǎng yīng yǔ ma*? Excuse me, do you speak English?" Chris asked.

"Yeah. What can I do for you?" The answer—spoken in impeccable English—didn't surprise Chris. English proficiency was one of the requirements for working in Unit 61398.

"I'm from the US, and I'd like to ask you some questions."

"This is not a good time for me." The hacker tried to shut the door, but Chris planted his foot in the doorway and leaned in.

"That would be a mistake. I know where you work on Datong Road. I know what you do."

"I don't care what you think you know."

"Do you want your bosses to know that you're working for us?" Chris raised his voice a bit when he said it.

The hacker glanced nervously around the landing at the doors of the other apartments, clearly afraid that one of his neighbors was overhearing the conversation.

"I could say that more loudly," Chris said, "in case your neighbors didn't hear."

Hsu froze for a moment, weighing two unappealing options, then said, "Come inside."

Chris stepped into the apartment, which was lined with inexpensive particleboard bookcases stuffed with science fiction and coding manuals. It was a first-decent-job apartment, a clear step up from student lodgings, but not yet the sort of place where an adult would live. An iMac on a desk in the corner was by far the nicest item in the room, and it was plastered with Japanese anime images.

As soon as the door closed, Hsu said, "You're going to have to leave, or I'll call the police." He seemed agitated, stepping back behind the kitchen counter to put some space between them, the confident, wisecracking fellow from the bus nowhere to be seen.

"Your name is Bai Hsu, right?" Chris asked.

After a moment's hesitation, he said, "Yeah. What's yours?"

When Chris in turn hesitated, Hsu added, "I know you won't give me your real name, so unless you show me your passport, this conversation is over."

Chris produced the passport and held it out for Hsu, never letting it out of his grip.

"Christopher Bruen," he said. "Well, Chris, I've got a feeling that if I call the police and give them your name, they're not going to let you leave the country. So tell me what it is that you want."

Chris explained what he was looking for—proof that APT1 was conducted by the People's Liberation Army and that they had stolen Zapper's proprietary algorithms.

"I don't know anything about that," Hsu said. "And even if I did I couldn't provide that kind of information to you."

"You're afraid of going to jail?"

"Yeah, I'm very afraid of going to jail. You're asking me to disclose state secrets."

"So the state *is* behind this?"

"I'm not saying anything to you."

"Look, we already know that the PLA is behind the hacks. And I'm going to explain to you why you should be even more afraid of me than you are of the PLA. We know all about the work being done on Datong Road. If you cooperate with us, no one will be able to trace anything back to you."

"What are you talking about? Nothing can be traced back to me, because I've given you nothing."

"If you don't help us, we're going to make it very clear to your bosses that you supplied us with information about the operation."

"That's a lie, and no one will believe it."

"The team at Zapper is pretty sophisticated. They're capable of making things look very bad for you."

"Not sophisticated enough to keep us out," Hsu said with a note of pride.

"No, I'll give you that."

"And even if you could send me to prison, I could make sure that you go right along with me."

"There's no need for anyone to go to prison. I just need some information. I'm going to guess that I wasn't lucky enough to have stumbled upon the one person who has all of the details about the Zapper intrusion. But I bet you know who I should talk to."

Hsu moved into the living room. "It's not fair to put me in this position," he said. "I had nothing to do with the Zapper hack. I didn't work on it personally."

"Okay, but you know someone who did, don't you?"

Hsu drew back the curtain and looked down on the pedestrians passing in the street, probably checking to see if someone was observing his apartment. "You could have been followed here."

"I don't think so."

"Of course you don't."

Chris remained silent, waiting for Hsu to make the next move. Just as nature abhors a vacuum, most people abhor silence and feel an irresistible need to fill it, even to the point of making incriminating admissions.

After a few long seconds, Hsu said, "I think they brought in two specialists to work on Zapper. Independent contractors. There were others involved in processing the extracted data, but those two guys seemed to be doing most of the penetration work."

"Do you have their names?"

Hsu seemed to recognize that he'd reached the point of no return. He took a breath and stepped past it. "Li Owyang and Bingwen Ma."

"Do you know where they live?"

"No, but I do know that you won't find them in Shanghai. When the operation was over and Zapper finally discovered the intrusion, they both left the unit. Li said that he was going to visit his sister, and I think Bingwen was going with him. He said she lived in Longhua, Shenzhen, and worked at the Commsen factory."

Chris was familiar with the Commsen factory in the Shenzhen district, north of Hong Kong, where hundreds of thousands of employees worked in massive facilities, manufacturing smartphones, tablet computers, and other devices, largely for US tech companies. Chris's own smartphone probably originated in one of those vast factories. It wouldn't be easy to track down Li Owyang's sister in that sea of workers.

"Do you know her name?"

Hsu shook his head.

"How about her address?"

"That's all I've got."

"Are you sure you don't know anything else about her? Anything at all."

"She worked on tablet computers. Li and I talked about it once. Her job involved—what was it?—signal integrity. I think that was it. There. Now will you please leave me alone?"

"Your name won't be mentioned, and you'd better forget that we ever met."

"Don't worry about that," Hsu said, already ushering him to the door.

Chris stopped short of the threshold. "Just a couple more questions and I'll be gone. You do work for the PLA, don't you?"

"I thought you already knew that."

"We were ninety percent sure."

Hsu looked him unsteadily in the eye. "I'll put it this way. Do you think I'd be this scared if it wasn't the PLA?"

"Okay, I'll take that as a yes. But what do they intend to do with the algorithms?"

"I don't have access to that sort of information. I'm just a technician. Please leave now. I mean it."

Chris nodded and left without another word. He wandered back through the ramshackle street, where the drunks were now a larger presence than the night-shift factory workers. A few hostile, distrustful glances were directed at him. In the tourist-friendly confines of the Park Hyatt and on major thoroughfares like the Bund, Americans seemed to be welcome enough. But here, far from the tourist zone, it appeared that opinions were divided as to whether he belonged.

He was going to need help to find Li Owyang's sister and the two hackers. It was time to deploy his secret weapon—Zoey.

6

The next morning Chris decided it was safer to connect with Zoey outside the hotel. Using the so-called Great Firewall of China, the Chinese government employed a number of methods for censoring Internet communications, including blocking access to many Western sites, but it couldn't screen all online content. To censor social networking sites and other online businesses, the Chinese government had turned to the private sector.

In order to remain in business, online companies were required to hire "editors" to monitor their sites and scrub potentially offensive statements. The editors, like white blood cells fighting infection, constantly scoured web postings for the latest signs of dissent or unauthorized expression, often disguised using coded language. As soon as one code word was identified and expunged, another would appear. For example, the imaginary date of May 35 was sometimes used to refer to June 4, the date of the Tiananmen Square massacre. Despite the never-ending game of Whac-A-Mole, the end result was a system more efficiently repressive than the government could have managed by doing the job itself.

Another common technique was "packet filtering," which terminated a text/data communication when a certain number of controversial keywords were detected. In his conversation with Zoey, Chris intended to avoid controversial keywords like "Unit 61398," "APT1," and "Zapper algorithms." Nonetheless, he figured that there was a greater likelihood that the PLA would be monitoring Wi-Fi connections originating from the Park Hyatt, a popular venue for foreign visitors.

Chris found a tea and coffee shop off of the Bund with Wi-Fi and the right noise level. Not so quiet that the café's other denizens could easily overhear, but not so crowded that there would be people close at hand to eavesdrop. He used their prearranged secure website to connect with Zoey via encrypted Skype connection, an approach designed to evade the Great Firewall.

When the Skype connection blinked on, he was faced with the welcome sight of Zoey, who was in her natural habitat—the firm's forensic lab. A large coffee cup blocked part of the foreground.

"Nice to see you," Zoey said. "Are you okay?"

"I'm fine, but I've reached a bit of a dead end."

"Time to use your lifeline."

"That's right."

Chris proceeded to describe his meeting with Bai Hsu and his search for Li Owyang's sister in Shenzhen.

"That's pretty good progress, considering you just got there."

"Thanks, but I don't know where to go from here. I could go to Shenzhen and ask around for the sister, but I don't think that's very likely to be productive."

"Commsen," Zoey said. "I've read about that place. Talk about your needle in a haystack."

"Can you help me narrow things down?"

"Maybe. If these two hackers, Li Owyang and Bingwen Ma, are so good that the PLA would bring them in as special contractors for that project, then I can't imagine they wouldn't leave a footprint in certain circles."

"Your circles?"

"Well, yeah. I'm going to reach out to some Chinese dissidents that I'm acquainted with. They're hacktivists, but they're bound to know some of the people who've gone to work for the government."

"It can be a fine line between black-hat and white-hat hacking," Chris said, thinking of the variety of pros that Paul Saperstein had recruited to defend Zapper. "At least in the US. Think it's a similar deal in China?"

"Well," Zoey said, "both sides are competing for the same talent pool, so when someone's as good as these two probably are, word gets around. The problem is that if they've done anything interesting it was probably under a handle."

"Be careful."

"*You* be careful. I'm the one sitting back here in my office in San Francisco sipping my Peet's, and you're the one messing with the PLA."

Chris wanted to talk to her about the apartment key that he'd given her before leaving, and what that meant for their relationship. But that was a conversation better conducted face-to-face, not over Skype. "How are things back there?" he asked instead.

"Well, I'm getting calls every other hour from the team at Zapper wondering if you've got anything for them. What should I say?"

"Tell them I'm following a lead, and that I'll let them know when I have something. I'd better sign off before someone notices this encrypted transmission."

"Okay," Zoey said. "I'll see what I can find. I'll leave a message on the secure site when I have something."

"While you're working on that, I'm going to head for Shenzhen."

"Just a sec," Zoey said, raising a hand as if to stop him from signing off. "Let's just say that I do find the address for Li Owyang's sister. And it leads to the hackers. What are you going to do? It's not like the PLA is going to return the algorithms."

"True. I don't really know yet. At the very least I'd like to come back to Saperstein with hard evidence of who stole the algorithms and why. Something he can use to pressure the White House into pressuring China."

"Yeah," Zoey said. "Because the Chinese government is so susceptible to external pressure. Look, just be careful out there. And I'm expecting you to bring me back an egg roll, okay?"

7

The Number Three Detention Center in Shanghai was a massive, tan two-story complex that could have been confused with a manufacturing facility but for the high wall studded with barbed wire around the perimeter. The squared-off arch over the building's entrance was emblazoned with the red-and-gold insignia of the People's Republic.

Tao passed through metal detectors operated by paramilitary guards in blue uniforms with winged badges that made them look like airline pilots. He waited anxiously in the antiseptic visitation area until Wenyan was escorted to a seat on the other side of the glass. Tao always dreaded the first glimpse of his brother. Like time-lapse photography, the transformation occurred with unnerving rapidity. With each visit, Wenyan looked thinner, more dead behind the eyes.

Some might say that Wenyan was lucky he had been granted the rare privilege of receiving visitors, but there was a reason for that. Wenyan had friends—of a sort—in one of China's most powerful families.

Three years ago, Li Chen, the wealthy son of the president of an automobile factory, killed a pedestrian while drag racing through the streets of Beijing. The victim, a thirty-two-year-old mother of two from a rural town, was hurled twenty yards and died on impact.

Li Chen was said to have joked with his rich friends and smoked cigarettes while he waited for the police to arrive.

Tao's brother, Wenyan, had worked in the same car factory run by Chen's father. Putting together transmissions on an assembly line had been a decent job, and Wenyan had hoped eventually to rise from the factory floor to a lower management position. One day Wenyan finally caught the eye of Mr. Chen, but it was not for the meticulousness of his work.

Chen, who usually remained upstairs in his office, paced around the factory floor in a visibly agitated state, examining the faces of his workers, all of whom assumed that a wave of layoffs was on the way. Chen stopped before the station of Wenyan Zhang and invited him up to his office for a "conversation." As Wenyan told the story, you could practically hear the thrum of the assembly line skip a beat as everyone tried to observe the exchange without staring. Wenyan knew that this could be many things—a firing, a promotion, an accusation of theft—but it was unlikely to be a conversation.

Once the door of his office closed behind them, Chen began by noting the close resemblance between Wenyan and his son Li. Then he made the astounding proposal that Wenyan serve Li's four-year prison sentence for vehicular manslaughter in exchange for a fee of roughly a hundred eighty thousand yuan, or thirty thousand dollars.

Wenyan had been speechless. He'd never really believed the stories about the practice of *dǐng zuì*, or "substitute criminals," which had been associated with the Chinese criminal justice system since the nineteenth century. He also had not been left with much of a choice.

For one thing, Chen was talking about a substantial amount of money. In addition, Chen said he would fire Wenyan on the spot if he refused the offer. Finally, the wealthy and party-connected Chen vowed that if Wenyan did not serve his son's sentence, Wenyan would never be hired for any job that had a future.

Chen closed by rationalizing the practice of *dǐng zuì*, likening it to a cap-and-trade policy for crime. Wasn't he still paying for his son's crime, and paying market value at that? But Wenyan understood that Chen's most dire threat remained unspoken: to refuse the offer would almost surely mean losing his life.

Tao was a year and a half older than Wenyan and sometimes jokingly referred to him as "the spare," an allusion to China's one-child policy, which in practice was more of a guideline than an immutable rule. Tao and his brother had the same strong chin and wide-set eyes, but they weren't often confused with one another. While Tao had a laconic demeanor that hardened his features, Wenyan had a mobile forehead and expressive eyes that displayed every thought that fluttered through his consciousness. Tao always used to say that it was as if Wenyan walked around with his wallet in his hand.

These were Tao's thoughts as he watched the prison guard place Wenyan in the chair and activate the microphone.

"Li," Tao said, using his brother's assumed name with a slight grimace.

"Every time you say it, you make that face you used to make when you took cough syrup," Wenyan said with the approximation of a smile.

"How are you doing?"

"As well as can be expected. At least I have a job."

Tao knew all about Wenyan's "job," which consisted of being marched every morning at 5:00 a.m. to a prison factory to make earbuds for airlines. The workday ended at 7:00 p.m., and if he ever stopped because he was ill or exhausted he would be beaten, Tasered, pepper-sprayed, and placed in an isolation cell.

"One year down," Tao said. "You've made it this far. You can make it the rest of the way."

"I can't think like that. You can't count the days here."

"You'll get through this. They can't break you."

Wenyan looked him in the eye. "Oh yes they can. It's dangerous to think otherwise. You just have to hope that they don't want to."

"You're performing a service for a very powerful family. The people who run the prison must know that."

"True, and it would be inconvenient for the Chen family if I died in here. It might make it difficult to explain why their son, Li, is still alive. Have any photos surfaced?"

"No. I think Chen must have gotten to everyone who was on the scene." Tao had learned that the practice of *dǐng zuì*, like so many other things, had been transformed by the smartphone. In at least one similar case of vehicular homicide, bystanders had photographed the perpetrator using their phones. When a substitute criminal was imprisoned for the crime, photos of the perpetrator and his replacement were posted online by outraged citizens.

Unfortunately, if any bystanders had snapped photos of Li Chen laughing and smoking with his friends as the woman's body was carried away, they had not been made public. Tao regularly searched the Internet for those photos, even though he knew that such activity might bring a government agent to his doorstep.

"Let's talk about something else," Wenyan said. "How's Super Dan doing?" Wenyan was a fan of Lin Dan, or Super Dan, a professional badminton player widely acknowledged to be the greatest ever—a sort of Michael Jordan with a shuttlecock.

"He took the gold again at the London Games. First men's singles player to successfully defend his gold medal."

Wenyan grinned. "He's just the best ever, man."

"And he's married now."

"Fang?"

"Yeah. When they have kids, I guess we know who'll be bringing home the gold in badminton around 2030 or so." After trying to keep their relationship quiet for some time, Super Dan had married

Xie Xingfang, nicknamed Fang Fang, herself a world-champion badminton player.

"Good for them."

"During the London Olympics, he was wearing a double *F* tattoo on his arm."

"I know you couldn't care less about Super Dan, so thanks for paying attention to this stuff. What else is going on out there?"

"Well, season four of *Game of Thrones* was awesome. I bought a bootleg DVD." He and Wenyan were able to watch the episodes without subtitles because their parents had cobbled together what little disposable income they had to buy their sons English lessons. They saw it as their ticket into China's emerging middle class, and they had not been wrong.

"No spoilers, okay?"

"When you get out, we'll do some binge watching and get you caught up."

Wenyan gave a pained smile, as if the thought of simply sitting in a darkened room and watching a television show was too great a pleasure to even contemplate. Tao could see that Wenyan might not make it through his sentence. It made him more certain that he had done the right thing when he had approached Chen personally and offered his services.

The idea had occurred to Tao ten months ago. One day he had simply arrived at the auto factory and asked to see the company president. After giving his name at the security desk and waiting for fifteen minutes, he was informed that Mr. Chen was not in the office that day.

Two days later Tao returned, and this time, to his surprise, he was told that Mr. Chen would see him. He didn't even have to wait. Two security guards frisked him for weapons and then escorted him, walking close at his side. They crossed the factory floor, where men in white coats with sparking welding torches scrambled beneath auto chassis suspended from the ceiling by massive, bright-yellow conveyors.

Tao was led up an iron staircase to the management offices, passing through several anterooms, before he arrived at a door flanked by frosted glass windows with a plaque that read "Mr. Longwei Chen."

Mr. Chen sat like a pasha behind an expansive, uncluttered mahogany desk. He did not rise when Tao entered. Chen was a compact man in his midfifties with thinning hair and a face that was heavily creased, particularly around the eyes, giving him an aspect of perpetual watchfulness, like a wooden owl posted in a garden to keep predators away. It was probably a useful attribute for a factory manager.

Tao's eyes immediately went to the silver-framed photo of Li Chen on the corner of the desk, next to photos of Chen's two other children and wife. Li Chen did resemble Tao's brother, if it were possible to wipe away the insolent, privileged smile.

"The resemblance is striking, isn't it?"

"Very."

"I hope you know that I value the service that your brother is providing to me and my family. Now what brings you here today?"

"I have a proposal for you."

"Yes?"

"I'd like to speak in private," Tao said, nodding to the guards. He knew that Chen would not want to openly discuss the fact that he had paid someone to serve his son's prison sentence.

"He's okay, right?" Chen said to the guards.

"He's clean."

Chen nodded, and the two guards left the office.

"Okay, so what is this proposal? And don't try anything foolish, because the guards are right outside the door."

"I would like to offer myself as a replacement for my brother. You can see that I bear a strong resemblance to him—and to your son.

Wenyan is not going to survive another three years in that prison. And if he dies in there, it will create an awkward situation for your son. I'm stronger than my brother, and I can do the time."

Chen waved his hand dismissively. "What, you think it's easy to place a substitute criminal in prison? There are certain prison officials that are willing to turn a blind eye so long as things aren't too flagrant. But you can't make fools of them. You are wasting my time."

Tao knew that his window was closing fast and that in moments the guards would hustle him back to the sidewalk. "Then I can provide other services," he said.

"What are your skills?"

"I'm an electrician. I work on new houses and office buildings."

"I have plenty of electricians on my payroll."

Tao's mind raced. There must be something that he could say that would help his brother. "I am willing to do what is necessary. *Whatever* is necessary."

Chen studied him. "And what exactly does that mean?"

"I mean that if you have the ability to shorten my brother's sentence, then I would do anything that you wanted. I'm not squeamish."

Chen laid his hands carefully on the desk. "I might be able to shorten that sentence, but it would not be easy, and it would be costly. I'd have to call in favors. You would need to provide a service of exceptional value to justify that."

"I will do anything that is in my power."

"Then let me ask you, Tao Zhang, have you ever killed a man?"

8

As Chris watched the flat landscape roll past on the train from Shanghai to Shenzhen, he reflected on how small the world had become. Small enough that Chinese hackers could test the doors and windows of corporate America on a daily basis. Small enough that within twenty-four hours of learning of the breach, Chris was in Shanghai looking up at the retro-futuristic towers of Pudong. He gazed out the window and listened to Bach's The Well-Tempered Clavier on his iPhone, trying to ignore the man in the adjoining seat eating something pungent from a paper bag. Bach's meditative, pristine compositions were the best remedy that he knew for cognitive dissonance. They reminded him that there was order and reason in the world, all appearances to the contrary.

It was a truism that a smaller world was a good thing. In theory, it enhanced understanding among disparate cultures, allowed the First and Third Worlds to cross-pollinate. But Chris wasn't so sure that the world hadn't been better when everyone had lived their lives within twenty miles of their birthplace.

Today's hyperconnected way of life was in many ways messier and more fractious than what had gone before. A century ago, in order for opposing worldviews to clash, someone had to dispatch an invading army. Now zealots anywhere in the world could launch attacks large and small against the US so long as they had the requisite technical skills. Of course, US companies had the same strike capabilities, which was what put Chris on the train to Shenzhen.

The late-afternoon sun glared whitely through a malignant cloud that enveloped the horizon—China's famous air pollution. The PRC was largely made up of plains, which sent roiling waves of dust into the atmosphere under the best of circumstances. But, given the unregulated growth of Chinese industry and dependence on coal, the best of circumstances were gone for good.

The government-run weather service referred to it as *mái*, which meant "haze" in Mandarin. Up until around 2006, it had been known as *wù*, or "fog," and that was still how most PRC citizens referred to it. As in so many aspects of Chinese life, the government generated edicts and official pronouncements, but certain aspects of human behavior could not be dictated.

China's air-quality readings were divided into five classes. Classes one and two were categorized as "blue sky." On a level-five day, citizens were told to stay indoors and avoid exertion. To Chris's still unpracticed eye, the grimy view from his train window rated at least a four.

The train rattled along through the suburbs of Shanghai, passing dirty concrete housing complexes, then dirty concrete factories, and then green fields, all of them shrouded in a filthy-looking *mái*. Over the course of an enervating eighteen-hour trip, the green fields once more gave way to smokestack factories and red tile–roofed apartment buildings, and then he was in Shenzhen.

When the train arrived in Shenzhen, Chris checked into a hotel. As the sun sank, he walked over to take a look at the Commsen factories. Commsen Technology Group, which was the trade name for Dong Mai Precision Manufacturing Company, was the world's largest electronics contract manufacturer, producing most of the US market's popular smartphones and tablet computers.

Chris passed enormous redbrick dormitories that housed Commsen workers. Even though the workers reportedly lived eight to an apartment in bunk beds, judging by the new buildings under construction Shenzhen appeared to be experiencing a housing shortage. In the streets outside the dormitories, vendors had set up stalls selling food, clothing, toiletries, and other essentials.

Aside from vendors manning the stalls, nearly every person in sight appeared to be a Commsen worker. They were easy to spot because they wore green polo shirts with "Commsen" on the collar. Chris was reminded again of Bentonville, Arkansas, the corporate headquarters of Walmart and a similarly extreme example of a company town.

Chris walked on past the dormitories to the gates of the factory itself as the sun set in a spectacularly bloody end worthy of a Peckinpah film. As any resident of Santa Monica could tell you, the one positive byproduct of air pollution is lovely sunsets.

The boxy factory facilities were seven stories tall and massive, extending as far as he could see. Nets were strung above the first floor of the buildings. At first Chris thought it was some sort of postmodern architectural flourish, but then he realized that these were the famous suicide nets that had been the focus of so much Western media coverage. The news stories reported that working conditions in the Commsen factories were so stressful and demanding that there was an unusually high rate of suicide, with workers leaping from the upper floors.

Zoey had informed him that only last week a Commsen employee committed suicide, leaping from the roof and getting enough distance to avoid the protective net. The reasons for the employee's death were not known, but it was speculated that it might have something to do with Commsen's recently introduced "silence mode" policy, which required—under threat of termination—that workers not talk on the job. The eerie quiet of the enormous factory must have made an already-miserable workplace even more excruciating.

Workers streamed out of the factory gates as a shift ended. Commsen operated two facilities in the area—one in the Guanlan neighborhood, which employed a hundred sixty thousand workers, and this one in the Longhua neighborhood, which employed two hundred forty thousand. Chris studied the workers' faces. Even if he had known what Li Owyang's sister looked like, the odds of spotting her in this ocean of green-shirted Commsen workers would have been minuscule.

It might help if he could get inside the factory, but there was no way to do that without a security badge. As with the PLA's facility on Datong Road in Shanghai, all Chris could think to do was keep his eyes and ears open and hope for some opportunity. It wasn't the most promising of plans, but it was all that came to mind.

Chris noticed that he was not the only one observing the factory workers. At the edges of the parking lot that fronted the factory gates were squads of PLA soldiers wearing brimless helmets, unnecessary camouflage uniforms, and bulky black earphones with stems for microphones. Some of them were carrying riot shields. The soldiers seemed to be standing by for now, but they looked ready for action. Zoey's research indicated that there had been incidents of unrest recently at Commsen factories. If the government felt the need to call in the equivalent of an army, then this unrest must have included more than a few disgruntled employees.

Chris watched the scene for an hour, but the soldiers didn't appear to be readying to move. Finally, weary from the daylong train trip, Chris decided to return to his hotel. Given the military presence, something was about to happen here, but likely not until morning.

9

When Chris returned to the Commsen factory at 8:00 a.m., hundreds, perhaps thousands, of soldiers had assembled, most of them with clubs and riot gear. Many were stationed in a park a couple of blocks away from the factory. They seemed relaxed, confident in their overwhelming force.

He bought a breakfast sandwich at a Starbucks and watched the soldiers mill about and talk. To call Commsen a factory wasn't quite accurate. It was more like a city, and he was on its main drag, which, in addition to the Starbucks, included a bank, a grocery store, and a dry cleaner. Since many of the workers had little time to do anything else but sleep, it was important to provide easy access to all essential services. Big New York law firms operated on a similar principle, footing the bill for takeout dinners to ensure that associates remained at their desks late into the evening.

Everything was quiet until about 10:30 a.m., when he heard a muffled roar from the factory across the street, like a distant, cheering football stadium after a score. In a matter of minutes, the soldiers were ordered into formation and began suiting up. Battalions of PLA soldiers marched in quickstep formation past the window of the Starbucks. Their boots in unison on the pavement outside shook his table. The troops filed past the factory gates and streamed through several entrances, with riot shields and batons raised.

Soon workers began running outside through the exits that weren't blocked by the soldiers. Some of them already had bloodied heads, and others were crying from tear gas. Chris realized that he had been presented with an opportunity. The factory's security was suddenly nonexistent.

He left the coffee shop and began to walk behind the advancing soldiers. He followed a PLA squad inside the factory and was greeted by a scene that looked like one of Breugel's depictions of hell. There was so much going on that it was difficult to focus the eye. The noise was deafening, the sound of hundreds shouting, screaming, crying.

The factory floor was a vast high-ceilinged space about the dimensions of an indoor stadium. It was crisscrossed by assembly lines manned by employees in white scrubs. In the open center area of the factory, a pitched battle was taking place that appeared to involve several hundred workers, all writhing together like one organism. The workers were fighting the PLA, but they were also fighting each other.

The soldiers advanced on the scrum from several directions, knocking workers to the concrete, clubbing them, stomping them. If the battle had been fought on open ground, Chris was certain that the troops would have quickly neutralized the situation, but the factory equipment and assembly lines blocked their access. What was astounding was the scale of the scene, like some Cecil B. DeMille epic run amok. While hundreds of workers were fighting, thousands of PLA soldiers were attempting to suppress the incident, a display of crushing force and an indication that the government viewed this as something that might grow into a far larger revolt.

It was hard to tell what was going on in the chaos. Workers were hurling tools, electronic devices, and whatever else came to hand. To an outsider, the incident seemed like nothing so much as a free-for-all brawl.

A young woman in a green Commsen polo shirt hurried unsteadily past Chris, bleeding from a gash on her forehead. Two male workers throwing punches at each other fell sideways into Chris, sending him staggering. He tried to make his way to a quiet place at the edge of the factory floor away from the melee.

He found a spot away from the fighting near the administrative offices that ringed one side of the factory and called out to anyone in earshot, "Does anyone here speak English?" He didn't trust his Mandarin under these deafening conditions.

The cubicle-level administrative workers simply ignored Chris, too engrossed in observing the riot.

"I need to find someone here. Please, can anyone help me?"

A small, pudgy man with dark bangs that fell nearly into his eyes finally responded. "All right, okay. Who are you trying to find?" Chris recognized the man's type on sight—the reluctantly competent office drone.

"Her last name is Owyang, and she works on tablet computers. Something to do with signal strength."

The man scuttled back into his cubbyhole office like a hermit crab and perched behind his monitor. "Let's see," he said as his hands flew over the keyboard. "Owyang. Tablets. Signal strength." He moved his face in close to the monitor to scrutinize the results. "Got it."

"Where is she?"

"Well, her workstation is over there," he said, pointing to an area about fifty yards away near another assembly line. "But I doubt that you'll find her there now. As you can see, we have a bit of a work stoppage here."

"What's her first name?"

"Mei-Hua."

"Do you have a photo?"

"Yeah, I've got her personnel file up on my screen. Take a look. But I thought you knew her."

"I know her brother."

"You're with one of the US client companies, right?"

"As a matter of fact, I am," Chris said, a statement that had the virtue of being true. Zapper used Commsen to manufacture its tablet computers.

"I thought so. I hope you'll remember that I helped you when you speak to my bosses. I'm Fengge."

Chris furrowed his brow to indicate that he was making a mental note, which he promptly tossed into his mental wastebasket.

Encouraged, Fengge added, "Let me help you get out of here. That girl you're looking for won't be there, and some of my coworkers aren't too crazy about Americans."

"I'm going to take a look just the same," Chris said. "Thanks."

He made his way across the factory floor toward Mei-Hua Owyang's workstation, trying to stay as far away from the rioters as possible.

The crowd suddenly surged in his direction, and a PLA riot squad baton struck his shoulder. If the blow had landed on his skull, he might have been knocked unconscious.

The PLA troops secured their gas masks, and then he heard the whump and clatter of tear gas canisters being fired. Chris stuck his mouth and nose into the elbow of his shirtsleeve and kept moving.

It was then that he saw her. Mei-Hua was crouched beneath a conveyor belt, trying to shield herself behind some cardboard boxes. She was wearing a white smock instead of the standard-issue Commsen green polo, which probably indicated technical expertise.

Between them a PLA soldier smashed a riot shield into two workers and struck at them with his baton. She was trapped there until the struggle stopped, but she was also being enveloped by the tear gas, which was billowing across the factory floor like dry ice smoke at a heavy metal show.

Chris stepped around behind the PLA soldier, then lowered his shoulder and barreled into his back. He managed to shove the soldier and the two struggling workers forward about five yards. No one even turned around to look at him as they fought on. It was enough for Chris to reach under the conveyor belt and extend a hand to Mei-Hua.

There was a look of panic on her face, but she took his hand. What choice did she have with the clouds of tear gas growing thicker by the minute? He grabbed Mei-Hua's arm and pulled her to her feet. They headed for the nearest exit, both of them coughing and crying.

"Do I know you?" she asked in Mandarin.

"No, but I'm going to get you out of here," he replied, also in Mandarin.

She nodded, recognizing that this was not the time for questions. "Okay," she replied in English, a swift accommodation to his crude Mandarin.

The exit was now jammed with workers, tears streaming down their faces. Fortunately, the PLA troops were not pressing their advantage, concentrating on those who were still fighting in the middle of the factory.

At last they made it through the double doors and into the smoggy sunshine. They spent a few moments with their hands on their knees, filling their lungs and dabbing at their stinging eyes.

"Why did you help me?" she finally asked.

"I don't know really. I guess because I could. What was happening in there?"

"There are always a few malcontents that cause trouble. The vast majority of the workers are happy with their jobs at Commsen."

She was giving him the party line, and why wouldn't she? She didn't know who he was.

"I have nothing to do with your bosses. You can tell me what actually happened. I won't tell anyone. I'm just curious."

She squinted at him through bloodshot eyes. "Gangs from two neighboring districts have never gotten along. It probably dates back centuries. It started as a fistfight between two guys from those factions, and it just blew up. Of course, things were already at the breaking point in there."

"Your English is very good."

"Thanks. My parents would be pleased." Like the other hackers working at Datong Road, Li Owyang was undoubtedly fluent in English. It figured that his sister was also proficient.

"How bad is it in there, in the factory?"

"Well, there are worse places to work, but it's not good. The work is so intense and precise, and they expect you to do it so quickly. It was bad when the sales of smartphones and tablets were booming, but it's worse now that the market has leveled off."

"Wouldn't that be a good thing from your perspective?"

"You'd think so, but now the US tech companies have started spreading the work around to other manufacturers. A more limited supply of work means that we end up being forced to work even harder so that Commsen can compete." She paused. "So who are you, and why all the questions?"

"As it happens I'm an attorney from the US. My client is deciding whether to give some manufacturing work to Commsen or one of its competitors."

"We didn't make a very good first impression, did we?"

"No. But don't worry. I won't get you in trouble."

"You'd better not. If my bosses found out I said anything, I'd get a lot more than a slap on the wrist. I really have to be going. Thanks again for getting me out of there."

Mei-Hua turned and walked away toward the dormitories. Before he lost her in the crowds emerging from the factory, Chris set out, following her. If the two hackers were still staying in her apartment, then she should lead him right to them.

10

Chris followed Mei-Hua through the crowds, who were all trying to get as far away from the factory violence as possible. She hurried through the plaza across from the factory and past the dormitories that housed the Commsen workers.

People poured out of the shoddy, prefabricated apartment buildings, buzzing about the riot and attending to the wounded, many of whom had severe head lacerations. Some of the male workers seemed to be threatening to return to the factory and make a stand against the PLA, but even Chris could tell that was bluster. The government had dispatched what seemed to be an entire army to suppress the eruption, and opposing such an overwhelming show of force would have been suicidal.

Beyond the dormitories were more drab apartment buildings. Mei-Hua ducked inside the vestibule of a two-story concrete building that seemed to consist of two units, one on the ground floor and one above. Chris took up a position on a bench in a children's playground carpeted in brown grass a block away. He had his smartphone ready to photograph anyone who emerged from the building.

After about twenty minutes, Mei-Hua emerged from the apartment and walked off down the street. Chris decided that it was best not to continue following her. He was betting that this was where she lived and where the two hackers were staying.

Chris considered what he would do if he actually did come face-to-face with Owyang and Ma. There was not much point to trying to retrieve the stolen algorithms. They had undoubtedly already been shared with PLA representatives or whatever Chinese entrepreneurs intended to exploit them to create some new, doppelgänger, PRC version of Zapper. If he could obtain a copy of the algorithms, it would be useful only as evidence of who had perpetrated the hack. Chris figured that the best he could do would be to get photos of Li Owyang and Bingwen Ma. If he could gain access to their apartment, he might be able to obtain evidence proving their links to the PLA and the Datong Road operation. But attempting some sort of break-in seemed too risky.

He sat on the bench for an hour, but no one else emerged from the apartment building. He began to wonder if there might be a rear exit. In any event, Chris couldn't spend all night occupying the bench in this deserted playground. He was suspicious-looking enough as it was.

Footsteps crunched on the dead grass behind him. Probably a parent and child making use of the playground slide before it grew dark. But before he could turn around to check, Chris felt something nudge his back.

"That's a gun," said a male voice behind him in Mandarin. "Just stand up slowly. Don't turn around. We're going to cross the street and go inside that apartment you're so interested in."

11

Like all risk takers, Chris desperately wished that he had folded his hand a few minutes sooner. He had promised himself not to put his life on the line for this assignment, but that was exactly what he had done.

As Chris was marched across the street and up the stairs of the apartment building by the man with the gun, he cursed his poor judgment and struggled to suppress a rising panic. It would be so easy to disappear in a place like this. If he went missing, Zoey, his law firm partners, and Paul Saperstein and Zapper would make inquiries through all of the official channels, but the trail of clues would soon go cold, and he would simply vanish into the vast expanse of China.

When Chris faced the door of the top-floor unit, the man reached past him and knocked, all the while keeping the gun on Chris. A young man with soft features and shoulder-length hair answered the door. Chris saw the shock register on his face when he saw Chris had been brought there at gunpoint.

"What's going on? Who is this?" he said in Mandarin.

"I don't know yet. Are you going to let us in, or are we going to have to do this in the hallway?"

The young, doughy-faced hacker opened the door, and the man with the gun gave Chris a hard shove, sending him stumbling into the center of the room.

"Turn around."

Chris faced the man with the gun for the first time. He was in his mid- to late forties, with a hard, lined face. He was wearing a blue, short-sleeve silk shirt that showed his sinewy forearms.

"Bingwen!" called the hacker. "Get in here, man!" Clearly, the doughy-faced kid with the wispy moustache was Li Owyang, Mei-Hua's brother. He was wearing a black T-shirt with the word "Metadata" printed on it in the style of Metallica's logo.

The apartment was littered with fast-food containers and beer cans. A second young man appeared from one of the bedrooms at the rear of the apartment, long limbed and skinny, with a pale, acne-pocked face. Bingwen Ma.

"Put that gun away, will you?" Ma said.

The man with the gun ignored him and addressed Chris. "Why were you watching the apartment?"

"I was just sitting in the park. Can we speak in English? My Mandarin's rusty."

"No one sits in that park," Owyang said in English.

"I was just getting my bearings. After the riot at the factory."

"What were you doing at the factory?" the gunman asked, also in English.

Chris decided that it was best to stick as close to the truth as possible. "I'm a lawyer with a US law firm. My client sent me here to examine the Commsen factory, because they're trying to decide whether to use it for a manufacturing project. They had heard some disturbing stories about the facility."

"That sounds plausible," Ma said.

"I'll decide what's plausible," the gunman said. "You didn't see the way that he was staring at this place. Hand over your wallet."

Chris slowly removed his wallet. Slowly, because he was doing an inventory of what was in there that might indicate his true objective.

The gunman rifled through the contents of the wallet and removed Chris's business card. He handed it to Owyang. "Zapper him."

Owyang went to a laptop and began reading the search results. Chris felt sick because he knew what they would find.

"This guy's a privacy and security expert. There are articles about how he hunts down hackers."

Chris decided that there was no point in trying to carry on with the lie. "I represent Zapper. They know that you all were involved in the theft of their intellectual property."

Ma and Owyang exchanged startled looks that pretty much confirmed the accuracy of that statement.

"You've been misinformed," said the gunman.

"I don't think so."

"Who told you to come here?"

"That's privileged."

"We'll see about that."

"How does he know about us?" Owyang asked.

"Shut up!" said the gunman.

"That kind of sounded like a confession to me," Chris said. "Look, my colleagues in the US know where I am right now. They know everything that I know about the Zapper intrusion. The smart thing to do would be to put away that gun and just let me walk out of here."

"I don't think anyone knows you're here," said the gunman. "But we're going to know all of the details soon enough. What you know, what you don't know. Who knows you're here. We're going to know everything that we could possibly want to know about you—because you're going to tell us."

While he was saying this, the gunman was searching the kitchen for something. Items rattled and clanged as he combed through the drawers.

"What are you looking for?" Owyang asked, sounding anxious.

"I'll know it when I see it," the gunman said.

"Shouldn't you be calling this in to your bosses?" Ma added.

"I'll get to that after I've completed my interview," the gunman said. "I'd like the opportunity to handle this part myself." Finally, he smiled and lifted a rolling pin from the drawer. "I didn't expect to find one of these here," he said.

"I bake," Owyang said. "It relaxes me."

The gunman measured the heft of the rolling pin, smacking it into his palm. Chris couldn't help but follow each motion with his eyes.

"I know who you are—Li Owyang and Bingwen Ma," Chris said. "You're both going to be held accountable for anything that happens here."

"How about me? Do you know who I am?" asked the gunman, swinging the rolling pin at his side like a batter in the on-deck circle.

"No, I don't."

"That's too bad. Because I'm the one you really need to worry about."

The gunman tucked the pistol into the small of his back underneath his shirt and advanced on Chris.

"You don't have to do this," Owyang said.

"No, you're right. I don't. I could start putting bullets in him—in his foot, his hand, his knee." To Chris, he added, "Bet you'd prefer the rolling pin to that."

"These are the choices?" Chris asked.

The gunman gave a humorless smile and then swung at Chris. Chris raised his right forearm to block the blow and felt the rolling pin crunch bone.

Reflexively, he pulled his damaged arm down and cradled it with the left arm, the pain obliterating all reason. That gave the gunman a clear shot for his next blow, which struck the base of Chris's skull. A searing flash exploded behind his eyes. He went down hard and fast next to a low coffee table, a corner grazing his forehead and drawing blood.

Ma said, "You should give me the gun while you do this, Park."

"Are you kidding?" the gunman said. "You've never fired a gun in your life."

Another blow struck Chris's ribs, and the air went out of him. Chris was barely conscious, and his vision was blurred. One more blow to the head and he would be unconscious or dead.

Park's face swam into view as he bent down to take stock of the damage.

"Now we can have a proper conversation. Who knows that you're here?"

"Paul Saperstein and everyone at Zapper."

"Let's try again." Park brought the rolling pin down on Chris's left hand.

From his prone position, Chris saw the tip of a ballpoint pen on the edge of the coffee table above him. Reacting to the pain, barely thinking, Chris reached up with his right hand and grabbed the pen.

"What are you doing?" Park said. "You ready to write up your confession?" He gave Chris a cruel smile. "I'm afraid it won't be so easy as that."

Park was still grinning when Chris jammed the pen into the side of his neck. Blood immediately began to well around the barrel of the pen. With a pained, incredulous look, Park drew the pen slowly from his neck. Blood immediately began to spurt from the wound in time with the man's racing heart.

I must have hit an artery, Chris thought distantly as Park stood straight and wandered around the room, blood geysering between his fingers. Owyang and Ma started following him around like they wanted to help but didn't know how.

"Put pressure on it!" Ma cried.

Owyang had grabbed a towel from the bathroom. "Just stop moving and we'll wrap this around it."

Park didn't seem to hear them. He turned from the other side of the room to gaze at Chris again like he had just figured out the last thing he wanted to do. Then he staggered over to Chris and fell upon him.

Chris tried to squirm away, but Park got his hands around his throat and began squeezing with surprising strength, their faces only inches apart. Chris's Mandarin wasn't good enough to discern whether what was coming out of Park's mouth was speech or simply inarticulate screaming.

Chris gasped for air as he stared into Park's contorted features, not sure which of them would draw his last breath first.

But then Park's grip on his throat began to loosen. A few seconds later, Park's hands fell away, and he fell silent.

Chris tried to get out from under the dying man, but he was too damaged and dazed to move him.

Owyang and Ma crept in closer, horrified looks on their faces.

"We should get the gun," Owyang said.

"I'm not going to get it. You get it," Ma replied.

"The American's not dead yet. We need to finish this."

"I think he can hear us, you idiot. Just do it."

"*Just do it*," Owyang mimicked. "You need to get it through your head that you are not my boss."

"All right, fine. I'll get the gun. But you're going to owe me."

Chris heard their conversation faintly, but he couldn't see them, because his vision had grown cloudy, and he felt that he was somehow drifting away from himself. Blacking out, he realized.

No. He had to retain consciousness, because as soon as the two hackers stopped bickering, one of them was going to kill him.

Chris cast about Park's body and found the pistol still tucked in the small of his back under the shirt. He gripped the gun and pointed it at Owyang and Ma.

"Get him!" one of them screamed.

Chris saw the figures moving in close and felt the fear like pain masked by anesthesia. He squeezed the trigger. Then he squeezed it again and again, too far gone to even aim properly.

The sound was deafening in the small apartment, and he smelled cordite. He kept pulling the trigger even after the chamber was empty.

Click. Click. Click.

Then whiteness bloomed before his eyes, and he lost consciousness.

12

Zoey didn't like answering to anyone, and she didn't like taking tests. When she was called down to the Zapper headquarters to present her findings to the company's all-star security team, that was what it felt like—a test. Zoey had never done well on a standardized test in her life—probably because she was not standardized.

But as she was led back to the Einstein Auditorium, a large room with amphitheater seating, and took her place at the podium, Zoey recognized that this was not a standardized test; it was a challenge. Zoey liked challenges, and she liked proving doubters wrong.

Chris had told Zoey all about his late-night meeting with the new Zapper security team, but she was still a bit taken aback when she saw the faces of a dozen or so of the world's top security and computer forensic minds staring up at her from the audience. SoNar. Carina Blount. Doug Reeves. Sergei Timoshev.

Dez Teal stepped up beside her, testing the microphone with a tap. "Team, team, we're going to get started now. This is Zoey Doucet, who works with Chris Bruen and runs Reynolds Fincher's forensic lab. We all owe her a debt of gratitude because she assembled much of the evidence that led us to target the PLA facility on Datong Road in Shanghai as the likely source of the intrusion. We thought it would be useful for Zoey to level-set, walk you through her findings so that we're all on the same page."

Zoey caught the glances and eye rolling in the audience. Use of the term "level-set" suggested that she had gained a lead on the assembly of high-priced data security talent, and they were not used to being brought up to speed. They were paid to bring other people up to speed. It promised to be a tough room.

Zoey opened her laptop and projected it on a large screen behind her. "Thanks, Dez. I'm going to walk you through the evidence that led us to conclude the Datong Road facility is the base of operations for the Third Department, Second Unit of the PLA."

She proceeded to flash one obscure document in Mandarin after another on the screen. The job listings that indicated Unit 61398 was hiring English-speaking hackers. The academic articles that suggested the unit was a source of expert information on covert communications and network security. The China Telecom correspondence offering a "national defense discount" for installation of fiber-optic communications infrastructure.

The first interruption came from Sergei Timoshev, who was sitting in the front row. "Excuse me, please."

"Yes," Zoey said. "It's Sergei, right?"

"This is all very—circumstantial. Clearly."

"True, but Chris has already uncovered additional *concrete* evidence that we were right about Datong Road. So it seems that we're past the point of questioning the findings of our initial investigation. *Clearly.*"

Sergei's eyes narrowed. He wasn't used to being mocked. "And where is this new concrete evidence?"

"In China. With Chris. We'll be able review all that when he returns."

"Then not so concrete, is it?"

"What is your—?"

Dez stepped in and interrupted Zoey before things got out of hand. "Thank you, Zoey, for that excellent summary. Now let's move on to some of the leads that you're currently pursuing."

Zoey knew that this was going to be the most difficult part of her presentation. It would be easy to criticize and poke holes in what was coming next, but if her instincts were right, then it was too important to withhold.

"Well, just in the past twenty-four hours I've found something that troubles me. It's not solid, but I thought you all should know so that you can consider it and maybe build on it." She hit a key on the laptop to display a string of text on the screen. "This is a message board chat between someone we believe to be a manager of Unit 61398 and some sort of contractor. We've had it translated from Mandarin."

"How do you know that this person is a manager?" It was Carina Blount, of Blunt Object Consulting.

"That was established by reviewing many posts by this individual over the course of several weeks. Time and again, but usually in subtle ways, he demonstrates manager-level knowledge of the unit's operations. I'd be happy to produce those materials after the presentation if you'd like to review them."

"Yes, I would," Blount said.

Zoey picked up a laser pointer and focused it on a line of the chat message. "Here, the manager is chatting with the contractor about the Deep Web and Silk Road."

Silk Road was a popular website offering illegal goods and services, located in what is known as the Deep Web, a vast collection of websites and databases that search engines like Zapper have not indexed for their search results.

She moved the pointer. "Here, the contractor refers to Silk Road and says, 'Isn't that where Red Sun has set up shop?' The manager responds, 'If you want to continue this conversation, then we need to move to an encrypted channel.'"

Zoey turned back to the audience. "That got me wondering who or what Red Sun was. So I combed through Silk Road until I found this on a page called "White Wolves Professionals." She hit a key to display a screenshot of what could have been any slickly designed corporate website, except that it was filled with efficient-looking men aiming high-powered rifles and handguns, their faces in shadow or turned artfully away from the camera.

"'White Wolves Professionals' offers the services of hit men, and here is a page dedicated to a contract killer who goes by the name Red Sun."

The webpage for Red Sun included another anonymous photo of a man with a high-powered rifle, probably lifted from a gun catalog. The text read simply, "Professional hits—clean, experienced, anonymous. Standard pricing in bitcoin."

As Zoey went on to demonstrate to the room, pricing was listed on another "White Wolves" page, ranging from twenty-five thousand dollars for a "citizen" to two hundred fifty thousand dollars for a CEO, and fifteen million dollars for a head of state.

"So what are you saying here?" Timoshev asked. "Do you really think the PLA, with all of its trained soldiers and spies, would need to hire a contract killer?"

"I'm not drawing any conclusions, just showing you what I found," Zoey said. "But I suppose if you wanted to build a theory, you could say that maybe the PLA would use a contract killer like this Red Sun for a job where they wanted complete deniability and virtually no electronic evidence trail. As we all know, that's the beauty of the Deep Web, TOR, and Silk Road."

When searching the Internet, most users merely dipped their nets in the sunny shallows of a wide sea of data, never plumbing the dark reaches of the Deep Web. But in order to enter that world, where criminals transact their business in anonymity and with impunity, the price of admission was merely the download and installation of some free software.

The Deep Web had been born in 1996 as a project of three scientists at the US Naval Research Laboratory, who presented a paper titled "Hiding Routing Information" at a workshop in Cambridge, England. The paper outlined the features of a system initially known as "onion routing" that would permit users to access the Internet without ever revealing their identities to web servers or routers. The special browser used to access the Deep Web, known as TOR (for The Onion Router), was highly anonymous because it used onion-like layers of encrypted connections.

In onion routing, a connection to a particular server, such as the one offering Red Sun's services as a killer for hire, was routed through a chain of other computers, or nodes, with each node peeling away another layer of encryption. At any link in the chain, it was impossible to tell where the message had come from or where it was going, ensuring an extraordinary degree of anonymity. Payment for Red Sun's services was equally anonymous because all transactions on Silk Road were conducted using bitcoin, an online form of currency that could be translated into dollars.

Timoshev shook his head in disbelief. "You know this Red Sun, and all of the hit man ads on Silk Road, are probably just shams, pranks."

"Perhaps."

"And why would a manager of Unit 61398 be chatting on a message board?" Blount asked.

"It was an IRC board, so he believed that there would be no record of the chat messages. Also, they were off duty and weren't talking about official business. They just slipped up a few times and dropped some hints."

Internet Relay Chat (IRC) boards were a popular mode of communication for hackers because they were not hosted by an Internet service provider, so records of the chat messages were not stored.

Timoshev resumed the questioning. "And are you telling us that, in all of Silk Road, this so-called killer was the only person using the name Red Sun?"

"I was getting to that," Zoey said. "There were some other references to Red Sun on Silk Road. It's also the name of a brand of heroin, and a couple of online drug dealers have taken Red Sun as their alias."

"So what makes you think that this manager wasn't simply a drug addict?" Timoshev asked. "Isn't it a little—melodramatic—to think that he's talking about a contract killer?"

"Based on the context of the messages, I thought it was more likely to be a reference to a hit man. I guess you could call it an instinct."

More eye rolling from the audience.

"So really, Zoey, what *is* the point of presenting us with this?" Carina Blount asked. "Are we supposed to be scared?"

"You're supposed to draw your own conclusions," Zoey said. "But if Chris succeeds in China and brings back evidence that would be damaging to the PLA's economic espionage program, a program that they've clearly invested a huge amount of money and resources in, then that sounds to me like a situation where they would want to strike back hard while maintaining complete deniability. Knowing that, and then seeing a connection between the PLA and this Red Sun character, well, yeah, that scares me."

At that point the presentation broke down as the assembled experts piled on with a barrage of questions and criticisms. Zoey had been expecting it, but she still found herself unable to respond politely, and Dez swiftly brought the session to a close before the company's high-priced assemblage of security talent came to blows.

Zoey had known that the presentation wouldn't end well, but she didn't regret having brought forward the information about Red Sun. The thought of the PLA working with a contract killer *did* frighten Zoey, and she thought that it should scare everyone in the room. At least now they couldn't say they hadn't been warned.

13

When Chris finally came to, he was shocked to find himself staring into the face of the gunman, Park, inches from his own, eyes open. The dead man was still sprawled on top of him, and his blood covered everything around them.

Repulsed, Chris pushed away from the body and stood up. He was unsteady on his feet, and his head ached with every movement. His hands were shaking, and he was nauseated from the adrenaline and the smell and feel of the bright, sticky blood, much of which had soaked through his shirt to his skin.

Smog-burnished sunset light streamed through the curtains, suggesting that an hour or more had passed. On the floor beneath the window were the bodies of the two hackers, Li Owyang and Bingwen Ma. Owyang had taken a bullet to the forehead, and Ma had been struck twice in the chest. Several more stray bullets had pocked the plaster walls.

The metallic smell of blood seemed to thicken the warm, still air in the apartment. Chris felt sharp electric pain in his right arm and side. If he had to guess, he would say that he had a cracked rib and a fractured forearm.

He found it hard to grasp that he had been responsible for the deaths of these men, but he knew that each of them had been prepared to kill him. But once his pain-clouded mind had absorbed the terrible facts of his situation, panic began to set in. It was the same panic Chris associated with one of his recurring nightmares, in which he had done something horrendous and irreversible. But in this moment, as in the recurring nightmare, one thing was certain— he needed to start running.

Chris realized that Mei-Hua could return to the apartment at any time. He had to get out of there, but first he would finish his assignment. He had come too far and paid too high a price to do otherwise.

He found a laptop and shoved it in his computer bag, even that simple motion bringing a stab of pain. There would be time to review its contents later, but Chris suspected that it would hold evidence that Owyang and Ma were involved in the Zapper hack.

Chris removed the gunman's wallet. An ID badge showed that his name was Xi Park and he was some sort of security officer in the People's Liberation Army. He had probably been assigned to protect the hackers or escort them to their next assignment. The PLA and the Chinese government would be using all available resources to track down the hackers' killer because they would immediately suspect that this was retribution from the US for the APT1 intrusions.

At a sudden sound in the hallway outside, Chris froze. He heard keys jangling on a chain, so he picked up Park's gun again and faced the door. A woman's voice cursed softly in Mandarin, and there was the sound of a package being placed on the floor. It could be Mei-Hua, but he wasn't sure.

The sound of a key turning in a lock.

But it was not the door to that apartment. It was the unit across the hall. Chris's heart rebooted, and he began to breathe again.

He photographed Park's face and IDs with his smartphone. He photographed the bodies of Ma and Owyang. He recognized that it was risky to carry the laptop and photos with him, because they were all the evidence needed to arrest him for three murders. If he felt that his pursuers were closing in, Chris would abandon it all with the computer bag.

Before Chris could leave, he would have to do something about his clothes, which were smeared with blood. He searched the closets and found a shirt, pants, and hooded jacket that fit him. Chris shoved his bloody clothes into a trash bag from the kitchen. He would toss it into a dumpster once he was several blocks from the scene.

He pulled the hood up over his head, stifling a cry of pain. If someone saw him, perhaps they might mistake him for Owyang or Ma, though he was taller than both of them.

Chris turned the doorknob and ventured out onto the landing. No one in the stairwell.

Chris crept down the stairs, stepped onto the sidewalk, and walked quickly away from the building, keeping his head down. When he was a half block away, he glanced back to see if he was being followed. It was then that he saw Mei-Hua returning, carrying a brown paper grocery bag. She passed him on the opposite side of the street and did not see him. He watched her enter the building.

A minute later Chris heard Mei-Hua screaming. He strode quickly away toward the train station, anxious to get out of earshot.

*   *   *

Headed south on a clattering train to Beijing, Chris once again watched the apartment buildings, with their red-tile roofs, give way to factories, which in turn gave way to fields. He had taken the first train out of the station, regardless of the destination. The important thing was to quickly put as much distance as possible between him and that blood-spattered apartment. He wanted to cradle his damaged arm, but he let it dangle painfully at his side so that he would attract less attention on the street.

Chris noticed a spot of dried blood on his hand and rubbed it away with his thumb. He had spent ten minutes in the train station restroom cleaning himself up, but he kept finding traces he had missed. He knew he would find more things he had missed, and that frightened him.

Chris removed the laptop from the backpack and opened it up, then examined his aching forearm, which was covered with an enormous violet bruise. With effort, he tried to ignore the broken bone and focus on the laptop. It was definitely Owyang's computer; the desktop image was a photo of him with a pretty girl at a graduation ceremony. Chris paused because he knew he was at a critical juncture. He wanted to immediately review the contents of the laptop but didn't want to muddy the forensics.

If he could get the computer back to his forensic lab in San Francisco (which was admittedly a big if), then Zoey would be able to access the files, which were almost certainly encrypted. If they contained the sort of information that he expected, then US-Chinese relations were about to become a lot chillier.

Chris couldn't stop replaying the deaths of Li Owyang and Bingwen Ma. He didn't feel any guilt over Park's death. After all, the PLA officer had been in the process of beating him to death with a rolling pin. Given that Park was a trained and deadly professional soldier, Chris could only attribute his survival to sheer blind luck.

But it had been obvious that neither Owyang nor Ma knew how to handle a gun. He also knew that if he had blacked out a moment sooner, they would have figured it out, and he would be dead. Even though it was self-defense, he wondered if he had a choice. Perhaps he could have aimed lower, taken them down with shots to the legs.

Owyang and Ma reminded Chris a bit too much of himself when he was an immature teenager who got in over his head in a hacking scheme. He knew from experience just how quickly the excitement of getting behind a firewall could turn criminal, and dangerous.

Chris had been on the verge of blacking out, so it was hard to reconstruct exactly what he'd been thinking in that critical moment in the apartment. As he assembled the working version of events that would become his memory of the incident, he became increasingly convinced there had been a choice and that he had made the wrong one.

Did Chris decide to kill those two men either because he was afraid or hurt or angry—or maybe, and this was the part that bothered him the most, simply because he wanted to? He would probably never know precisely what impulses were at work in the split second when he squeezed the trigger. Chris knew already, though, that he would continue to revisit that moment, even though the actual sense memory of the incident would only degrade, like an analog tape played too many times.

The night came, and he leaned his head against the cool, vibrating Plexiglas of the window and tried to sleep.

Some time later, he started awake. He eyed the faces of the passengers around him and found one man on the opposite side of the compartment watching him. Hopefully because Chris was a Westerner far from the beaten tourist track and not because he had killed three men in Shenzhen.

In his mind he returned to the apartment, retracing every one of his actions. Rather than questioning his decisions, he now began to wonder whether he'd left any clues that would set the PLA or other Chinese authorities on his trail. The deaths of Park and the two hackers were unlikely to be treated as a routine robbery-homicide. The PLA would probably give the apartment a thorough CSI-style forensic exam, and he had not been meticulous or clear-headed enough to remember everything. Not even close.

The best that he could hope for was a decent head start on his pursuers. He doubted he would be able to keep his plane reservation. The PLA would probably have his identity figured out before he could reach Shanghai, and put him on every watch list.

Chris flipped open his personal laptop, and the screen seemed to single him out in the dark train car like a solo spotlight. Fortunately, the train had wireless, so he attempted to send Zoey a message through their secure website.

After an agonizing wait, Zoey responded. The letters raced as she typed. He could sense her anxiety coming right through the screen.

ZOEY: You okay, Chris?

CHRIS: No, but I'm safe for the moment.

ZOEY: What happened?

CHRIS: Found Li Owyang and Bingwen Ma, but they had a PLA escort. They're all dead.

There was a long pause before the reply. She chose not to ask the obvious question of whether he had killed them.

ZOEY: Are you injured?

CHRIS: No, I'm on a train to Beijing. I think they're going to be pursuing me. Maybe they already are.

ZOEY: What can I do?

CHRIS: Need help getting out of China. Probably don't have much time.

ZOEY: Let me think.

CHRIS: I'll need new papers.

ZOEY: Right. Have an idea, but need to run it down. Sit tight and I'll get back to you.

CHRIS: Are you okay?

ZOEY: Don't worry about me. I'm fine. Just know that we're going to get you out of there. Even if we have to send in Seal Team Six.

CHRIS: Thanks, Z.

ZOEY: Thank me when you're home. Try to get some sleep.

The connection terminated.

Communicating with Zoey helped calm him a bit, but he found sleep impossible now. He gazed through the scratched Plexiglas window at the outline of a factory under construction. In the moonlight, the superstructure of the building looked like the bones of some great beast that had been picked clean by carrion birds.

A couple of hours later, he awoke to a pinging sound. He squinted in the white morning sunlight, which streamed through the train window. Outside were rolling hills and green fields. The pinging was a new email. From Zoey.

ZOEY: Go to the secure site. I have a contact for you.

Chris logged on.

ZOEY: I found someone who can help you. He's a dissident pro-democracy hacker named Guiren Song.

CHRIS: Are you sure he can be trusted? If he's a dissident, won't he be under surveillance?

ZOEY: It's possible, but he says he's not under active surveillance. Where are you right now?

CHRIS: Not sure exactly. I just woke up. But we're definitely not in Beijing yet. I'm in the countryside somewhere.

ZOEY: Good. The train is going to stop at a place called Badaling. Part of the Great Wall is there. That's where you get off.

CHRIS: And then what?

ZOEY: Buy a ticket to the Great Wall and go to the second parapet to the right of the entrance. You'll meet Song there.

CHRIS: How will I know him?

ZOEY: He'll be wearing sunglasses and a blue baseball cap.

CHRIS: What happens then?

ZOEY: We should let him tell you that. We've got a plan for extracting you, though. Second parapet to the right of the entrance, okay?

CHRIS: Got it.

A half hour later, the train was approaching Badaling. In the distance Chris could see the Great Wall stretched across the rugged green hills like a pale snake, its notched walls resembling a saurian spine. Chris knew that he was far from safe, but he began to breathe a little easier knowing that someone would be waiting for him and that they had a plan.

The train shuddered and slowed. *Probably routine*, he thought. Then the train came to a complete stop well short of the Badaling station. *Maybe there's some obstacle on the tracks.*

Then Chris saw activity in the car ahead. Railway agents were requesting the papers of train passengers—but only those who were male and non-Chinese. The Chinese authorities knew that he was on the train.

Chris rose slowly, careful not to look like he was fleeing, and made his way to the back of the car and away from the inspections. As he entered the next car, he saw another railway worker making his way toward him down the center aisle, inspecting passports.

He was trapped.

14

Chris was unable to go forward or back. His only option was to exit.

The pneumatic doors were set into an alcove at the rear of the car, so the approaching ticket agent couldn't see him when he ducked inside. Chris pushed open the doors and looked up and down the tracks. No railway workers were outside, so he jumped down, skidding in the gravel of the embankment. Once more the pain crashed over him like a wave enveloping a surfer.

Chris scrambled to his feet and ran away from the train. He needed to make it over the nearby hill before one of the railway workers looked out the window and spotted him. With each step he expected to hear a shout in Mandarin behind him or maybe even a gunshot.

As soon as he crested the hill, he threw himself painfully on his stomach and looked back at the train. No one was following.

After a few minutes Chris descended the green hillside dotted with white and yellow wildflowers into a ravine that paralleled the train tracks. He set off walking toward Badaling, which looked to be about a mile and a half away. Fifteen or twenty minutes later, he heard the train begin rolling again. He hoped that Song wouldn't stop waiting for him on the wall when he figured out the train had arrived without him.

As Chris approached Badaling, the Great Wall loomed ever larger before him, and its enormity began to sink in. He imagined the sheer volume of human toil that had been expended in transporting the enormous stone blocks and bricks across the mountainous terrain, then recalled the army of tech workers at the Commsen factory in Shenzhen. China had always had sheer numbers on its side.

He broke into a jog as he made his way along the ravine. It was a warm spring day, and sweat began to sting his eyes. The pain from his cracked rib, which he had begun to tolerate, ratcheted up to an excruciating new level.

If Song gave up on waiting for him, then Chris might not make it out of China. He could imagine the dissident nervously eyeing the oncoming tourist crowds, wondering whether he would be met by Chris or the PLA. Who could blame him for bailing out if Chris failed to show on time?

Finally, he reached the outskirts of the town, climbing out of the ravine and putting as much distance as possible between him and the train station. The Badaling portion of the Great Wall was one of China's premier tourist destinations, so the crowds were thick and would provide welcome cover.

When he saw the scale of the Great Wall up close, Chris was reminded that it had been a military fortification defending the borders of the Ming Dynasty long before it became a tourist attraction. If he had been greeted by this seemingly impregnable and never-ending barricade as a fourteenth-century barbarian looking for plunder, the imposing sight would have been enough to send him back to foraging for a living.

Chris passed through a courtyard with an unmanned police kiosk, a battery of ceremonial cannons, and a pole bearing a red-and-yellow PRC flag snapping in the wind. He paid his entrance fee and walked under an ornamental wooden arch and up a stone path to the wall. Whoever had chosen the site for the rendezvous knew what they were doing. It would be hard to pick out anyone in the throngs and, unlike most of the places he had been on the trip, here Western faces did not stand out in the slightest.

Once he was on the broad stone walkway atop the wall, he turned right and headed for the second parapet. The steps climbed precipitously up the mountainside to a forbidding tower that was white stone set against a background of lush, green mountain vegetation and unusually clear blue sky. Chris attached himself to a school of tourists making their way to the tower. He wanted to race past them, but he knew that would only draw attention. He glanced back to look for a blue baseball cap in case Song had already abandoned their meetup.

It was then that he saw that he was being followed.

His pursuer wore a gray uniform, and he was stocky, gasping a bit at the exertion of ascending the steps. He didn't look to be a PLA soldier and was more likely a parks worker who had been deputized into the manhunt.

The man quickly looked away, but there was no question that he had been staring directly at Chris. Perhaps he was just a pickpocket who saw him as another tourist mark. But pickpockets didn't usually wear uniforms. Chris's heart rate spiked. As in a chess end game, he had only a few possible moves now. If he didn't make the right ones, he would be captured in a matter of minutes.

A French tour group clogged the path ahead as they listened to their guide intoning from a book. Chris ducked into the band and used them to momentarily block his pursuer's view.

The heavyset man was now gesturing to a gray-uniformed colleague, who set out after Chris at a more athletic pace. Realizing that he had very little time left before he was apprehended, Chris glanced desperately up at the second tower—and there stood the man in sunglasses and the blue baseball cap: Guiren Song.

Hiding in the tourist group wouldn't protect him for much longer, so he bolted for the tower.

It wouldn't be accurate to say that things slowed down in that moment, but Chris certainly saw everything with a painful clarity. The man in the blue cap was younger than Chris had expected and had the blocky build of a wrestler. He had already spotted Chris, but more to the point he had also spotted Chris's nearest pursuer.

Song nodded at Chris and then took a quick step back into the darkness of the stone arch, which led inside the tower. When he reached the parapet, Chris followed him in. As soon as Chris was through the archway, Song grabbed him by the front of his shirt with both hands and brought his face close.

"I want you to listen to me carefully," he said in unaccented English. "I won't have time to say this again."

Chris nodded.

"Go down these steps and you'll find a garbage truck parked directly below us. Climb in the back and cover yourself up. You'll be driven away from the wall."

"Where will I be taken?"

"No time for that. Go."

As Chris descended the ancient stone stairway, Song turned and exited through the other side of the parapet. If he was lucky, the pursuers would not have spotted him with Chris or emerging from the tower.

Chris ran down the steps, taking them two and three at a time, feeling each shock in his knees. Near the bottom of the stairwell, a garbage truck had backed up into an alcove at the base of the tower, just as Song had said. He could see the back of the driver's head in the cabin up front, but he didn't turn around.

Chris tossed his laptop over the back gate of the truck and then attempted to climb after it. Despite his fractured forearm, he finally managed to pull himself up on the gate and throw himself into the mound of trash after a couple of agonizing failed attempts. As Song had instructed, Chris burrowed down into the sea of bottles, cans, and fast-food containers. At least it wasn't wet, and the smell could have been worse. Passersby couldn't see him, because the truck was shielded in the alcove.

Almost immediately after he had buried himself in the garbage, he heard the grinding of gears, and the vehicle lurched forward. Chris carved out an air pocket in the trash mound that allowed him to breathe and look up at the sky.

The truck rumbled through the visitor center that surrounded the Great Wall and stopped at the gated entrance. This chokepoint was the place where capture seemed most likely. Chris hunkered down deeper in what appeared to be a mountain of inscrutably labeled Chinese soda cans. He waited a few seconds. Then a few seconds more.

This is taking too long.

And then they lurched forward and were moving again, leaving the Great Wall behind.

He began to breathe easier as they picked up speed through the streets of Badaling. From his vantage point, Chris could see the tops of commercial buildings and, farther and farther in the distance, the Great Wall snaking among the mountains, as it always had and always would.

The driver left the surface streets and got on a freeway. The entire contents of the truck bed now seemed to be vibrating like overheated molecules about to undergo a chemical reaction. It was like being trapped in some hellish, filthy version of a Chuck E. Cheese ball pit.

Chris had no idea who was driving, but he hoped that he could be trusted. At this point he really had no choice but to have faith that

Zoey and the team at Zapper had found reliable partners to aid in his extraction.

The vehicle slowed a bit as it bumped along what felt like an unpaved road. They had probably reached the landfill or wherever the garbage was to be deposited.

There was shouting outside. Chris was alarmed, until he understood what they were saying. Protesters were shouting in Mandarin, "We were not consulted!" and "Send it back to Yangfang!" Apparently, the locals did not want this garbage dumped in their landfill.

The truck rumbled forward, and the shouting protesters were left behind, no doubt directing their protests at the next team of sanitation workers.

At last they came to a complete stop and the engine cut off.

"You can get out of there now," said a man's voice in English.

Chris clambered out of the truck bed, struggling for traction in the yielding sea of aluminum cans. When he was finally out and sprawled on the ground, Chris gazed up into the curious face of a skinny young man in the blue jumpsuit of a municipal garbage worker.

"I'm Quan Shao," he said in English, extending a hand. "We can't stay here."

"Where are you taking me?"

"Beijing. I'll explain everything when we're back in the truck."

Chris stood and for the first time got a sense of where he was. The landfill was a gray, blasted expanse that extended as far as the eye could see in rolling dunes of debris. He estimated it to be at least as big as twenty football fields.

The smell was assaultive.

Chris stepped up into the cabin of the truck, and they drove back out past the protesters, who hurled a few more shouts in their direction through the surgical masks they wore to minimize the stench.

"What's going on here?" Chris asked.

"Trash has just recently become a real problem for us. China became urban and industrialized practically overnight, which meant that people started eating more packaged foods, using more cartons, bottles, and cans—so a lot more trash. Americans have been living like that for a long time, but it was new here and it happened fast. Our landfills couldn't handle it all."

"So what are the protests about?"

"Party officials make decisions like where the trash gets dumped. The locals here in Changping believe that the party bosses screwed them in favor of Yangfang, another town eight miles from here. Changping has to accept Yangfang's garbage, and it's spoiling life here. This landfill is drawing such a huge amount of insects that it's affecting local fruit production."

"I guess I see their point."

The man parked the garbage truck in a lot on the outskirts of Beijing. They walked to a two-door Saab parked in the same lot, for which Shao had the keys. Shao then proceeded to drive him into the capital in the Saab.

They made their way on surface streets into Beijing, the commercial buildings growing steadily more dense and the streets more crowded.

"So where are you taking me?"

"My apartment. You'll get a new passport, and we'll tell you about the plan. Guiren Song will meet us there—if he makes it."

They rode in silence as they entered the outskirts of Beijing, which announced itself as nothing more than a series of unidentifiable commercial buildings and apartment towers with a bit more space between them than you would see in most US cities. To Chris, it looked about as glamorous and exotic as the anonymous San Francisco suburb of Daly City.

Beijing was organized as a series of concentric rings, marked by perimeter freeways. Chris read the street signs as they passed the

Sixth Ring Road, then the Fifth and the Fourth. These were all copies of the Second Ring Road, which had been built upon the ruins of a fortified brick wall that once encircled the city. The wall had been torn down by the communists in the 1950s and '60s, who were seeking to eliminate all traces of the old order, but it still made its ancient presence felt in the rings of clogged traffic that encircled Beijing like fatty deposits around a stuttering heart.

Shao left the Saab in a parking structure, and they walked to an apartment building on a bustling street just inside the Fourth Ring Road. As they ascended the steps to the third-floor landing, Shao glanced up and down the stairwell to see if anyone was observing them.

"Do you think we're being followed?"

"No, I don't think so, but we can talk inside."

The apartment bore all the trademarks of student lodgings. Thick textbooks filled with color anatomical drawings were open on the coffee table.

"You're a student?"

Shao paused for a moment, then said, "Yeah, I'm studying medicine at the Peking University Health Science Center. I'm going to be an immunologist."

"Is Song also a medical student?"

"It's best that you not ask too many questions about us."

"No, I understand." Chris realized that they were afraid he might be captured by the PLA before he could escape the country, and tortured until he gave them up.

"If you're a dissident, isn't it possible that your apartment is under surveillance?"

"I'm not on any watch lists yet. Song is, though."

"So you're a newbie."

"No, I've been at this for a while now, but I'm still under the radar," Shao said with a note of defensiveness. "You don't have to stand in front of a tank in Tiananmen Square to work for change. That's been done, and it wasn't all that successful."

"What makes you and Song take risks like this?"

"We're doing it because economic reform is not enough. If we stay on the course that the party has laid out for us, we'll end up with all of the worst aspects of your country and none of the best. You can keep your Big Macs. We'll take the *New York Times* and democratic elections."

"I can see how you'd want to make that deal."

"I want our nation to succeed and surpass your country, and I believe that we'll do that some day soon. But I don't think we need to do it by stealing your secrets. It suggests that we aren't capable of winning a fair fight."

Chris recognized Shao's proud nationalism as perhaps the defining trait of the Chinese people, and it spanned all demographics and ideologies. Regardless of whether you were a party official or a dissident protester, it was very likely that you believed China was destined to dominate the next century.

While they waited for Song, Chris cleaned up in the shower, and then Shao bandaged his injured arm and ribs. Chris was glad that Shao happened to be a med student. When Shao finished, the pain remained but felt manageable.

Within a half hour a knock came at the door. It was Song, looking surprisingly cool for someone who had just evaded arrest by seconds and inches.

Shao clapped him on the shoulder. "Chris told me what happened. I wasn't sure you'd make it."

Song walked across the room and collapsed into a chair, the stress finally showing.

"Did you get away cleanly?" Shao asked.

"I think so. They never saw me with him, so there was no pursuit. It was very close, though."

"You sure you didn't pick up any tails on your way here?"

"No, and you know I wouldn't be here if I had. I need a drink."

Shao produced a bottle of Suntory Whisky, and they sat down with Song at a table in the small kitchen and drank in silence until their nerves had settled.

After a few minutes of respectful silence, Chris asked, "Okay, so how do you propose to get me out of the country?"

"We have a fake passport you can use if you're stopped, but the idea is that you don't go through any checkpoints," Song said. "Every customs agent will probably have your photo, so it wouldn't do any good."

Song slid an authentic-looking blue Canadian passport with gold embossed lettering across the table. Chris flipped it open and saw that it contained an old photo of him with the name Henry Childs. The passport was stamped for entrance to China two weeks ago and also included a few other stamps for England and Spain. To his untrained eye, it looked very convincing.

"If I'm not going through customs, how am I getting out?"

Song drained his glass and poured another. "We know a captain of a container ship who's friendly to our cause. You're going to the port of Xiamen, and you'll be put inside a container vessel there and taken to Taiwan."

"How long will I be in there?"

"It takes about fourteen hours," Song said. "Xiamen is the closest port. You'll bring food and water. You'll be okay."

"What happens when I reach Taiwan?"

"We have someone there who will meet you and get you on a plane back to the US. You'll be getting another fake passport. It'll have an exit stamp from the PRC."

"How am I getting to Xiamen?"

Song stood and began spooning udon noodles onto plates for the microwave. "A driver will be here tomorrow morning to take you to Xiamen. It's probably not safe to be on the road at night because you're more likely to stand out. You can sleep here tonight."

Chris took a sip of whiskey. "Whether I make it out of here or not, I'm going to owe both of you a great debt."

Song and Shao gave a collective shrug as they ate their noodles.

"When I'm back in the US, is there anything I can do for you, for your cause?"

Song stopped eating. "You can get your story out about the PLA and what they're up to on Datong Road. This is our country, but sometimes the government needs to be embarrassed."

"You think it will make a difference here?"

"By itself, no," said Shao. "Not even close. But the first stroke of the ax never brings down the tree. That doesn't mean that you don't strike the blow."

"I'll drink to that," Chris said.

15

Chris walked through one of the *hútòng* neighborhoods near Tiananmen Square at nine in the morning, looking for the place where Song and Shao had told him that he would meet the driver who would take him to the port of Xiamen. Gingerly, he shouldered his pack, filled with provisions for his journey in the container vessel, as he made his way through the mazelike streets. It was easy to get lost in the *hútòngs*, which were narrow alleyways formed by rows of traditional *sìhéyuàn* courtyard residences. The *hútòngs* reflected a traditional way of community life that was fast disappearing as Beijing remade itself.

Just as he was admitting to himself that he'd become hopelessly lost and would miss his rendezvous, Chris spotted a series of white arrows painted on the sides of buildings and on the street. Apparently, he wasn't the only one who found it difficult to locate the second-rate tourist attraction that was his destination.

Even when he was standing in front of the place, he nearly missed it. It was the entrance to a small shop, with a sign over the doorway that read "Beijing Under Ground City." When he stepped inside into a tiny and nondescript room, his immediate reaction was to turn back. This couldn't possibly be the place. It looked like one of those obscure, empty shops where foreigners never understood what was for sale.

Chris resisted that impulse, stepping through a low doorway in the back that opened into a much larger area, where a man in military camouflage gear was selling tickets. It made sense that the entrance was so inconspicuous, given the site's original purpose. This was the entrance to Dixia Cheng, Beijing's vast underground city, a crumbling monument to Cold War paranoia.

In the spring of 1969, tensions between China and the USSR flared into armed conflict, which centered around a tiny island in the Ussuri River along China's eastern border. Eight hundred Chinese died in one battle in which the Soviets unleashed aircraft, tanks, and missiles. Mao Zedong took the Soviet threat so seriously that he began preparing an emergency evacuation plan in the event that the Soviets invaded Beijing. Sixty percent of Beijing's population was to flee to the hills, but the remaining forty percent of the population was to hide out in a Dixia Cheng (underground city) in the event of invasion, air raid, or nuclear war.

Chairman Mao put armies of Beijing citizens to work excavating the massive shelter, enlisting both adults and schoolchildren, a communal movement in keeping with the massive public campaigns of the Cultural Revolution. From 1969 to 1979, the underground city was excavated largely by hand. When it was completed, it was capable of housing three hundred thousand people for about four months and consisted of a network of tunnels as deep as sixty feet beneath the city, stretching about eighteen miles in length and spreading over a fifty-two square-mile area. The entrances to the shelter were hidden in small houses and shops like the one Chris had just passed through.

When the USSR disintegrated and threats of a Soviet attack disappeared, the underground city lost its purpose and fell into disuse.

Dixia Cheng eventually became a tourist attraction, but an obscure one, with most of its tunnels shut down.

What a strange place for a meeting.

Chris bought a ticket and descended into the hidden city, walking through echoing corridors to the appointed meeting place. Cold War paranoia seemed to seep through the arched concrete tunnel walls, which were damp with condensation. At this early hour there were only a handful of other tourists, mostly youngish Westerners with Lonely Planet guides. Chris passed a large dormitory-style room full of iron bunk beds with peeling Mao posters on the walls. There were rooms designed to house a roller-skating rink, barbershops, vaults where sunless crops like mushrooms could be grown.

Finally, Chris reached the spot where the driver was to meet him, the site of Dixia Cheng's movie theater. There were a couple of tubes of red neon glowing over the entrance, but that did not make the place look any more inviting. He stood in front of the cinema for a half hour as directed and began to suspect he had either been abandoned or betrayed. There were no other tourists around, likely because it was early in the morning and their meeting place so remote.

At last he heard quick footsteps approaching. It was a man wearing a faded khaki work shirt and jeans with black stains on the legs where he had wiped oily hands. He had a flat, expressionless face, and eyes that were sunk deep behind puffy lids. He would have made a good poker player.

"Bruen?" he said in a croaking voice.

"Yes."

"Let's go. But follow me at a distance."

Chris lifted his pack and followed the man through the tunnels. As they emerged back through the small shop that served as an entrance to the underground city, the camo-clad ticket taker took no notice of them. He was clearly not a real soldier. The outfit was probably some sort of nod to China's revolutionary past and the Mao era.

Outside, the morning sun was beginning to penetrate the smoggy haze that lay over Beijing. Chris's contact strode at a brisk pace for two blocks to a large fenced lot, where his truck was parked. Chris climbed up into the cabin of the vehicle, which appeared to be some sort of large moving van, and the driver got underway.

"How long will it take to get to Xiamen?" Chris asked.

"Depends on the traffic," the driver said.

"Why did you choose to meet me there?"

"Because almost no one goes there. And there are no cameras down in the tunnels. Up here, you never know who might be watching."

"I appreciate what you're doing here."

"No need to thank me," he said without removing his eyes from the traffic ahead. "I've been paid."

The truck crept through surface streets, which were congested by bicycles and the ever-present construction. Eventually, they reached a freeway heading east out of the city, cutting through the concentric circles of the ring roads.

Chris tried again to strike up a conversation. "Is the crew of the tanker ship in on this?"

"It's best that you not ask questions," the driver said.

"I just want to know if I should worry if someone sees me entering the container," Chris said.

"I'd worry about everything if I were you."

Chris was beginning to get an uneasy feeling about the driver, and it had nothing to do with that intentionally ominous remark. He didn't like the way the driver refused to look at him or speak with him. It was a sign of someone who wanted to distance himself from what he was about to do.

Another hour passed in silence as they followed the road along the Jiulong Jiang River as it broadened to its mouth and emptied into the Pacific. Hulking gray container ships lined the docks and, in the distance, the Haicang Bridge stretched across the harbor, as slender and tensile as the filament of a spiderweb.

Chris felt a rising anxiety as the truck pulled into the port and neared the docks. He had the unmistakable sense that he was being set up, despite having no evidence to back it up. And what choice did he have but to follow the plan? If he strayed from the carefully arranged path, he might never make it out of China.

He was going to have to decide in a matter of minutes whether what he was feeling was free-floating paranoia or an instinct that would save his life. What if the ship's route was longer than they had represented, long enough for his food and water to run out? What if the container wouldn't be opened for days instead of hours? If that was the case, then he would die of heat and dehydration inside that metal box like a dog left in a parked car.

Chris's mind raced as he tried to decide what he was going to do, toggling back and forth between the two options.

The truck pulled up next to the *CHSL Jupiter*, a docked container ship that looked several city blocks long. At that moment the driver turned to him and, for the first time since they'd met in the underground city, he smiled.

And that was his tell.

"Don't look so worried," the driver said. "Everything has been taken care of."

Chris merely nodded in response. He had only spent a few hours with the driver, but he knew without doubt that this man was not the type to offer reassurance. Rather, this was his way of closing the deal with someone he viewed as a clueless dupe.

The driver pointed to several steel containers the size of railway boxcars stacked beside the ship. "See the one on the bottom right there? It hasn't been sealed yet. You get inside there, and in about fifteen minutes or so that crane is going to pick up the container and lower it onto the ship."

"What do I do then?"

"You just sit there and wait. One of the crew will seal the container when it's onboard. He will not open it. You will never speak with him."

Chris figured that his only chance of escape would arrive when he was on board the ship. If he refused to enter the container, he had no doubt that the driver would turn a gun on him.

He felt exposed walking across the dock in the midday sun. Approaching the container, he saw that there was no padlock on the door. After glancing back at the driver to confirm that he was still watching, Chris opened the heavy steel door and stepped into the musty darkness. It took a while for his eyes to adjust, but slender strips of light filtered around the door's seams. The container was entirely empty. He sat down on the dirty floor to wait.

About ten minutes in, he was tempted to open the door to see if the driver was still there. Perhaps it was possible to run, but he finally decided that would be unwise. The driver would probably be watching the container until it was loaded on the ship.

He saw only one way out of his situation, and it wasn't a good one. But what other choice did he have? As he went through it again in his mind, he realized that it wouldn't do to keep carrying Li Owyang's laptop. He was going to need to remove the hard drive.

Fortunately, Chris carried the tools of his trade with him. He removed a set of small screwdrivers from his computer bag and went to work unfastening the bottom panel of the laptop to get at the hard drive. He quickly had two of the four screws out.

Outside, he heard the ignition of the crane turning over, then a metallic creaking sound that grew into a rumble. Moments later the container lurched upward into the sky, rocking sickeningly from side to side like a Tilt-A-Whirl. Chris was thrown and rolled on the floor until he steadied himself by lying spread-eagled. The laptop skidded across the floor of the container, and Chris scrambled after it. At least there weren't any unsecured crates inside the container or he probably would have been crushed.

He lunged and got his hands on the laptop. The container swung on a horizontal axis as it was hauled over the water to the ship. Chris tried to roll with the motion, holding the laptop aloft to protect it from being bashed against the wall. It was impossible to remove the tiny screws on the bottom of the laptop while the container was pitching and rocking.

The container plunged precipitously, until it landed on the deck with a bone-rattling, metal-on-metal jolt. At first Chris was so stunned by the impact that he wasn't sure if he'd retained his grip on the laptop. Now his window of opportunity was closing fast. If the captain was standing on the deck waiting to slap a padlock on the door, then he was trapped, and there was nothing to be done.

Chris hurried to remove the two remaining screws, struggling to calm himself and keep his hands steady for the delicate work. The last tiny screw came loose, and he popped out the hard drive. He sealed the drive in a Ziploc plastic bag and put it inside the front of his shirt.

Chris opened the door a few inches and looked out on the deck of the ship, an open, rust-red expanse dotted with the metal twist-lock spikes used to secure the containers to the deck. There were no crew members in sight, although the outline of a figure could be discerned in the darkened windows of the bridge tower, which rose from the opposite end of the ship.

He pushed opened the door of the container and stepped out onto the deck. There was no time for hesitation now.

Chris shut the door of the container and walked quickly across the deck to the railing. He threw the laptop and bag over the side of the ship and watched as they disappeared into Xiamen harbor. Chris's stomach clenched as he gazed down at the choppy, gray swells, but that didn't stop him from climbing over the railing and jumping feetfirst.

16

Stepping off the deck of the *Jupiter* was like jumping off the roof of a four-story building, and the impact knocked the air out of Chris's lungs when he hit the water. Beneath the surface of Xiamen harbor, he continued his flailing plunge. When his downward momentum slowed, he looked up, saltwater stinging his eyes, to see the sun reduced to a distant glimmer.

His shoes felt like lead weights now, and he wished he had removed them before jumping. There was no time to attempt that now. As it was, he wasn't sure he had enough breath to reach the air.

Chris began swimming, kicking madly. The sun didn't seem to be getting any closer. His cracked rib made every stroke painful.

For a few endless moments, his mind was blank as he struggled upward against the water, which fought and pulled at him like a human opponent. Finally, he burst into the air, filling his lungs and inhaling a fair amount of petroleum-laced saltwater in the process. He coughed, sputtered, and retched as he tried to keep his head above the choppy waves.

When he had recovered his bearings, Chris saw that he was about a hundred yards off the bow of the *Jupiter*. Any crew member who happened to be looking in his direction could have seen him, but he saw no one at the railings.

He confirmed that the plastic baggie containing Owyang's hard drive remained inside his shirt, then began paddling away from the *Jupiter* and back to the docks. His path led him alongside the endless, gray hulk of another container ship. With his clothes and shoes weighing him down and his injuries restricting his motions, Chris's swimming strokes had grown wild and not very effective. He swallowed more saltwater and coughed it up.

A life preserver splashed next to him, and he grabbed on to it. Then a rope ladder uncoiled beside him. Chris looked around frantically for other options and found none. This was no time to question what lay on the other end of the ladder. He gripped it and began slowly and painfully pulling himself out of the water and up the side of the ship.

When Chris reached the railing, hands reached out to grab him. He was hauled aboard, dripping, and laid out on the deck like the day's catch.

A half-dozen crew members crowded around to stare at him, probably trying to tell if he was crazy, injured, or both. Then the oldest of them—a small, wiry man in a dirty tank top—began shouting at him in a language he did not understand. He seemed indignant at Chris's apparent stupidity and the introduction of that stupidity to his ship. The man was clearly the captain.

Chris sat up and motioned that he did not understand. In Mandarin, he asked, "Do any of you speak English or Mandarin?"

A young crew member, who looked to be about eighteen, said, "I speak Mandarin."

"Tell your captain that I would like to speak with him in private—with you to translate."

The captain listened to the request and after a moment nodded. Then he barked a few sharp commands that sent the crew back to their tasks.

The captain and the boy led him to the captain's quarters in the tower, which was little more than a map-strewn cubicle.

As soon as the door was shut, the captain said something short and sharp.

"He says, 'Speak,'" the boy said.

"Yes, I got that," Chris said.

Chris told the captain that he was an American, who needed to get out of China by any means necessary.

The captain spoke and the boy translated. "Are the police after you?"

"Yes."

"What did you do?"

"Something that the government didn't like," Chris said, making a calculated gamble.

"He says the government doesn't like a lot of things."

Chris couldn't be certain, but he thought that the twist to the captain's lips might have been his version of a smile.

"That is very true."

The captain studied him, then said something, a fairly long sentence for him.

The boy continued, channeling the old man and unconsciously mimicking his laconic tone. "I don't want to know who you are or what you've done, but I'm going to let you stay on board if you want to go to Thailand."

"Thailand is fine. Tell him, 'Thank you.'"

The boy passed that along, and the captain shrugged in acknowledgment.

"And you're going to have to keep out of sight. There's a cot in one of the storage compartments, and you can stay there. Anapan— that's me—will bring you your meals."

"I appreciate the hospitality."

"He says you haven't tried the food yet." The captain turned to a newspaper that was spread across his small desk, signaling that their audience was concluded.

Anapan led him down an iron staircase into the bowels of the ship and the most depressing, dirty, claustrophobic space that he had ever inhabited. As unappealing as it was, Chris was so exhausted that he knew he would sleep as soundly here as he would on four-hundred-thread-count Egyptian cotton sheets at the Ritz-Carlton. But before he could pass out on his bunk, he needed to contact Zoey, who was probably worrying about him.

He had Anapan show him to a computer with Internet in a closet-size room that was available to the crew. Anapan referred to it as the "porn booth." As soon as he accessed the secure site, he received an instant response from Zoey.

ZOEY: Are you okay? What happened?

CHRIS: I got a bad vibe from my driver and jumped ship. I didn't trust him.

ZOEY: I guess your instincts were correct.

CHRIS: Why do you say that?

ZOEY: Because Song and Shao are in custody.

Chris found it hard to process the information. He had just left them that morning, and they had risked so much to help him escape.

ZOEY: Are you there? Are you okay?

CHRIS: Where are they being held? And what are the charges?

ZOEY: We don't have details yet. We may never know.

CHRIS: Were they injured?

ZOEY: Someone on the street saw them being taken away outside Shao's apartment by PLA soldiers. Their heads were bloody but otherwise they were okay. We think the driver must have given you up.

CHRIS: I owe them my life. We need to do something to get them out.

ZOEY: Where are you? Are you safe?

CHRIS: I'm on a container ship bound for Thailand. I think I'm safe.

Chris proceeded to provide the details of his destination in the Bangkok Port aboard the *Thailand Star*.

ZOEY: We'll have someone there to meet you when you arrive. It doesn't seem so important now, but I know that Saperstein will kill me if I don't ask—do you still have the laptop?

CHRIS: No, but I've got the hard drive. If the evidence is there, we still have it.

ZOEY: Then things may get interesting when you return.

CHRIS: Don't the Chinese have a curse, something about living in interesting times?

ZOEY: Yeah, well, they say a lot of things. They should just shut up.

Chris signed off, and almost as soon as he was back on his cot he plunged into a sleep so deep that he might have been drugged. As his eyelids grew heavy, he felt the forward motion of the ship cutting through the waves. The sense of momentum translated into his dreams, in which he was a bullet speeding to its destination.

17

Chris stood on the bow of the *Thailand Star* at sunset as it approached Bangkok Port, a cool wind in his face as the container ship sliced through the green waters of the Gulf of Thailand. The voyage from Xiamen to Bangkok had taken eight days. Chris had spent most of his time walking the ship's long decks and communicating with Zoey through the secure site. He had gotten some rest, and his bones had begun to knit, but he still had no new information about the fates of Song and Shao.

Chris had also had plenty of time to consider the driver's betrayal during the long voyage. At first he didn't understand why the driver had taken him to Xiamen at all. If he was working with the PLA, he could have pulled a gun on him at any time. Chris had reached the conclusion that the driver wasn't a PLA operative, just a sympathizer who had decided on the fly that he would rather betray the dissidents than complete his mission. The driver was too cautious to risk a direct confrontation, so he had been waiting until Chris was safely locked into the container vessel before turning him in.

The ship eased into the bar channel where the port was located on the left bank of the Chao Phraya River. In the distance, Chris could see the office towers of Bangkok, many of which favored a stair-step design that made it look like they'd had chunks carved out of them.

The ship passed beneath gigantic yellow gantry cranes that stood like sentinels guarding the entrance to the busy port. One of the docked ships had a city bus sitting incongruously atop each of its containers. The port was a crawling anthill of activity, with trucks arriving and departing, and dock workers steadying bales of copper wire as they were lowered from the cranes. Chris examined the scene closely, watching for any sign that the PLA was there to greet him.

He saw nothing that appeared out of the ordinary until he spotted a familiar face. Dez Teal, the executive VP of Zapper, was standing on the dock next to a black limousine. Chris never thought that the sight of Paul Saperstein's corporate minion could elicit such happiness.

Teal gave a little wave and a thumbs-up sign.

The ship docked with a tectonic thump. As Chris waited for the gangplank to be lowered, he realized that the captain was standing beside him with his translator, Anapan. The captain had traded his customary greasy tank top for a garish short-sleeve silk shirt. Apparently, this was his shore-leave attire.

"The captain has a question for you," Anapan said.

"Of course," Chris said.

The captain uttered a staccato sentence.

"He wants to know if we—I'm not sure how to translate this—fucked them up." Chris recognized Anapan's translation problem. The Thai language probably had as many terms for sexual intercourse as the Eskimos have for snow.

"Fucked up who?"

"The Chinese."

"Yes," Chris said. "I think we may have fucked them up good. Tell him, 'Thank you.'"

For the first time the captain's weathered face cracked into a broad smile, and he said something to Anapan.

"He says there's no need to thank him for that. The pleasure is his."

Chris shook hands with the captain and Anapan and headed down the gangplank to Dez Teal, who was pacing impatiently.

Dez rushed over to greet him as soon as he stepped onto the dock, pumping his hand. "Chris! It's good to have you back. We really thought we'd lost you."

"It's good to see you too, Dez," Chris said, the words sounding strange to him.

"Let's get you out of here," Dez said. "But first, you do have the materials with you, right?"

Chris reached into the plastic shopping bag he was carrying and produced the plastic baggie containing the hard drive.

"Excellent. Paul is very anxious to hear your story firsthand. We also want to get that hard drive to our forensic team."

"I could use a bed and a bath," Chris said.

"You can get both on the Gulfstream. Believe me, you won't be roughing it from here on in."

They climbed into the limo and drove alongside the Chao Phraya. On the opposite bank of the river were the spires of the Buddhist temple Wat Arun, adorned with multicolored shards of porcelain.

"Have you examined the contents of the hard drive?"

"No, I would have messed up the forensics if I'd tried to do that outside the lab." Chris didn't want to talk about China, because it would lead to the story of the three men that he had killed. Chris gazed out the window at the temple across the river, its dome glowing in the sunset.

"Gorgeous, isn't it?" Dez said. "It's called Wat Arun, the Temple of the Dawn, but this is actually the best time to see it."

Chris glanced at him as if to ask, *Who made you a tour guide?*

Dez added, "I've been waiting for you to arrive for four days. Had a chance to do some sightseeing."

On the way to the airport, they crept through the congestion that surrounded Khao San Road, a pedestrian thoroughfare a block from the Chao Phraya that was a mecca for backpackers. The neighborhood was teeming with hostels, cheap restaurants, and vendors hawking tourist trinkets and skewers of street food.

"Any more news about Song and Shao?"

"We have a source who says they're in a detention facility outside Beijing. That's all we know so far."

"Is the State Department working on this?"

"No, State doesn't feel that they can reach out directly to the PRC, because they don't want to acknowledge what you and Zapper were up to over there."

"Does that really matter at this point? The mission is over, and we're going home."

"It matters to the State Department because the Chinese will think the mission was government sanctioned. And it certainly matters to Zapper. The press would have a field day if they knew about this little exploit. People know us as the search engine that they rely on every day. We're not supposed to be engaging in covert ops abroad."

"You know, the press might think you were heroes for striking back against the Chinese."

"Perhaps that might be true if you hadn't killed those three men in Shenzhen." Dez grimaced as soon as he said it. "Sorry, that was insensitive of me."

"It's okay," Chris said. "It's the truth."

"I want you to remember that everything you did in China is subject to attorney-client privilege. You cannot make any public statements. No attempts to draw media attention to Song and Shao."

Chris chose not to respond. If there were a way for him to help Song and Shao, then he'd do it, regardless of attorney-client privilege.

Exhausted, Chris sank into the leather upholstery of the limo and stared at the tumultuous street life. Impossibly young backpackers in boy-girl pairings spun away from Khao San Road onto side streets like stray isotopes, still hoisting beers and vaguely dancing to a distant, pulsing dubstep beat. Chris tried to remember what it was like to be so young and unscarred.

Dez may have continued speaking; Chris wasn't sure. About a half hour later, the limo pulled onto the tarmac of a private airport in front of a massive Gulfstream jet. Dez and Chris boarded the plane and were greeted by the uniformed pilot, who nodded and said, "Whenever you're ready, sir."

The cabin of the Gulfstream G650 was bigger than most New York City apartments, all cream-colored leather and gleaming, burled mahogany.

"You ever flown on one of these?"

"No, it's a little out of my price range."

"One of the perks of working for Saperstein. It's the only way to travel. It can climb to forty-one thousand feet, above the commercial air lanes, and it has a top speed of Mach .925, nearly the speed of sound. Much faster than a commercial jet. We'll be back in Menlo Park in no time."

"Like I said, I just want a shower and a bed."

"Help yourself to the shower in back. I'll have the flight attendant make up one of the seats as a bed."

After he had showered and closed his eyes, Chris found it more difficult to sleep than he had expected. He was visited by the image of the two hackers, the amateurish assassins, closing in on him in that stuffy apartment in Shenzhen. He was raising the gun, and he knew exactly what he was doing as he pulled the trigger and sent them staggering backward in a fine mist of blood. He was pretty sure that wasn't exactly what happened, but it felt like the truth.

Guilt, emotion, and trauma had already muddied the waters of his memory, so Chris knew he would never really have a clear picture of the event. Now it was only a matter of deciding which version of the story he would choose to accept as the truth. But he couldn't shake the sense that he had wanted to kill those two young men and, if that were true, he wasn't sure what that said about him.

Chris believed that nearly twenty years of practicing law had not impaired his sense of good and evil, but in his professional life he was rarely called upon to make moral judgments. He was an advocate who helped his clients achieve their objectives, which were usually more about mundane matters like money or control, striking a financially favorable deal, or exercising leverage to achieve a business objective (which was usually also about money). Those issues were not about good or evil—they were about stronger arguments and weaker arguments, leverage and its absence. But if he had a choice in that terrible moment, then pulling the trigger in that apartment in Shenzhen *was* a matter of good and evil. The problem was, he no longer knew whether the choice had been his. In the absence of any certainty on that point, he was left to wonder how good he was, and how evil.

18

When the private jet touched down in San Jose, another limo was waiting to whisk them to Zapper's corporate campus in Menlo Park. Thanks to the lux accommodations of the Gulfstream G650, Chris actually felt ready to face the expected grilling from Paul Saperstein and his team of security experts.

Dez Teal ran interference as they entered the Zapper corporate offices and brushed past various security desks and midlevel corporate officers. It was only Zoey, standing in the middle of the hallway with feet firmly planted and a "thou shalt not pass" look, that brought them to a stop. She clearly hadn't slept or changed T-shirts in a couple of days, and her hair was pulled up in a ponytail, but Chris thought she looked amazing nonetheless.

"Paul is waiting," Dez said, as if that explanation would dissolve any obstacle.

"Paul can wait," Zoey said.

Dez looked to Chris for help.

"I actually need to speak with my colleague," Chris said. "Give us just a second." He motioned to an empty conference room off the hallway. "In private."

Dez nodded in resignation. "Not too long, please?"

Chris and Zoey entered the conference room and shut the door behind them. Zoey immediately body checked him into the wall and gave him a long, hungry kiss. Dez must have heard the thump in the hallway.

Chris winced.

"Are you okay?" Zoey asked.

"Cracked rib and a fractured forearm. Never mind right now." They finished the kiss and, when they finally pulled apart, Chris said, "I missed you too."

"You nearly got yourself killed," she said.

"But I made it back," Chris said. "Hardly a scratch on me."

"I'd like to put some scratches on you."

"That sounds like fun, but it will have to wait."

"I don't care if you have an audience with the boy king. You're going to have to stop putting yourself in harm's way like that."

"I had no idea it would turn out that way."

"Next time, send an associate. Isn't that what you guys do when there's a difficult, unpleasant job?"

"I think HR might have issues with that."

"We're not done with this conversation."

"I know."

Chris reached in his pocket and handed her the hard drive.

"What's this?"

"It's the hard drive of the laptop that I found in the apartment where Owyang and Ma were staying. I think you should take it back to our lab for analysis."

"And you still haven't reviewed the contents?"

"I wanted to keep the forensics as clean as possible, which is one more reason to do this in our lab."

"Right. Everyone here will be fighting so hard to claim credit that it could compromise the work."

"I'll see you tonight."

"Yes, you will."

Chris and Zoey returned to the hallway, looking disheveled. With a raised eyebrow, Dez conveyed that he had noticed but chose not to comment.

Dez led Chris into Saperstein's airy corner office, which looked out on the green expanse of the corporate campus. Chris had been expecting to be greeted by the entirety of Zapper's all-star security team, but he saw only Saperstein and Marty Lewin, Zapper's general counsel. Marty was a Silicon Valley legend and had served as the "adult supervision" to a host of tech giants as they negotiated the treacherous path from the garage to the NASDAQ.

"Welcome back, man," Saperstein said, shaking Chris's hand. "Are you okay?"

"I'll be fine," Chris said.

Saperstein seemed agitated. "I had no idea what I was sending you into over there, and I want you to know that I truly appreciate what you did. We all do."

"Thanks, Paul. Things got out of hand, but it was never my intention to escalate the situation."

Lewin took this as his cue. "Chris," he said with a curt nod.

"Marty." Chris knew that it was not Lewin's job to congratulate him. He was there to manage a crisis that had the potential to become an international incident.

Lewin motioned for Chris to sit at a table by the window. "I know that you need time to rest and regroup, but we're going to need to debrief you now, at least get the basics of the story down. The State Department will also probably need to be informed. It was fine to keep State in the dark when this was just an exploratory trip, but now that a PLA officer and two contractors have died, we're going to have to tell them."

"I understand," Chris said, taking a seat. If the Chinese government started making public statements about what happened in

Shenzhen, Saperstein and company couldn't afford to have the government believe that Zapper was holding back.

Chris recounted the entire chain of events, slowing it down to
provide every terrible detail of the confrontation in the apartment
in Shenzhen and the deaths of the PLA officer and the two hackers,
Li Owyang and Bingwen Ma. When he was done, there was a pro-
tracted silence.

"I don't know what else he could have done," Saperstein said.

"Well, it's a little early for conclusions," Lewin said. "But if the
public heard that story, a lot of people would probably be sympa-
thetic. No one likes to have their property stolen, and having a government backing the theft makes it all the worse."

"The problem is," said Saperstein, "if the public hears this story,
they're going to know that our algorithms have been compromised.
I don't want to think about what that might do to our stock price."
Zapper was one of the most widely held stocks, so a plunge in its
price would impact the savings of many individual investors and
perhaps the market as a whole. Saperstein also stood to personally
lose hundreds of millions of dollars if the stock price crashed.

"Of course," Lewin said. "But it may not be possible to keep this
out of the press. What happens next may depend on what's on that
hard drive. Do you still have it on you?"

"I gave it to Zoey for analysis in our forensic lab."

Saperstein shot an exasperated look at Lewin.

"That's disappointing," Lewin said. "Why didn't you just hand it
over to Dez Teal?"

"Zoey and our lab have made more progress on this investigation than anyone else on your team. I thought it was right that she
should get the first shot at this."

"We expected you to have it with you," Saperstein said. "It's
secure, though, right?"

"Yes, very."

Saperstein shrugged, letting it go. "Okay, but we're going to need that analysis right away. Let's assume for a moment that this is the smoking gun that links the PLA to the systematic theft of US intellectual property. What do you think would happen if we shared it with the White House?"

"Given China's role as the US's major creditor, they might choose to sit on it," Chris said. "While State would probably love to embarrass China with that sort of information, they might decide that the potential financial repercussions would be too great. If you insult the guy you owe money to, it's more likely he's going to call in his marker. The Chinese government has probably already assumed that my visit to China was endorsed, and maybe even sponsored, by the US government. If the president and State Department play that sort of information for leverage with Beijing, then that would probably just confirm their assumption that the US government was behind this operation from the start."

"Because that's how *they* do things," Saperstein said.

"Yes."

"And if China believes that the US government sent you there to kill a PLA officer and two of its agents as some sort of retribution." Lewin paused. "Well, who knows what sort of shitstorm that might provoke."

"What happens if the State Department takes the conciliatory approach, reaching out to China and sharing everything they know?" Saperstein said. "They could just decide to apologize for our actions. Make us the scapegoats."

Chris nodded. "If State goes that route, they would renounce our actions, disclaim all responsibility for the matter, and probably bring legal proceedings against us."

"On what charges?" Saperstein asked, clearly alarmed.

"Chris could be extradited back to China," Lewin said, "where he could face murder charges. The US attorney general could also probably come up with some basis for an enforcement action against Zapper, something along the lines of unfair business practices."

"If the press reported that Zapper had sent someone to China to kill the people who stole their algorithms, then you would instantly become the new poster boy for corporate malfeasance," Chris said. "It might even be fatal to the company."

Saperstein nodded. "But I still think the risks are greater if we hold out on the State Department. We have to tell them. Then the best we can hope for is that they bury this, and the Chinese do the same. Maybe this is just too embarrassing for all concerned."

Lewin turned to Chris. "Is there anything else that you need to tell us about what happened in China? We have some hard choices to make here, and we can't have any more surprises."

Chris contemplated his nagging doubts about the shooting in Shenzhen but knew that was not what Lewin was looking for. In fact, it was probably the last thing that Lewin wanted to hear from him.

"No," Chris said, "that's everything."

Lewin stood to indicate that the meeting was over. "Okay then. Thanks for being so forthcoming. Paul and I will need to talk now about how to proceed from here."

Saperstein leaned across, shook Chris's hand, and looked him in the eyes. "You put yourself on the line for us in China, and I will never forget that. We're going to support you in every way possible."

"I appreciate that," Chris said.

As Chris left Saperstein's office, he had the queasy feeling that his fate was about to be decided. He liked Saperstein, but in Saperstein's world when someone said they were going to support you in every way possible, it usually meant you would never hear from them again. And when they said they would never forget what you had done, it usually meant they already had. Lewin would make sure that all future inquiries from Chris were directed to legal counsel.

As he walked out of the Zapper headquarters amid a throng of young programmers, Chris suddenly felt very alone.

19

Tao received the email on his smartphone as he was sitting in a darkened movie theater in Shanghai watching a generic American action movie that featured an extraordinary number of car crashes. When he saw that the email originated from his Silk Road account, he left in the middle of the film so that he could view the attachment on his home computer. Tao walked up the theater aisle, enveloped in a Dolby maelstrom of squealing tires, rending metal, and fireball explosions that briefly froze the moviegoers in their seats like Pompeians caught in the Vesuvius eruption.

"Then let me ask you, Tao Zhang, have you ever killed a man?"

As he walked home, Tao recalled those words spoken to him in that wood-paneled office in Shanghai by Mr. Chen, the automobile factory manager, because they set him on the path to becoming a professional hit man.

Professional hit man. Sometimes he still had trouble believing that such people existed outside of books and movies and that he was one of them. Tao occasionally found it necessary to retrace the path that had led him to his vocation. Tao liked to entertain the notion that if he could find an implausibility, or a choice that he would have made differently, then he would somehow be transported into a different reality. One in which he didn't kill people for a living.

On most days Tao was a midlevel manager in an auto parts distribution company with no apparent ties to the PLA, the Ministry of State Security, or any other state agency. Mr. Chen had arranged the position for him through a friend, and for several months all he did was move boxes of carburetors and distributors in a warehouse and manage the company's inventory. But one day he received a call at home offering free one-on-one training sessions. At first he thought this was just a zealous telemarketer trying to sell him an expensive gym membership, and he hung up. But the man called again, more insistent this time, and it became clear that Mr. Chen and his friends were finally making contact. This was how they would decide whether he had the makings of someone who could be useful to them.

The training sessions were conducted by Bo Han, a former PLA officer, at a firing range on the outskirts of Shanghai, and after hours at a Wing Chun martial arts studio. Han never wore his uniform and never said that he was acting in any official capacity, but he gave Tao first-rate training in the deadly arts.

Although Han was not the sort to praise a pupil, Tao knew that he was doing well when the pace of training accelerated. Within a matter of months, Tao had learned the basics of firearms, hand-to-hand combat, explosives, poisons, and surveillance. Tao was not so arrogant as to think he had mastered these disciplines. There was always more to learn.

Once he was properly trained and the sessions with Bo Han concluded, Tao would never again meet any of his clients in person. That was possible through the impeccable anonymity of the Deep Web and the website known as Silk Road.

Silk Road was an enormously popular and successful online bazaar for criminal goods and services, offering everything from drugs to fake passports to hacking software—to hired killers.

When Tao had completed his training, he was instructed by Han to set up shop on the "White Wolves Professionals" section of the Silk Road, where professional hit men offered their services. He was told to identify himself as Red Sun so that his bosses would know they were dealing with Tao.

The White Wolves were a loose aggregation of putative hit men. As with eBay, you took your chances when you contracted directly with a private party. Some of the so-called hit men were probably outright frauds who would take your down payment and run. Tao doubted that many adhered to his standards of professionalism.

Tao had performed three hits so far, over the course of two years. Han told him he would never meet the people giving him his assignments. The anonymity of Silk Road would ensure that they could never be linked to Tao, and vice versa. While anyone hiring a hit man has an obvious desire for anonymity, this was doubly true of the people who trained and hired Tao. If there were even an implication that a state agency utilized the services of a professional hit man, then the diplomatic and political fallout would be disastrous. Tao was called in for the jobs for which even the PLA needed plausible deniability and they needed enough distance between themselves and their operative to ensure that even the covert branches of other governments couldn't make the connection.

On Tao's last day of training with Han, the workout had been particularly strenuous, focusing on martial arts. Wing Chun, the quick-handed style Han favored, combined striking and grappling and was effective for close-in fighting. It had taken time, but Tao had finally perfected the all-important Wing Chun stance, which Han compared to a stalk of bamboo—firm but flexible, rooted but yielding. It was all about adaptability and improvisation, and those were useful traits for a hired killer, even outside the context of hand-to-hand combat.

The gym's air conditioner was busted, and the air inside the gym was humid and still. At the end of the session, Tao sat cross-legged on the mat, his hair plastered to his forehead with sweat. Han sat next to him. Even though the workouts were designed to put the onus on Tao, his teacher was also breathing heavily.

They sat like that on the floor for a while as their heart rates came down.

Finally, Han said, "You're going to be good at this work, Tao. I can tell."

"It's not work I would have chosen," Tao said. "But if I'm going to do it, I should do it well."

"It's like hunting," Han said. "A hunter who is unskilled makes a mess of things, wounds the prey, causes unnecessary suffering. Some deaths are better than others."

"I understand, but I need to know one thing."

"Yes?"

"How long will I have to do this? When will my brother be set free?"

"I don't know the answer to that, but if you do your job, you'll get what you want. The men on the other end of this will honor the bargain."

Tao looked him in the eye. "And do you know these men? Is this something that you know about them?"

"The bargain will be honored." But Han glanced away as he said it, and Tao knew that he didn't really know.

Tao was bound to kill men he didn't know for other men who he didn't know, all in the hopes that someday mercy would be shown, and his brother and he would be released from this bloody pact. As Bo Han said, some deaths were better than others.

* * *

You would think that hanging up your shingle on the Deep Web as a paid assassin would attract a fair amount of user traffic, but it didn't seem to. Despite the anonymity of the Deep Web, even those who wanted someone dead were generally smart enough to avoid reaching out to a complete stranger to do the job. Although juvenile pranksters were probably tempted to email him just to see if he was really a hit man, even they must have sensed that it was best not to mess with whoever was behind the handle Red Sun.

That was fine with Tao. He was only interested in carrying out hits that originated from Mr. Chen and his group of powerful crony-capitalist friends, the ones that would bring his brother Wenyan closer to freedom.

Tao's apartment was in a gray high-rise apartment building that seemed less like a place where people lived and more like a place where they were stored. His unit was a one-bedroom flat on the eighteenth floor, where nothing was ornamental or personal, aside from a few photos of his brother and family.

Tao booted up his computer, opened the message's attachment, and found information on the target: a photo and his home and work addresses—in the United States. There was also the information for a contact in San Francisco who could provide him with assistance if necessary. The target, whose name was Chris Bruen, looked a little like a rumpled professor. An accompanying message informed him that Bruen was an attorney for the US-based search engine Zapper and that he had killed two PLA-affiliated hackers and a PLA officer as retribution for the extraction of certain Zapper trade secrets. Apparently, he wasn't as benign as he appeared.

Tao didn't usually get this much information about the reason for a hit, and it made him suspicious. Perhaps his client wanted to impress upon him the importance of the assignment, let him know the stakes were higher this time. There was a political component to this, and if the FBI or another foreign law-enforcement agency became involved, then this was going to be his most difficult job yet.

If this was a high-value target, then that should mean he would receive extra credit if he was successful. Tao wondered if this might be the hit that cleared the ledger and set his brother free. As soon as the idea came to him, he discarded it. If he allowed himself to carry that hope, it would crush him when it didn't come true.

Tao's payment was also included in the message, in the form of a digitally signed transfer of fifteen thousand dollars in bitcoins, half of his contract price. If Tao had been in it for the money, he would have been highly skeptical of accepting payment in the wildly fluctuating online currency.

Bitcoin transactions were all accounted for in a master transaction log, known as the blockchain. The blockchain's ledger verified and time-stamped all bitcoin transfers to make sure the same bitcoin couldn't be spent twice by its owner. The blockchain was maintained by a decentralized network of computer operators, known as miners, who received bitcoins in return for the contribution of their work and computing power to maintaining the system. Bitcoin transfers were encrypted, but not as elaborately as the Deep Web, with its onion-routing system. Nevertheless, it was very difficult to link a bitcoin transaction to a real-life identity. Bitcoin and Silk Road had made murder for hire available to anyone who wished someone dead. God help the world if that information became more widely known.

Tao found himself looking forward to visiting the US. Like most people he knew, he had grown up on American TV, movies, and music. He realized that he had never really thought of the US as a place where people actually lived and worked. It had always existed for him in his mind as some sort of obscenely opulent music video.

But what he was really looking forward to was getting back to work. It had been nearly two weeks since the hit on Ryuichi Naruse in Tokyo. When he had looked into Naruse's eyes on that blossom-strewn cobblestone path in Shinjuku Gyoen National Garden, he knew that something had changed about his relationship to his work. It was there in his brain like a tumor, but he didn't yet know whether it was malignant or benign.

In San Francisco he would find out.

20

As Chris swiped his security badge and walked through the door of the law firm's computer forensic lab, Zoey swiveled around in her chair to face him, backlit by an array of glowing computer monitors.

"We've got it."

Most of the Reynolds Fincher offices boasted breathtaking views of San Francisco Bay and Embarcadero, but in the forensic lab the floor-to-ceiling windows had been replaced by whiteboards—a security measure that served as a reminder that, even on the thirty-eighth floor, you were never safe from prying eyes.

On one of the whiteboards, Zoey had created a diagram of the evidence that they'd assembled while tracking APT1 over several months. Photos of the Datong Road facility in Shanghai were taped to the board, with black magic-marker lines radiating outward to scribbled hacker handles, photos, and bits of correspondence.

Chris greeted her with a kiss and sat across from her. "That's good news. Would you care to be more specific?"

"The smoking gun."

"A little more specific than that too."

"There are email exchanges here between Li Owyang and a Security Officer Yu that clearly provide the link between Owyang and Ma and the PLA. They also show that the PLA targeted Zapper."

"How are the forensics?"

"It would be nice to have the entire laptop, but this is clean. No one could say that the hard drive was tampered with, and we have clear dates and times for everything. It's irrefutable."

"I'm not sure that matters."

Zoey frowned. "What does that mean?"

"Saperstein and Marty Lewin are concerned about making this thing public. They're afraid that if word gets out that their algorithms have been compromised, the market won't like it."

Zoey shot him a frustrated look. "But, but—the Chinese stole from them!"

"Don't get me wrong. They want it to stop, but they'd rather deal with this quietly through diplomatic back channels. The State Department may threaten the Chinese with the embarrassment of disclosure, but everyone would prefer that it not come to that."

"But they *should* be embarrassed," Zoey said. "What they've been doing is outrageous. It gives hacking a bad name."

"Let's see what you've got," Chris said, sitting down next to Zoey.

"Here," she said, pointing at the screen, where an email string was displayed.

OWYANG: I'm surprised that you're hiring outside contractors.

YU: It's an important assignment, and we have heard very good things about your skills.

OWYANG: You've heard correctly. What's the target?

YU: Zapper.

OWYANG: Big time. What do you hope to get?

YU: We want the most high-value information available, which will probably mean having a persistent presence behind their firewall. We'd like to extract the proprietary algorithms for their search engine—that's the prime target—but we would also like to see financial projections, board minutes, strategic planning documents.

OWYANG: Very ambitious.

YU: Of course, they must never know that they've been hacked.

OWYANG: You don't ask for much, do you? I know some of the members of their security team. They're not lightweights.

YU: We know it won't be easy, and that's why we're bringing in you and Ma to supplement our considerable resources. Of course, you will also use members of our Datong Road team.

OWYANG: You want us to teach your team our latest tricks.

YU: Yes, and we're paying you handsomely for that service. You are aware that we don't have to pay you?

OWYANG: Yes, of course. We're proud to serve the national interest.

YU: Good.

Reading the email exchange, Chris felt sick to his stomach. Owyang and Ma hadn't even been willing participants in the Zapper hack. They clearly did not have the option of saying no to the PLA. He wondered once again whether he could have somehow avoided killing them. When he recalled the incident, the entire sensory experience enveloped him: the heat; the close, still air in the apartment; the sickening smell of blood. Chris knew he must be suffering symptoms of post-traumatic stress disorder, but recognizing it didn't make it feel any less crippling.

Zoey placed a hand on his knee. "Chris? You okay?"

"Yeah, just thinking it through."

"I think it's more than that," she said.

"Well, yeah, it is."

"But you're not going to tell me, are you?"

"Something I'm still trying to process."

"You're not that mysterious, you know. You're thinking about Owyang and Ma, aren't you?"

Chris's pained silence could not have been clearer.

"You aren't to blame for their deaths."

"Aside from the fact that I pulled the trigger."

"You know you didn't have a choice."

"See, that's the thing. I'm not so sure about that anymore."

"Yeah, well I am. I know the kind of person you are, and I know you're not capable of something like that. I wouldn't be with you if you were."

"Thanks," Chris said.

Zoey stood and came to his side, hugging him against her hip. "Dude, you need to stop torturing yourself."

He nodded. "I'll try."

She stepped back and, in an obvious effort to change the subject, held up a black flash drive. "So copies of all of the emails between Oywang and the PLA officer are on this drive. What do you propose we do with it?"

"We have to turn everything over to Zapper and the State Department. It's not our call to make."

"I don't like it," Zoey said. "Very unsatisfying. We have APT1 dead to rights. There are public records showing that Yu is a high-ranking PLA security officer, and the emails are from a governmental domain."

"I've been wanting to nail APT1 for years, just like you. But I don't want you keeping any copies of the hard drive or those emails."

"That goes without saying," Zoey said.

"I mean it."

"I know you do."

Chris checked his watch. "I gotta go. Richard Grogan wanted me to have lunch with him." Grogan was chair of the firm's corporate group.

"Grogan. Must be serious."

"Maybe he just wants to have a friendly chat. Promote collegiality, that sort of thing."

Zoey rolled her eyes. "Yeah, I'm sure that's it."

*   *   *

Chris chose Yank Sing, arguably the best dim sum restaurant in the city, for his lunch meeting with Richard Grogan. The place had a few advantages for this sort of occasion. First, the food was excellent. Chris was particularly partial to the shrimp dumplings and green onion cakes. Second, Yank Sing was a place where you could get in and out very fast because, almost as soon as you sat down at the table, the wait staff began running dim sum carts up to your table.

Grogan was in his early fifties, with salt-and-pepper hair and deep-set, alert blue eyes. He was an outstanding M&A attorney, but those same qualities also made him an annoying person to talk to. He never gave anything away without a quid pro quo, and he never let anyone off the hook. If Grogan was taking the time to have lunch with him, then Chris was certain of one thing—he must have something Grogan wanted.

"So how goes it?" Grogan led off.

"Good. Things are good."

"I was afraid we were going to lose you earlier this year. What an unfortunate mess that was." Grogan was referring to an incident six months ago in which Chris and Zoey had been suspects in a joint FBI/CIA investigation of a cyberterrorism threat involving a highly sophisticated computer virus known as Lurker. "So you're back in the old routine now?"

"Like nothing ever happened." That wasn't exactly true, Chris thought. He still held a bit of a grudge over the way the firm had summarily suspended him from the partnership at the first whiff of suspicion from the FBI.

"Glad to hear it," Grogan said. "I also heard something about a trip to China for Zapper."

"That's right. I'm advising them on an intrusion."

"China, cyberterrorism, hackers—my practice seems pretty dull in comparison."

"Oh, it all sounds a lot more exciting than it really is."

"That's not what I've heard. The Zapper team seems to be buzzing about your trip to China. Apparently, it's viewed as a big success."

"I'm glad they feel that way."

Grogan paused, clearly hoping Chris would share details of the mission to China.

"I'd love to fill you in, but Zapper has bound me to strict confidentiality, even within the firm," Chris added.

"Of course. Understood."

Grogan recognized that Chris had cemented his position as Zapper's primary lawyer with the trip to China, and that was why he had invited him to lunch. And as if that weren't maddening enough for Grogan, he wasn't even permitted to know what Chris had done to gain that status.

A waitress appeared with a cart full of covered trays. Grogan waved her away, but Chris countermanded the signal, saying, "Trust me, you want the barbecue pork buns."

Grogan leaned forward, suggesting that he was about to get to the point. "I want you to know how much I value you as a partner here."

"Thanks. That means a lot coming from you."

"I'm aware of the very close relationships you have with many of my clients, so I thought it would be good for us to take a little time to catch up. Present a united front and all that."

"Sure. Good idea." Chris thought he knew now where this was headed.

"I know you've forged some close bonds with Paul Saperstein at Zapper, Dave Silver at Blue Cloud, and quite a few others."

"Well, going through a major security breach together can be a bonding experience."

"Exactly. I imagine so. And so my point is that I want to make sure that you're happy here, getting what you need."

"Like I said, I'm good."

"For what it's worth, I didn't like the way the firm handled your recent situation."

"I appreciate that. So you voted against the suspension?"

Another person would have paused at that remark, but with Grogan it was more like the barely perceptible shifting of gears in an expensive car. "No, I felt I didn't have any choice but to vote for it, but I thought things could have been handled much better."

Chris shrugged. "Thank you for that at least."

Grogan was well aware that Chris was very close with many of the firm's top tech-sector clients, clients for which Grogan was the RA, or responsible attorney. RA credit for a client like Zapper was a significant matter because that company accounted for tens of millions of dollars in billings for the firm. As the RA for Zapper, Grogan pocketed a decent percentage of those revenues in compensation. Chris was designated as the AIC, or attorney in charge, for the matters that he handled, but there was less financial reward for that.

The problem for a person in Grogan's position began when a partner like Chris's relationships with important clients became so strong that Chris could take the client with him if he chose to leave the firm. Grogan feared that, after being suspended from the partnership over the recent incident, Chris might leave Reynolds Fincher with several of his major clients in tow. If Chris did that, Grogan stood to lose millions in compensation.

"I want you to know that I'm going to talk you up when I file my annual report with the Compensation Committee. I'm going to let them know just how integral you are to my practice and my clients. If there's something else I can do to support you, you just let me know."

"Well, you could always give me some of your RA credit."

They stared at each other over plates of sea bass and Peking duck. And then Grogan laughed heartily. A little too heartily. "I almost thought you were serious there. Good one, Chris."

"It was, wasn't it?" Chris smiled and dug into his food. Now Grogan was really going to start worrying about keeping his clients.

*   *   *

When Chris returned to the forensic lab after the lunch with Grogan, Zoey asked, "So how was your meeting with Grogan? What did he want?"

"Well, I don't think our conversation had the effect that he had in mind."

"How's that?"

Chris paused for a moment—so long that Zoey snapped her fingers to get his attention. "Hey, you still with me?"

"Have you ever thought about us having our own place?"

Zoey looked startled, "Are you talking about a house?"

"Um, no. Not at the moment anyway. I'm talking about our own law firm. Your own computer forensic lab."

Zoey swiveled around in her chair now, her back to the monitors. "Is this talk talk or serious talk? Because it would be cruel to lead a girl on that way."

"It's just talk—for now."

Zoey turned back to her array of monitors. "Hmm. That must have been some lunch. Did he pay?"

"No, but I think he might."

21

Tao Zhang had never seen so many Americans in one place, except on television during the World Series. As he advanced through the customs line in the hangar-like international terminal of the San Francisco airport, they were everywhere: wearing their National Football League jerseys; speaking in their braying accents; punching the buttons of their smartphones and tablets with their stubby fingers; playing Angry Birds; wiping the spittle from their blond, great-headed toddlers; eating McDonald's hamburgers, which appeared to be just as inedible here as they were in Shanghai, with their bird-shit spatters of Day-Glo-colored condiments; and authoritatively expressing themselves, as if their every trivial preference was a governmental edict.

Yes, that was really it, the trait that defined them as Americans— that confidence and authority. It was how you could always distinguish them from the self-effacing Canadians. It was bred in the bone, that attitude, which came from being told from birth that you lived in the greatest nation on earth.

But what if that ceased to be true? What would they do then? How would they behave? Now that was something Tao would pay good money to see.

And that day was coming. He didn't believe in communism or the party or his government, but he believed in China—as a people, as an overwhelming force of nature; as a giant that had been weak only because it had been constantly told that it was weak.

Even before he received this assignment, Tao had known that China was stealing America's intellectual property and trade secrets—anyone with access to the Western media had heard those claims. Tao didn't consider such an appropriation as theft—more like reparations for generations of the West's meddling with and oppression of China. If this hit was another way in which the PLA was drawing a line in the sand against the US, then that was fine with Tao.

"Is your trip for business or pleasure?" the customs agent asked, snapping him out his reverie.

"A bit of both."

He made his way through the terminal, with its motif of DNA-like strands of white piping, and rode a bus to the rental car company. He chose the most nondescript-looking car imaginable, a white Ford Focus, and drove north from Burlingame into San Francisco on a bright, cool day. The air was remarkably clear, and the midafternoon light was crisp. No filthy *mái* shrouded this city, although he had heard that he would feel right at home in smoggy Los Angeles to the south.

Not one to waste time, Tao went directly to Bruen's workplace before he had even checked into his hotel. Bruen's law firm was in Four Embarcadero Center, which was near the waterfront and the landmark Ferry Building, the fourth in a series of massive, tombstone-like, white office towers lined with narrow, vertical windows.

Tao took a seat on a concrete bench outside the office tower and waited. It was a good vantage point for surveillance. There was only one set of doors and one security desk for the building, so it would be easy to spot Bruen when he left work in the evening. Because the office was situated in the middle of a shopping center, he wouldn't appear conspicuous if he occupied the bench for long periods of time. There was also a Peet's coffee shop nearby with a view of the doors, so he could alternate his position if necessary.

After Tao had waited in the coffee shop for an hour and a half, Bruen finally pushed through the revolving door, lugging a heavy laptop bag. Tao recognized him immediately from the photo he had been given in Shanghai. Bruen was hard to mistake: tall—well over six feet—with a shock of unruly dark hair, and a long face with a thin nose and heavy-lidded eyes. He strode past the coffee shop window with the power-walking gait of someone who billed by the hour, and at a high rate. After waiting a couple of beats, Tao set out after him.

Bruen headed south on Battery Street. Tao knew that he lived within walking distance of the office in a loft south of Market Street, and that appeared to be his destination. Bruen kept a fast pace with his long legs, and Tao had to work to keep up, threading through the early evening crowds pouring out of the office towers.

Bruen took a left on Market and walked down to the Embarcadero, where the lights of the Bay Bridge glimmered in the dusk. If he was heading home, then he was taking the scenic route. Runners passed by with springing strides, relishing the cool of the evening and being out from behind their desks.

The target stopped at Red's Java House, a white clapboard shack suspended on pylons over the water. He emerged a few minutes later with a paper bag that already showed grease stains, containing what Tao assumed was an unhealthy takeout dinner. He was hungry, and his stomach rumbled in response.

After a few more blocks, Bruen arrived at his apartment. The lights came on in the loft, which had floor-to-ceiling windows that weren't covered with curtains at the top.

Tao walked up a nearby street that climbed a hill, looking for an angle that would allow him to see into Bruen's apartment with binoculars through the gap above the curtains. He had to back away over a hundred yards, but he finally found his vantage point. He removed a set of minibinoculars from his bag and focused until he saw Bruen moving about in his apartment.

Of course, Tao couldn't stay there for long. A man standing on the sidewalk gazing through binoculars at an apartment building would quickly draw attention. But if he could manage to park on the street in the spot next to where he was standing, he could probably take a clean shot with a high-powered rifle.

The notion was entirely impractical, and he instantly dismissed it. He would never set up for a rifle shot in such an exposed position. Nevertheless, this was Tao's thought process when he was hunting a target. He took pleasure in meditating on the assignment, exploring every angle until he had settled on the perfect strategy. Improvisation often produced the best results, and it didn't pay to fall back on familiar tactics. If he became predictable, then he wouldn't last long enough in this line of work to help his brother.

Tao took another look through the binoculars and saw that Bruen was now sitting at an upright piano in a corner of the loft. His hands fluttered over the keyboard. From his hunched posture and the speed of his fingering, Tao assumed that he was playing some classical piece, something precise and complex. He wondered whether Bruen was an improviser or a planner.

Tao didn't even have a gun yet, so nothing was going to happen tonight in any event. This was just about reconnaissance, becoming familiar with Bruen's habits. And he knew that he wouldn't be shooting through the window of the loft, as interesting as it was to contemplate how that might be accomplished. No, that would look like an assassination and would attract far too much attention.

His initial thought was that he would get him using a handgun when he was walking in this less busy neighborhood in the evening.

Tao imagined for a moment that the lens of his binoculars was a rifle scope as he focused on the spot just below the hairline at the base of his skull. *There.* Reflexively, his trigger finger twitched.

Tao's thoughts were interrupted by the buzzing of his cell phone. It was a text from his US contact. Time to begin in earnest.

22

Zoey knew that she shouldn't have made a copy of the flash drive. Chris would be pissed off if he found out. Make that *when* he found out. And Paul Saperstein and the team at Zapper would be livid.

When she made the copy, she wasn't even certain yet that she would do anything with it. She just knew the PLA should not be allowed to rob US companies blind with impunity. As her hacker friends liked to say, information wants to be free. And, to her way of thinking, this information, which proved irrefutably that the PLA was behind the APT1 attacks, was screaming to be released.

So far the State Department had received a report summarizing the contents of the flash drive, but the original remained in her forensic lab. *Her forensic lab.* She still loved the sound of that more than she probably should. And a stunt like this was the sort of thing that could cause her to lose that job.

Although she rarely acknowledged it to Chris, she was happy in her new position. Although she considered attorneys to be a noxious subspecies, now that she worked among them every day, she had to concede that some of them had redeeming qualities. She enjoyed the work, compiling the evidence to stop thieving employees and ruthless hacking crews. And she was good at it. For once in her life, she was able to use all of her talents and get decently compensated for doing it.

Zoey knew that she had a tendency to sabotage herself in the workplace, but that usually happened when she hated the job. Over the past ten years, she had worked in a dozen semimenial jobs, including stints as a math tutor, a security consultant, a writer of graphic novels, and a bartender, holding no job more than eight months at a time. She hoped this wasn't a case of her self-destructive instincts kicking in.

And her talent for self-immolation wasn't limited to the workplace. She was also adept at blowing up any relationship with a man that had the potential of turning into something stable and promising. And she would categorize her relationship with Chris Bruen as promising. Unlikely—perhaps. Maddening—definitely. But also promising.

Since she'd started sleeping at Chris's place, she had learned a few things about him. He wasn't over the death of his wife, Tana, but he was as close as he was probably going to get without someone else. Whether he could get fully beyond his loss remained to be seen. From what Zoey had learned about Tana, she thought that she would have liked her, despite the fact that they were very, very different people. She had decided that was a good thing, because if she had been too much like Tana he would probably always think of her as some sort of weak-tea version of her.

Chris had developed some quirks in his years of living alone, and she knew that she had as well. The question was whether they had become so set that they couldn't be adjusted to accommodate another person. For example, he would wake up in the middle of the night and play a short passage of Bach over and over again to lull himself back into drowsiness. That wouldn't be so bad, but he hummed to himself while he played. It was the humming that was starting to get to her.

What would her hacker compadres say when they learned that she was seriously dating a lawyer? And not just any lawyer—oh no. Chris was a former DOJ prosecutor, someone who had put more hackers in jail than almost anyone else. For black-hat hackers, Chris was on every conceivable enemies list. If word of their relationship got around, she was going to have to wear a disguise to the next DefCon conference.

She realized that disclosing the emails regarding APT1 would place an enormous strain on her relationship with Chris, but she felt she had no choice. If you had to sacrifice your ideals for your partner, what kind of relationship was that? Even though the whole "information wants to be free" thing had become a tired slogan, in this case there was truth to it. The Chinese theft of US intellectual property was a problem of national importance. Who gave the State Department the right to sit on that information?

Zoey knew Matt Geist, a journalist for the muckraking *San Francisco Sentinel*, a free weekly newspaper that took a particular interest in tech industry issues. Geist would love this story, and he and his publisher, a holdover from the Berkeley Free Speech Movement, were ballsy enough to run with it in the face of State Department intimidation. He was also just reputable enough that the mainstream media would not ignore him.

Zoey copied the flash drive and placed it in a letter-size envelope. She couldn't trust it to the mail. She needed to meet with him in person.

Zoey held the phone in her hand for several minutes before punching in the number. She knew Chris would justifiably view this as a betrayal. She also believed that it was the right thing to do and consistent with the ethical principles that had guided her during her years as a hacker. Old Zoey and New Zoey warred for a moment more—and then she placed the call to Geist.

As soon as the number began ringing, she mouthed the word "boom." *Way to go, Zoey, blowing up your life again just when things were getting good.*

"Geist." His voice sounded blurry. There was a substance involved, but she couldn't tell what it might be.

"It's Zoey."

"I was just thinking about you."

"You don't need to do that, okay?"

"Then why are you calling me? What news from the hacker underground?"

"I have news all right. I've got a story for you. But you're going to have to convince me that you are capable of pulling it together before I tell you."

"I'm with my former editor, and we are drinking with purpose tonight to mourn a lost way of life. We are journalists, and we hold our liquor."

In the background, a gruff voice added, "Damn straight. And the liquor holds us."

"That doesn't even make sense," Geist said to his drunken companion.

"My shit is just too fucking deep for you to fully comprehend it right now."

"If you say so."

"Geist!" Zoey said loudly into the receiver. "I think you're going to want to hear what I have to tell you. If you're not too busy mourning a lost way of life."

"So what do you have?" Geist was making a game effort to regroup.

"I can't tell you over the phone."

"What, you want to meet in a parking garage at midnight too?"

"You'd like that, wouldn't you?"

"You know that nothing gets me wetter than a conspiracy theory."

"Well, dry your panties," said Zoey. "I'll stop by your place at 9:00 a.m."

"Better make it eleven."

"Okay. Drink some water before you go to bed."

23

Visiting San Francisco's Chinatown felt a little like coming home for Tao—if his home had been turned into a ride at Disneyland. He walked under the tiled arch at the base of Grant Avenue and was greeted by Chinatown in all its garish nighttime glory. Glowing red lanterns were strung overhead across the street, and pagoda towers lined the avenue. Even the streetlamps were exotic jade-green fantasias.

As Tao wandered the side streets, he saw that Chinatown actually had a dual nature. Part of it was a Disneyfication, a put-on for the tourists looking for their clichéd notion of Eastern exoticism. But behind the facade, he could see that an authentic Chinese community existed alongside the stores selling trinkets. The tea-smoked ducks hanging in the window of a butcher shop could have been sold on the street where he lived in Shanghai.

A group of uniformed waiters smoking cigarettes on the steps of Old St. Mary's Cathedral eyed him as he walked past. While no street in China looked quite like this, it was close enough to make him feel a bit homesick. In a strange land, it was at least an approximation of something familiar.

The text had instructed him to come to Chongqing Bazaar Antiques at nine thirty and ask for Wan. From the outside, the shop looked like any of the other places selling ceramic foo dogs.

A bell jangled as he stepped inside, but no clerk responded. The shop was empty. Tao made his way through a maze of antique chests, painted screens, lamps, and enormous ceramics vases, proceeding to the cash register in the back. When he reached the register, he rang the bell on the counter, which jangled noisily in the silent store.

Tao waited for about a minute, beginning to wonder if someone was setting him up. Maybe his mission had been aborted. Maybe he was now a loose end to be eliminated. He tried to settle himself and not let his thoughts run wild.

A hushed female voice came from behind him. "Can I help you?"

He turned quickly and saw a tall woman of indeterminate middle age with glossy, shoulder-length black hair. She was wearing a tasteful, Western-style blue silk dress and a scrutinizing look.

"Wan?"

"Yes, *Ms.* Wan. You're not what I expected."

"What was I supposed to look like? Chow Yun-Fat?" She wasn't exactly what he was expecting either. He had expected Wan to be a man.

She smiled politely. "You're right, of course." Stepping past him, she entered the office that was behind the register. "Please come with me."

Tao glanced back at the front of the store, concerned about the privacy of their meeting, but he saw that the front door was shut and the "Closed" sign was up. He followed her inside.

The office was uncluttered and functional, dominated by a massive teak desk. Unlike the rest of the shop, there were no antiques. The woman went to a floor safe behind the desk, dialed a combination, and removed a Beretta 92FS nickel-plated pistol.

She placed the gun on the desk with a thump. "Satisfactory?"

"Very, so long as it's clean."

"It's untraceable. Feel free to assume that I know my job."

"I don't know you. So it's a little early for me to be making assumptions."

She stared at him impassively, neither arguing nor conceding the point. "I have a message for you. You have new instructions."

"The same target, right?"

"Yes, but you must do something extra. There's a flash drive. A copy of the hard drive Bruen stole. It contains some files that would be very embarrassing if they became public. Bruen brought the material back with him from China, and he has it in his firm's forensic lab. In addition to the hit, you need to retrieve any copies of the flash drive that you can find."

"Can you tell me what's on the drive?"

"Emails between a Security Officer Yu and the hacker Li Owyang. They constitute proof that the PLA has been stealing secrets from US companies."

"That will be more difficult."

"Yes, that's understood. But you're not expected to obtain all of the copies. The US government probably already has one, but they are unlikely to make it public. Others may not be so discreet. The primary mission is still Bruen, but if you can retrieve any copies of the flash drive, your fee will be increased substantially."

"Bonus points."

"If you like. You should know that if there are any complications, you can come here. But only if it's absolutely necessary. And if you allow anyone to follow you back here, you will wish that you hadn't."

"I'm not anticipating any complications."

"They never do."

Tao picked up the gun and placed it in his satchel. "I'll let myself out," he said.

"Use the back way," she said. "Good luck."

Tao pushed open a metal door onto the alleyway, which smelled of rotting seafood and garbage. He strolled the length of the alley and did not rejoin Grant Avenue until he was three blocks away from the antiques shop.

He wondered if Ms. Wan was a spy, but he was pretty sure she would consider that an overly dramatic word to describe her role.

Tao didn't understand how the PLA knew about the flash drive now, when they seemingly hadn't known about it when giving him his assignment. Perhaps their hackers had penetrated Bruen's law firm. Or perhaps they had found someone close to the project and made them talk. Tao wondered if there was another contractor working the job, a fail-safe in case he didn't succeed.

Tao walked until he had left Chinatown behind and entered the neon of the strip clubs and Italian restaurants of North Beach. He needed to think about the logistics of his assignment, but bloody thoughts preoccupied him.

What he would do to Bruen with a knife.

What he would do to Bruen with the lit burner of a stove.

What he would do to Bruen with a power drill.

The thoughts were not unwelcome. He had never found pleasure in his work in this way before, but since the hit on Naruse in Tokyo, things had changed. He had changed, and was changing still. Many Chinese people believed that there was no such thing as mental illness, or that it was reserved for the criminally insane, but Tao had a more informed view of the subject. In the human mind there was at least as much darkness as there was light, and that fact might as well be embraced. To do otherwise, Tao believed, was to willfully misunderstand those around you.

Tao tried to put his more twisted thoughts aside, save them for later. He needed to focus on the job and his primary motivation of freeing his brother. At least he told himself that was his primary motivation.

24

The Mission District was what was sometimes referred to as a "transitional" neighborhood, which meant that a familiar battle was being waged there, with history and tradition on one side and money on the other. As usual money was heavily favored to win. Zoey walked along Valencia Street, which was still pretty equally divided between bodegas and new upscale restaurants catering to the young bohos who flocked to the area.

She had met Geist when she was tending bar at the Bottom of the Hill. He had been a regular who had found his perfect barstool, drawn there by his enthusiasm for indie bands, Jameson, and, eventually, Zoey. He'd asked her out a few times with polite, self-deprecating persistence, but she'd never said yes. It wasn't that Zoey didn't find him sweet and appealing, but she had decided he was a little too much like her—too much the beautiful loser. She hadn't realized it at the time, but she had been looking for someone like Chris.

Zoey had been serving Geist drinks for almost a year before he learned that she was a hacker. Geist had started talking about a story he was working on involving a major corporate security breach, and Zoey couldn't resist lending her expert opinion. After that Zoey had been Geist's source on several articles over the years, but never anything as big as this.

As Zoey climbed the steps of Matt Geist's Hoff Street apartment building, she assumed that the journalist would be hung over, but she hoped he wouldn't be in the grip of a full-on bender.

It took several knocks and a little shouting, but Geist finally came to the door. He was wearing gray sweat pants and a ratty robe that was as colorless as his face.

He ran a hand through his curly, black-going-to-gray hair. "I thought you said eleven."

"It is eleven."

"It feels earlier."

"I bet it does. Can I come in?"

"Yeah, sure," Geist said, turning and leading the way. He lowered himself carefully onto a couch that was approximately the same color as his robe, making it appear as if he had been swallowed by the upholstery. One side of the apartment was lined with wall-to-wall vinyl records like wainscoting.

"Is your editor friend still here?"

"No, his wife carted him away last night. I would have done it myself but . . ."

"I'm sure that was for the best."

Zoey sat in a chair across from him and set a brown paper bag down on the table between them. "I come bearing coffee and breakfast burritos."

"Bless you, my child."

Zoey waited as Geist devoured a burrito and got some caffeine in him.

"So what was all that last night about mourning a lost way of life?" Zoey asked.

"It's what we print journalists do. Piss and moan about the good old days—when no one knew what a blog was. We were paid poorly then too, but at least we had jobs. I was going to say we had respect, but I'm not sure how much of that we had back then either."

"Who's your drinking buddy?"

"Dan Halliday, my first editor. We were Gannetroids together in the early nineties at the *Des Moines Register*."

"Gannetroids?"

"The *Register* was owned by the Gannett newspaper chain."

"It's tough when the thing that you love isn't valued by the world at large."

Geist seemed to be growing more alert with every sip of coffee. He raised his eyebrows at her over the rim of his cardboard coffee cup. "You know something about that too, don't you?"

"Let's just say that if I had been interested in stealing social security numbers I would have saved a lot more money by now."

"Now why couldn't we just love something like corporate law or real estate or accounting?"

"You can't choose who or what you love," Zoey said, thinking of Chris. "And no one loves accounting."

Now that Geist had begun to show signs of life, Zoey said, "So, are you ready to hear my story?"

"I'm breathless with anticipation."

Zoey proceeded to recount her tale of the PLA squad dedicated to hacking US companies, and Chris's mission to disrupt its efforts.

As she spoke, Geist raised himself up to an upright sitting position and began leaning forward. When she was done, he said, "That's a good story, but so far it sounds like that's all it is—a story. Do you have something more?"

Zoey pulled the flash drive from her pants pocket and slid it across the nicked-up table, littered with copies of *Mother Jones* and *The Nation*.

"What's on this?"

"The smoking gun. The email exchange between the PLA officer and Li Owyang. It's forensically sound."

"Does anyone know that you have this?"

"No, but if it appears in print, they will figure it out pretty fast."

"I'll have to review the contents of course."

"Of course."

"But if it is what you say it is, then—it's a very big story."

Now and then Geist broke stories, but they tended to be stories he had to try to convince the world to care about. Zoey could see his excitement building as he realized that this was a story that didn't need to be sold. For this one, the world would come to him. Every network news show would want to interview him. This was the kind of story that could turn around a career.

"You're glad I woke you up now, aren't you?"

"I think I am, yeah."

"I'd like to remain anonymous. I'll probably lose my job over this anyway, but if my name appears in the story then I'm definitely out."

"I can do that. The State Department isn't going to like it if we print this."

"No, they won't. You'll probably need a lawyer."

"The *Sentinel* has one on retainer. We're the kind of publication that needs lawyers. He's going to be very excited to defend this one."

"As excited as you are to get the story?"

"Is it that obvious?" Geist smiled. "Even if I end up in jail at the end of this, I'll still owe you one."

25

Tao had suspected that the PLA had hacked Bruen's law firm, but he was certain of it when he got the call that morning from Ms. Wan on his burner phone.

"Bruen's friend Zoey Doucet has made a copy of the flash drive," Wan said. "She's going to share it with a journalist named Geist. You need to make certain that doesn't happen."

"Where is she now?"

"In the law firm's offices. Where are you?"

"Exactly where I'm supposed to be. I'm in front of the entrance to their building, waiting for Bruen to appear. What do you want me to do?"

"Retrieve the flash drive—at all costs. No one will second-guess you if things get messy."

The only way that the PLA could know the content of Doucet's communications with the journalist was by intercepting her phone calls or emails. He imagined that a major US law firm had good security, but it was hard for any system to defend against a sophisticated, concerted assault by the PLA's hackers.

As if on cue, Doucet emerged from the office building. She walked a block to the entrance to the BART station and descended the steps to the trains. Tao followed her at a distance and, when she boarded a train, stepped onto the rear of the same car.

She exited at the Sixteenth and Mission station and climbed the escalator to the street. Emerging outdoors, Tao found Mission Street to be teeming and alive; it reminded him of the riotous backstreets of Shanghai. By contrast, the pristine white office towers of Embarcadero Center seemed as lifeless and calcified as old bones.

He followed her through the Mission, past the bodegas and dollar stores, past the hip cafes and the vintage clothing shops, past graffiti murals and taquerias, past garages and community centers. People walked with the loping pace of ordinary life, not the manic, overcaffeinated bustling of the Financial District. There were fewer people here attempting to walk with their eyes glued to a phone or device.

Doucet arrived at an apartment on Hoff Street that must belong to the journalist. She was carrying a brown paper bag and two coffees from a Mexican place where she had stopped along the way.

Tao fingered the Beretta in his jacket pocket and considered whether he should move in immediately and do the job right there in the street, but decided against it. There were too many pedestrians passing nearby, particularly considering he would need to search her for the flash drive after he took the shot.

No, he assumed that Doucet was bringing the flash drive to Geist, so it would be with him when she left. It made much more sense to wait until she was gone and then pay Geist a visit. He would have a controlled environment in the apartment and all the time necessary to locate the flash drive, even if that meant going to work on the journalist.

After Doucet disappeared into the building, Tao got himself a coffee and sat on the stoop of another apartment building down the street to wait for her to leave.

About a half hour later, Doucet emerged from the apartment and strode away in the direction of the BART station. Five minutes after she turned the corner, when he was fairly certain she would not return, Tao stood and crossed the street. He entered the tiny lobby of the building and saw from the mailboxes that Geist's apartment was on the second floor. Tao climbed the flight of steps, not attempting to quiet his footsteps. If he was listening, Geist would hear him coming.

He rapped on the door.

An eye appeared in the peephole. "Who's there?"

"You're Matt Geist, right?"

"Yeah."

"I'm a friend of Zoey Doucet's. She just left something here and asked me to come and pick it up. She didn't have time to come back. Had to get to the office." Tao's English was good, but a bit stiff.

He heard the chain on the door slide. When the door opened, Geist was wearing a ratty bathrobe and holding a coffee. He was animated, even though his eyes were bloodshot and he looked the worse for wear.

"Matt Geist," he said, extending his hand.

"Henry Yang," Tao said.

Geist led him into the living room, which, in the small apartment, was about two paces from the front door. "What are we looking for?"

"Thing . . . for makeup."

"You mean a compact?"

"Yes, right."

"Did she say where she left it?"

"Somewhere near where she was sitting."

Geist walked over to a chair near the sofa and ran his hand along the edge of the cushion. "Not finding anything. You know, I don't know how well you know Zoey, but I never thought of her as the kind of girl who carries a compact."

When Tao didn't respond, Geist turned around for a reaction. By that time, Tao had set his bag down on the floor and removed the Beretta.

"No, you're probably right," Tao said.

"You're not a friend of Zoey's, are you?" Geist said.

"No, I'm not."

"What do you want?" Tao could see Geist's head clearing, could see him focusing. He was not nearly as panicked as he might have been. "If you're looking for money, you came to the wrong place."

"I'm not looking for money."

"What are you looking for then?"

"I think you know."

He could see that Geist was putting it together. "I have no idea what you're talking about."

"Don't make this more difficult than it needs to be."

Geist started to punctuate with his hands, a nervous mannerism. "Look, take whatever you want. Not that there's much here. But there's a cop who lives downstairs, and he's going to hear a gunshot."

Tao grabbed a straight-backed chair from the dining table and set it in front of Geist. "Sit down."

As Geist lowered himself into the chair, his eyes darted about the room, looking for a weapon, looking for an exit.

Keeping the gun trained on the journalist, Tao reached into the bag again and produced vinyl rope and a roll of duct tape.

"Tape your feet together," Tao said, tossing the roll at his feet.

"There's no need for this," Geist said. "I'll give you what you want."

"I know you will," Tao said.

After Geist's feet were secured, Tao went around behind him and tied him to the chair.

"Just tell me what you want."

"You know." There was a violent ripping sound as Tao tore a strip of duct tape off the roll. He leaned in close to Geist's face. "I'm going to cover your mouth in a minute, and that's when the talking is going to stop for a while. When I remove the tape, you're going to tell me where I can find it."

"Find what?"

"The flash drive."

"What flash drive?" Geist didn't say it like a question; he spat it through clenched teeth like a curse, like he knew it was going to be followed by a blow.

The journalist probably saw the flash drive as a way to salvage his career, which couldn't be going very well, judging by where he was living. Tao wasn't displeased that it was turning out this way. He might have done it even if it hadn't been strictly necessary.

"So that is your answer?"

"That's right, you ridiculous fucking cartoon of a black ops fuck."

"You're going to hurt my feelings talking like that."

For some time now, a black tide had been rising inside Tao, along with a realization. Although it had taken him a while to admit it to himself, he had come to love his work as a hit man. He would do it even if his brother wasn't in a prison in Shanghai. In fact, he would do it even if no one was paying him. Of course, if no one was paying him, then that would make him a serial killer, wouldn't it? Fortunately, there was no need to apply such a distasteful label, because he was one of those lucky few who had the privilege of earning a living doing something that he loved.

Tao took the strip of duct tape and pressed it gently over the journalist's mouth. Geist's eyes were still bloodshot, but they were wide open and electric now. This was the moment Tao had been chasing: the moment of recognition, the moment of his control and the victim's subjugation.

When he had gazed into Naruse's eyes on that cobblestone path in Tokyo, the feeling had hit him like the first glimpse of the woman that you would marry. But he needed to know if the feeling was more than fleeting heat lightning. Now he knew that it was something that he could have again and again. And he would have it regardless of consequences, regardless of morality, regardless of human life. It was like the addict's first hit of heroin, or the pervert's discovery of the sexual kink that quickens his pulse and darkens his heart.

26

Later that afternoon, Zoey tried calling Geist at home and at the *Sentinel*'s offices, but he was nowhere to be found. She wanted to gauge his reaction after he had reviewed the contents of the flash drive, get a sense of how long the story would have to be vetted by the lawyers and editors before it could be published. Zoey was also anxious to know how long she had to speak with Chris about her actions before the *Sentinel* article appeared. That conversation was going to be difficult enough, and she didn't want him to learn about it first in the press.

She wasn't quite sure how bad Geist's drinking really was, so there was the possibility that he might have had too much hair of the dog and ended up passed out in his apartment. Maybe his editor buddy had returned and the revelries had resumed.

As the day progressed in the computer forensic lab without any word from Geist, Zoey grew more worried. Geist had seemed genuinely excited about the story, so it seemed unlikely that he would flake out.

"You seem preoccupied," Chris said. "Everything okay?"

He was one to talk. Chris had been immersed all day in studying the mechanics of how the Chinese hackers had gotten behind Zapper's firewall.

"I'm fine, thanks," Zoey said. She knew that she needed to tell Chris about her disclosure of the flash drive, but she couldn't bring herself to do it just yet.

When Zoey still hadn't heard from Geist at the end of her workday, she set out for his apartment. It was a breezy early evening—jacket weather—as she retraced her path to the apartment building on Hoff Street.

She felt a foreboding as she climbed the steps to the second floor. Zoey knocked tentatively on the door. There was no sound from inside the apartment.

"Geist! It's me, Zoey."

No response.

After rapping on the door and waiting, Zoey tested the doorknob. It wasn't locked, and that made Zoey even more worried.

She stepped into the apartment, which was dark except for the pale-red light from a liquor store's neon sign across the street, which filtered through thin curtains. The first thing she noticed was the smell. Zoey had never been at a crime scene, but she recognized the smell of blood. She had just never experienced it so intensely.

As her eyes adjusted to the darkness, she made out the figure bound to the chair in the center of the living room.

It was Geist, and he wasn't moving.

"Matt." Again, louder: "Matt!"

Zoey fought back a gag impulse and managed to avoid throwing up. She thought that maybe the red light through the curtains was playing tricks on her vision, so she turned on a lamp.

With the lights on, she could see that Geist's right leg was a bloody mess. It looked like someone had tried to perform major surgery on him with a hacksaw and without removing his pants.

She now saw that a large pool of blood surrounded Geist, and she jumped backward to get away from it.

She tried to calm herself enough to look again and saw the bullet wound in his chest. He had been tortured, then killed.

His leg was in the shape it was in because he had refused to give up the flash drive—for as long as he could stand it anyway. It had been Geist's shot at big-time journalism, and he had clung to it for as long as he could.

Zoey instantly recognized that someone had followed her from the office to Geist's apartment that morning. Maybe that same person was following her now.

She rushed to the door, locked it, and put on the chain. However, that wasn't going to be enough to deter anyone who was capable of this carnage. Zoey dialed the San Francisco Police Department on her cell, her trembling fingers fumbling the numbers.

After she hung up the phone, it dawned on her that the man who had done this must have hacked her work phone or email. Why else would he kill Geist? He must have known that she had given Geist the flash drive. There was only one way that he could have known that.

She stood frozen, staring at Geist's body, until the police arrived, knowing that he would be alive if she hadn't offered him the story. She could have looked away, but she felt that she deserved to have this grotesque image seared into her memory. She was going to have to carry it with her for a long time to come, and she was going to suffer for that—and she knew she deserved to suffer for that.

27

Tao knew exactly how he was going to kill Chris Bruen. In fact, he had gone over the plan in his mind so many times that he was able to visualize it as if it had already happened. It was called positive visualization.

Bruen would be walking home to his apartment from the law firm's offices. He would be south of Market on a deserted stretch of Beale Street. There would be few passing cars and even fewer pedestrians on the sidewalk. The night would be falling, but the streetlights wouldn't be on yet. It would be that half-light time of day when the moon was already bright in the sky even though it wasn't yet dark.

Tao would be wearing jeans, a gray hoodie pulled up over his head, and a Giants cap. He had followed the route several times, looking for CCTV cameras, and there were none that should pick him up. Even if he had missed one, his face would be obscured.

He would be carrying his Beretta in the pouch in the front of his sweatshirt. He would walk quickly up to Bruen from behind, his hands buried in the sweatshirt's front pocket. When he was just a couple of feet from his target, he would draw the Beretta in a smooth motion.

Bruen would be nearing the corner of Beale and Howard Streets, very close to an alley that opened to the right. Tao would stride up and speak Bruen's name. When he turned around, Tao would shoot him in the chest.

A bullet in the back would be easier, but that wouldn't look like a failed robbery. In a robbery attempt, the victim faced the thief. And Tao couldn't follow his customary practice of putting a bullet in the target's head once he was down for the coup de grâce. That would also look too much like an execution.

It was important to be accurate with the placement of the bullets. Or artfully inaccurate.

First, there would be one bullet straight to the heart. Then a shot to the gut. Just to make sure that he bled out. And finally one wild shot to Bruen's foot, which would convince the police that the assailant was a street robber who had just gotten lucky with that first shot to the heart.

Tao sat on a bench outside the Reynolds Fincher offices, waiting for Bruen as he had before, running the scenario through in his mind. He knew that thinking too much could be counterproductive. Planning and positive visualization were fine, but if you became too fixated, then you wouldn't be adaptable enough when things went wrong or differently.

Once more Bruen pushed through the revolving door, heading home. Tao rose and walked away in the opposite direction, then doubled back to follow Bruen once he'd passed. The target descended the escalator to the ground floor, then proceeded through the shops, heading south toward Market Street and his apartment. Tao's pulse quickened as he moved through the shoppers and office workers, feeling the excitement of the hunt.

While standing at a crosswalk at California Street, Bruen looked backward in Tao's direction. Did he know that he was being followed? Tao didn't see how that could be the case. Was someone else following Bruen or meeting him? Tao scanned the streets for anyone who might be there for Bruen but saw no one with eyes locked on the attorney.

The streets of the Financial District all ran down to the waterfront in a series of long corridors. The orange glow of sunset cast into the open sky to the left, and to the right it was obscured by office towers. But the traffic was largely headed south, the cars filled with East Bay commuters stacked in long lines, waiting to ascend onto the Bay Bridge. Beale Street was not one of the streets that turned into a parking lot at rush hour, so it was vital that Bruen followed his usual route home.

Bruen crossed Market Street, the broad thoroughfare that cut across San Francisco from the Embarcadero to the Castro, and headed down Beale Street, which was a mix of three- and four-story offices and sleek, new high-rise condo towers. There were few pedestrians on the street and Tao stood out, but thankfully Bruen didn't look back again.

Tao gripped the gun in the pouch of his sweatshirt and quickened his pace. Bruen was nearing the alleyway that would provide his escape route after the shot. He drew his Beretta and held it down at his side, but just as he did so he heard a car engine approach from behind him with a tubercular rattle.

An ancient, sky-blue VW Beetle raced up the street, passed Tao, and came to a stop beside Bruen.

"Get in!"

It was Doucet. She leaned across and opened the passenger-side door.

Tao's window of opportunity was slipping away, and he was prepared to let it go. You couldn't force these things.

But before Bruen could climb into the VW, he looked back down the street and saw Tao—and the gun dangling at his side.

Bruen jumped inside the car and shouted, "Go! There's a man with a gun."

Tao stepped into the middle of Beale Street so that he would have a straight shot through the rear windshield.

The first bullet shattered the glass. The second and third struck metal with the clanking, empty sound of tin-can target practice.

If they had driven straight up Beale Street, there would have been ample opportunity to kill them both. They would have been dead before they reached the cross street. But Zoey jerked the steering wheel to the right and drove down the alleyway that Tao had intended to use as his escape route.

He ran up to the entrance to the alley and fired a couple more shots, but it was too late. He watched the VW drive away, sputtering like a glorified lawn mower, until it turned onto First Street, merging into the traffic waiting to get on the Bay Bridge.

For a moment, he considered walking up the street and shooting them while their car was stalled in traffic, but he quickly dismissed that as a foolish move. If he shot two people in the middle of a line of a hundred cars, he would be seen by many, and there was no telling how many people might decide to climb out of their cars and pursue him. He would probably have to kill several bystanders in the process, and that was simply not professional.

He cursed softly, then walked away. Residents of the nearby apartment and condo towers would have heard the shots, so the police would be arriving soon.

When Tao reached the Embarcadero, he removed his sweatshirt and baseball cap and tossed them in a garbage can. He untucked his shirt and placed the gun in the small of his back. As he got lost in the crowds out for an evening stroll beside the bay, Tao knew that his job had just grown much more complicated.

28

Zoey screamed as the front and rear windshields blew apart in a shower of bright fragments. She hunched down over the steering wheel but kept her foot on the gas. The VW swerved and scraped against the wall of the narrow alley, sending up sparks.

Chris could hear the bullets clanking as they struck the car. Glancing back over the front seat, he saw the figure in a hooded sweat shirt and Giants cap standing in the middle of the alley, legs braced in a Weaver stance and calmly firing away. He ducked down behind the seat.

They were almost out of the alley. Almost at First Street. Chris's pulse raced and strained as erratically as the VW's engine.

The car emerged from the alley, and Zoey had to slam on the brakes as they faced a stream of bumper-to-bumper traffic headed for the Bay Bridge. Zoey forced the car into the traffic to a fanfare of car horns.

"Should we get out of the car and run?" Zoey asked.

Chris had a better view back down the alley. "No. He's gone. I don't think he'll follow into a crowd like this."

"Who was that?"

"I don't know," Chris said.

Zoey was gripping the steering wheel so hard her knuckles were white. "We need to get out of here!"

The traffic advanced a bit, so that Chris could no longer see down the alley. He kept his eyes on the alley's entrance. If the man in the sweatshirt came striding out, it would be all too easy to step up to the car window and gun them both down.

"Is he coming?"

"I can't see now," Chris said. "I'm going to get out and look. You stay here."

Chris opened the door and stepped out of the traffic and over to the entrance to the alley.

He glanced around the corner, but the alley was empty now. He rejoined Zoey in the car, which had barely advanced in the traffic.

"He's not coming for us."

"Unless he's looking for a place up ahead to take a shot."

"Well, yeah."

Fifteen endless minutes later, they'd flowed with the heavy traffic onto the Bay Bridge, heading east, away from San Francisco. Chris looked at Zoey and saw the tension visibly drain from her body as she put distance between them and the shooter.

"Did you get a look at him?" Zoey asked, nearly shouting over the wind whipping through the shattered windows.

"Yeah. He looked Chinese. And he seemed very comfortable with a gun."

"Would you recognize him if you saw him again?"

"I think so."

"You think this is a response to killing those two hackers?"

"Yes, that's exactly what I think."

Zoey pulled off the bridge at the first opportunity, exiting onto Yerba Buena Island, a green, rocky outcropping in the center of the Bay. They drove across the isthmus that connected to Treasure Island, a man-made island and former naval base built from landfill for the 1930s Golden Gate International Exposition. They parked the car beside the road that skirted the island. On one side were the apartments that had once been housing for naval staff. On the other was a stunning view of San Francisco, across the bay but improbably close at hand, the lights of the Embarcadero office towers winking in the gloaming. But they were in no frame of mind to admire the view.

For a moment they just sat there, brushing glass fragments out of their clothes and off the seat. Chris felt a weariness settling over him, the aftereffect of the adrenaline spike.

"We can't go back to our apartments until we understand what's happening," Chris said. "That was not a random robbery. It seemed more like a professional hit. And if that's true, he's not going to give up."

"And if he was a professional, then someone hired him to do it."

"Right. Since this is probably about the hacking and the deaths of Owyang and Ma, then that killer was most likely paid by the Chinese government or some agency. Probably the PLA."

"Wait a second," Zoey said. "Remember that connection I found between a Unit 61398 manager and Red Sun, that hit man working through Silk Road?"

"Of course. That was a pretty thin thread—"

"And the Zapper security team beat me up pretty good when I suggested it. But it looks a lot more plausible now, doesn't it?"

"It does. We need to revisit that theory, spend some time on Silk Road."

Chris sat quietly for a few long moments, contemplating their next move.

Finally, he said, "We're going to have to go to the State Department tomorrow morning. We can seek some sort of protective custody. Tell them what we think is happening."

"And you think that's going to stop this?"

"I think it's our best shot. If the State Department communicates with the Chinese through diplomatic channels, lets them know that they know what they're up to, then they'll understand that there will be real consequences if they proceed."

"What if they don't care what the State Department thinks?"

"That's a possibility. The Chinese might think that I was sent by the US government to begin with."

"Then what?"

"Then we're either going to need some serious protection, or we're going to have to run."

"And what about tonight?"

"Tonight we need to find someplace to hide out until we can go to the State Department."

"A hotel?"

"I'm not even sure that's a good idea. Remember how sophisticated those hackers on Datong Road are. If they can crack the security of a company like Zapper, and hundreds more like it, then I think they're more than capable of tracking us down using our credit card and cell phone records."

Chris removed the SIM card from his phone, and Zoey did the same.

"What do you suggest?" she asked.

"I'm trying to think of a place where we could lay low tonight."

Zoey nodded slowly, thinking. "I know a place that's lower than low."

"You know, if you hadn't come along when you did, I would be dead right now," Chris said.

"As you know, my timing is usually not that good," Zoey said.

"What were you coming to see me about anyway?"

"We can talk about that later," she said, shivering as a chill wind blew through the car. "Right now let's get the hell out of here, okay?"

29

When Zoey and Chris entered the Bottom of the Hill that night, a boozy cheer rose from the bar crowd. Zoey had been a bartender at the grungy Potrero Hill music club off and on for years and was a favorite of both the bartending crew and the regulars. This was the place where Chris had first met her seven months ago while tracking down some hackers for a case.

"I knew you couldn't stay away," said a woman behind the bar with short jet-black hair and tattoos up her right arm.

"It's either the stiff drinks or the weak company, I'm not sure," Zoey replied. Then she broke into a smile, ducked under the wait stand and behind the bar in a move that was clearly still preserved in muscle memory, and gave the woman a hug.

"Good to see you, K."

"Same here, Zed."

The other bartender on duty, a man in his midthirties with two-day stubble and an approximation of a haircut, stood patiently by, waiting for his turn. When Zoey turned and saw him, he simply extended his arms wide and smiled sheepishly.

"Okay, Justin, but don't get all handsy about it," Zoey said with a grin.

After the hug, a patron slouched over a beer offered, "I like hugs too, you know."

"You stay on your side of the bar, Wiley," Zoey said.

The greetings went on like that for a while, and then her friends began to wonder what they were doing there.

"We need a place to crash, and I was wondering if anyone's bunking upstairs tonight in the Cave," Zoey said.

K shrugged. "I was planning on sleeping one-off up there tonight, but I would gladly give up the place of honor for you—and your friend."

"Thanks, Krissa." Then to the assembled parties, Zoey added, "This is Chris Bruen."

"Your new boss?" Wiley asked.

"You need to rephrase that," Zoey said.

"Colleague?"

"Better."

"The word 'boss' isn't really part of Zoey's vocabulary," Chris said. "But you already knew that, didn't you?"

Nods all around.

Krissa led them up a narrow flight of wooden stairs. "You don't have to say if you don't want to, but is everything okay?"

"We just need a quiet place for a night, maybe two," Zoey said.

"If you're looking to be off the grid, this is the place," Krissa told Chris.

Krissa swung the door open to reveal a tiny room with a bed, a couch, a couple of worn chairs, and a minifridge. The walls were plastered with posters from the club's shows, many of which had been signed by the artists.

"You know, this place is not just for bartenders and employees who've had a few too many. The Cave has been the crash pad for rock royalty. You know who's slept in that bed? Alex Chilton. Paul Westerberg. Lucinda Williams. Jack White."

"I'm impressed," Chris said. "But you change the sheets, right?"

"Every five years." Krissa lingered in the doorway for a moment. "So how's the nine-to-five world treating you, Zed? You know you can always come back here. There's always a spot. The music's been better than ever lately."

"No poaching," Chris said.

Zoey waved a hand at him, taking the question seriously. "It's actually not bad, K. I've got to admit that I'm surprised, but it's not bad."

"So you like the work? Hunting down hackers? I still have trouble getting my head around that coming from you."

"I know, but most of the ones that we go after are just criminals with a keyboard. Some are even violent."

"Is that why you're hiding out here now?"

"Yeah, well, sort of."

"Stay as long as you like. It's good having you around again."

"If I have time, I might come down there and do a shift for old times' sake."

"Cool," said K. "Hey, if you need a place indefinitely, my brother has a little house in Stinson Beach, and he's out of the country indefinitely. I know where he keeps the keys. No one would find you out there."

"I thought you liked having me around."

"Shut up, you know I do. I just mean that if you seriously need to lay low for a while, that would be a place."

"Thanks, Krissa." Zoey glanced at Chris. "We just might need that."

Krissa backed toward the door. "I'll let you guys regroup. See you later."

"I don't mean to be rude, but was there ever a thing between you two?" Chris asked as soon as the door closed. "Because I was sensing a certain vibe."

"There was something many years ago. Call it an experiment. It was brief—but intense."

"You are full of surprises."

"You have no idea. Speaking of which, there's something that I need to tell you." She paused like she was about to take a header off a diving board. "I made a copy of the emails from Owyang's computer."

"You shouldn't have done that, Zoey. Why did you make the copy?"

"So that I could share it with Matt Geist, a reporter for the *Sentinel*."

"Wait. You actually did that?"

"Yes."

Chris stood and gave her a stony look. "Why?"

"Because I didn't think it was right for the State Department to bury that information about the PLA's role in hacking US corporations. How are companies going to defend themselves unless they understand the nature of the threat?"

Chris tried to keep his emotions in check. He took a breath and then said, "You know that information was privileged. It was an ethical violation to disclose it."

"But you didn't disclose it, I did. And I'm not an attorney."

"I doubt the State Bar or our client is going to make those kinds of distinctions."

"There's something else that I need to say before we get too far into this. Geist's dead. Someone came to his apartment after I gave him the flash drive and murdered him."

Chris dropped to the couch. "Murdered? He was murdered? Why didn't you tell me that sooner?"

"I wanted us to be someplace safe before I told you."

"Do you know who did it?"

"No one has been arrested, but I'm pretty certain that it was the same guy who fired those shots at us in the alley."

"Jesus, Zoey." Chris wanted to rise from the couch, but he only made it halfway before falling back. "Do you know where the flash drive is?"

"No, I didn't see it when I was in the apartment with the body. But I wasn't in any state of mind to conduct much of a search."

"We probably have to assume that he got the flash drive."

"I think so. Geist would have told him anything that he wanted to know, judging by how he looked."

"Wait," Chris said. "How did he know that you had the flash drive and were giving a copy to Geist?"

"I was getting to that," she said. "He must have hacked my phone or the firm's email system. I think we have to assume that our usual methods of communication are not secure."

"I really don't know what to say," Chris said after a long moment of silence.

"C'mon, don't get all quiet. I'd rather you just say it."

"Well, if my partners knew what you did, they would fire you. And I don't want to fire you. I like working with you. But I understand why they would want you gone."

"I did what I thought was right—but I understand that it isn't something that I can do and work at the firm. If I feel the need to do something like that again, I'll at least talk to you first."

"That doesn't give me a lot of comfort."

"It's the best I can do."

"The original hard drive went to Zapper, right?"

"Right. And they've probably shared it with the White House by now."

"And you haven't made any more copies of Owyang's emails?"

"No. And I won't." After a moment of silence, Zoey added, "What's really tearing me up is that Matt Geist would be alive if I hadn't approached him with that story. It's almost like I killed him."

"No, it's not like that at all. As angry as I am at you right now, you shouldn't think like that." Chris said it to spare Zoey the pain of guilt, which he knew all too well. But the truth was, the instant Zoey told him about Geist's death he had thought the same thing.

"I know how pissed off you are at me, so you don't have to be nice like that. It confuses me."

Zoey got undressed and climbed into the legendary bed, leaving him to the less legendary couch. Chris could hear her breathing quickly in the dark for a while, clearly wide awake. She probably knew he was awake too, but they didn't say another word to each other that night.

Chris knew that they would need to present a united front the next day to the State Department, but he wasn't sure yet if that was going to be possible.

30

The State Department's outpost in San Francisco was in Spear Tower, one of the office buildings at the head of Market Street near the waterfront, close by the Reynolds Fincher offices. Judging from their website, the office mainly served as liaison to foreign consulates and diplomatic visitors to the West Coast.

It was 8:00 a.m., and the low clouds over the Bay were glowing like kindling catching fire. Chris and Zoey introduced themselves as walk-ins to the receptionist, who sat behind a mahogany desk under an imposing US seal. Chris attempted to convey the seriousness of their visit to the receptionist without saying too much. He and Zoey had already decided that they weren't going to mention Geist's murder unless they had to. They needed to avoid questions about what Zoey was doing in Geist's apartment, because the State Department did not give aid to those who leak state secrets—they had them prosecuted.

"Are we okay?" Zoey asked.

"I'm not okay with what you did, but at least I understand it. Let's leave it at that for now."

"Fine."

They were greeted by Russell March, a young, clean-cut junior diplomat in shirtsleeves and tie who looked to be fresh out of the Kennedy School. He led them into a conference room that looked out on the Bay Bridge, the shipyards of China Basin, and AT&T Park.

"Now, what can I do for you?" he said.

"We work for a law firm that represents Zapper," Chris said. "We helped them track down Chinese hackers who had stolen their intellectual property. We provided evidence linking that theft to the Chinese government and the People's Liberation Army. The State Department is aware of this. You can check with your colleagues."

"Wow, okay," said March, who clearly hadn't perfected his unflappable diplomatic game face. "So what brings you here?"

"Yesterday someone tried to kill us, and we believe it was a representative of the Chinese government."

"Again, wow. That's a serious charge."

"Yes, wow," Zoey said. "Wow, we were nearly murdered."

"We believe we're still in danger, and we're seeking some kind of protective custody," Chris said. "The man who came for us seemed like a professional. In fact, we believe that he's a contract killer known as Red Sun, who offers his services through the Silk Road website. We think he's going to try again."

Now March looked like he'd just downed a double espresso. "The director is going to need to hear this," he said, rising. "If you will please wait just a few minutes."

A half hour later, March returned with the director of the office, a man with prematurely white hair and a flat-line demeanor.

"Richard Berkheiser," he said, shaking their hands. "I'm so sorry to hear about the incident yesterday."

Marsh sat down next to Berkheiser at the conference table. It was clear the junior diplomat wouldn't be doing any more talking.

"Are you aware of Zapper's cooperation with the State Department regarding the Chinese hackers?" Chris asked.

"I had not been involved, but I just spoke with my colleagues in DC, and I think I'm up to speed. Now I'd like you to tell me what happened yesterday—from the beginning."

Chris and Zoey told the story again. Berkheiser took careful notes.

"You seem pretty composed for two people who've just been shot at."

"Well, you should have seen us yesterday," Zoey said.

"So you believe the man that fired on you was Chinese?"

"Yes, that's right," Chris said.

"Are you certain of that? It was dark, and the man was how far away?"

"About fifteen yards."

"And then when you looked back at him in that dark alley, you were in a car that was speeding away. In a situation like that, a visual identification can be difficult."

"We're certain," Zoey said.

"But you didn't actually see the man, did you, Zoey?"

"Well, no. But if Chris says he saw a Chinese hit man, then that's what he saw."

"About that," Berkheiser said. "It sounds like this man might have been stalking Chris for a robbery when you interrupted him by pulling up in your car."

Zoey bristled. "Then why would a robber fire shots at our car as we pulled away? He was trying to kill us, not rob us."

"There are a lot of mentally disturbed street people in the Financial District and particularly south of Market," Berkheiser said, leveling his cool gaze at them. "He might have been delusional for all we know."

"Are you saying that you don't believe our story?" Chris said.

"Not at all. Not at all. I'm just trying to ascertain the facts. Clearly, you two have been through a traumatic event. But my job is to determine whether this is something that requires a commitment of State Department resources as opposed to, say, the San Francisco Police Department. I'm just asking you the questions that my supervisors are going to ask me."

"I understand," Chris said, and he believed that he did. The State Department was not going to be inclined to acknowledge that the Chinese government might have directly or indirectly sanctioned a hit on two Americans. If Berkheiser accepted their story as told, then that would necessitate a series of next steps, each of which would be more diplomatically awkward than the last. You do not accuse your primary creditor of murder for hire without recognizing the economic and political consequences of that decision.

"Did you report this incident to the police?"

"No," Chris said. "Given the context, we thought that the State Department was the correct venue for this discussion."

"We appreciate your sensitivity to the situation, but I think this actually sounds like a matter that is best directed to the San Francisco Police Department."

"I'm not sure you understand," Zoey said. "There is a hired killer who is hunting us. That hit man was probably paid by the Chinese government. We are US citizens. How is that not a State Department matter?"

Berkheiser raised an index finger. "Let's rewind that because, with all due respect for what you've been through, there are some problems with those statements. First, I'm not hearing any evidence that we're talking about a hired killer. The connections to this Red Sun person are . . . tenuous. Even you put a 'probably' in front of your statement that the assailant was hired by the Chinese government. I think 'probably' is a very strong word, given the facts that you've presented."

"So you're not going to help us?"

"We are going to help you by referring you to the proper authorities—the San Francisco Police Department."

"If you don't believe our story about a Chinese hit man, even with all you know about the Zapper intrusion and the activities of APT1, then I don't think we can expect the SFPD to take our story seriously," Chris said.

"I wouldn't prejudge that," Berkheiser said. "It's their job to protect our citizens from street crime, and that's what this sounds like. If they believe that you need protection, then I'm sure you will get it."

"You know that what we're saying is true, but your bosses have told you not to act on it because it would be—awkward—for you," Zoey said, her face beginning to flush. "How awkward would it be for you if we ended up dead?"

"I understand that you've been through a trauma," Berkheiser said. After a beat, he added, "I even know that you discovered the body of that journalist Matt Geist."

"You knew all along," Zoey said.

Chris recognized that this was the point where he needed to intervene. "Then you also know that's further evidence we are being stalked by a killer."

"Once again that's not a connection that I would necessarily make. The police view that as a drug-motivated robbery-murder. If you don't mind my asking, Ms. Doucet, what brought you to that journalist's apartment in the first place?"

Berkheiser clearly had known before they arrived at his office that Zoey visited Matt Geist's apartment, and he already suspected that she had been attempting to leak the emails from Owyang's computer. If Zoey answered that question fully, then she would be revealing that she had attempted to publicly disclose information that, when it was handed over to the State Department, had become state secrets. The State Department would have already had the FBI arrest Zoey if they had even a shred of evidence to support their suspicions.

Before he could stop her, Zoey spoke. "Matt Geist was a friend. That's why I was there."

Chris was relieved that Zoey had spotted the trap. If she had told Berkheiser what she had told him, then she wouldn't have been permitted to leave the office. Chris might also have been detained as a potential accessory to the disclosure of classified state secrets. While that would presumably put them out of reach of the killer, it would come at a very high price tag, which might include a federal prison sentence.

"Fair enough," Berkheiser said, looking a bit disappointed.

"I think we're done here," Chris said. "Thank you for your time."

"Sorry we can't be of more assistance," Berkheiser said.

"I'm sure you are."

Chris stood. Zoey remained seated. She clearly had a lot that she very much wanted to say to Berkheiser, but knew that it would be a bad idea to do so. For once Zoey exercised discretion.

"C'mon, Zoey," Chris said. "Let's get out of here."

When they were back on Market Street outside the office tower, fog had now rolled in over the waterfront, and the light was gray.

"We're on our own now, aren't we?" Zoey asked.

"Yes, and we need to find a place to hide," Chris said. He felt exposed walking among the suits and tourists. He kept scanning the crowds for a glimpse of the man from the alley advancing on them through the sidewalk throng.

Chris had only had a moment or two in the alley to get a look at the man with the gun, but he would have no trouble recognizing him. He had a round face with bland, even features and black hair that was neatly cut but still fell down over his forehead. The man wouldn't have been memorable at all but for the grim set of his mouth into a tiny slot. It was the expression of concentration that someone might make while taking aim through the scope of a rifle.

Chris took Zoey by the elbow and steered her down the steps of the nearby Embarcadero BART station.

"Where are we going?" she asked.

"Someplace safer than here."

31

As Chris drove into Marin County with Zoey, he was struck, as he always was, by the sight of the Golden Gate Bridge. Whoever had decided to paint the bridge orange vermilion had known what they were doing. Even after all his years in the city, it was still dazzling to see the "International Orange" spires against the backdrop of the blue of the bay and the browns and greens of the Marin Headlands.

"I hope your friend was right about the key to that place in Stinson Beach," Chris said.

"Should be where she said it is."

"I just wish that we had a copy of that flash drive," Chris said. "It's the one thing that might have actually given us some leverage in this situation."

"Even if you had the flash drive, what would you do with it? Threaten to disclose classified materials? Sure, I didn't have a problem with it, but I don't see you going all Edward Snowden."

"If my government isn't willing to protect me from a hit man, then I'm no longer all that concerned about embarrassing my government."

"Now you're talking," she said.

"I just can't believe that they would leave us twisting in the wind like that," Chris said. "They understand what we're up against."

"It's all about plausible deniability. It doesn't mean they won't do anything about it. They just won't acknowledge us."

"Right." Chris nodded. "So who else can we turn to? The law firm can't help us. Not with this."

"What about Zapper?"

"We can try to reach out to Saperstein and Zapper, but I think they're on the same page with the State Department now. I'm not sure they'd be willing to acknowledge our story either."

"But Saperstein has the resources to help, and they don't have to issue a press release about it. Our lives are in danger because you completed the assignment that he sent you on. You've been his trusted adviser for years. He should step up."

"Maybe he would if I asked," Chris said. "But think about the hackers we're up against—what they've done already. The more people we try to involve in hiding us, the more danger we're in."

"Probably right," said Zoey. "If Zapper can't protect its most precious corporate secrets, then how are they going to protect the location of our hideout?"

Chris slipped a Bach CD into the dashboard player, and the small space filled with the mellifluous groan of Unaccompanied Cello Suite No. 1 in G Major as performed by Yo-Yo Ma. Even when the world seemed to be spinning off its axis, Bach's compositions restored the illusion that there was some kind of order to life, some perfect equipoise between thought and feeling, contemplation and action.

"That's nice," Zoey said. "But in a half hour I'm going to want to hear some Buzzcocks."

Chris pulled onto Highway 1, and soon they were on the narrow, winding road through canyons and gulches that led to Stinson.

Outside the passenger window, the vine-laced cliffs raced by so fast and close that the eye could not focus.

They came over a crest and looked down on a long, verdant canyon that tumbled to the Pacific, which was pocked like pebbled glass under a low and cloudy sky. The road began to slowly wind downward in a queasy roller-coaster ride. Each roadside sign warning of turns ahead was more twisted and contorted than the last.

"Have you ever been to this place before?" Chris asked.

"The house? No, but I've heard Krissa talk about it so much that I feel like I have. She loves it out here. She liked to come here when she was in a dark mood."

"I can see why," Chris said.

They were on the main drag of Stinson Beach, which consisted of about a dozen funky mom-and-pop businesses just a hundred yards away from the beach and the relentlessly crashing waves. They rolled through the town and, before they even had time to comment on how small it was, had reached the other side.

"Here," Zoey said, pointing at a dirt path.

They followed the rutted road through the pines and up the hill to a clapboard cabin. It once had been white, but the paint was coming off.

He parked the car, and Zoey led him around to an overgrown garden in the back. She went directly to a large gray stone in a patch of begonias that was engraved with the words "Give Up," mocking the vapid positivity of New Agey Zen garden stones. A tabby slunk away into the undergrowth at their approach.

She lifted up one edge of the stone and reached underneath. She came up with a key and smiled.

They returned to the front of the house and stepped onto the creaking front porch. Chris looked back down the path to see if anyone was observing them entering, but he saw no one, just the pines and eucalyptus trees swaying in the gusting wind. Over the treetops, past the main road, he could see that the sky had turned nearly black on the horizon, and the rain was falling far away, evidenced only as faint, pale etchings on the darkness.

The key turned in the lock, and Zoey led the way.

The air in the cabin was stale and still. The interior was nicer than he would have guessed from outside. There were a few worn but comfortable-looking pieces of furniture, two bedrooms, and a small flat-screen TV. A stone fireplace blackened by smoke stains occupied most of the rear wall. A kitchen window in the back looked out on the pleasant overgrown garden, the kind that appeared to have been consciously cultivated to look wild and unkempt.

Chris went to the refrigerator, opened the door, and was greeted by a pungent smell.

"We're going to need some provisions," he said. "And we'll have to clean this thing out."

"Krissa's not much of a housekeeper," Zoey said.

Chris removed his Glock 19 pistol from his computer bag, loaded it, and laid it on the kitchen table.

"I didn't realize that you were carrying that," Zoey said.

"Does it make you feel better or worse that I have it?"

"I'll think about that and get back to you. What are you going to do with a gun anyway?"

"For someone who has put as many people in jail as I did at the DOJ, it's pretty much mandatory. I have a permit for it." Chris stood in the living room and turned in a circle. "As a place to hide out, this is pretty good." He ran a hand through his hair. "But I've been think-ing about something you said."

"Uh-oh."

"You were probably right that Zapper couldn't hide the location of this place even if they knew it. The PLA no doubt has a team of hackers supporting this hit man, and they are highly skilled. With the PLA's sophistication and unlimited resources, they can get whatever they want."

"Right. So?"

"To hide, we'd have to stay entirely off the grid, and that's not an easy thing to do for an extended period."

"So what are you saying? We're no match for a professional killer backed by the resources of the PLA, so let's give up?"

"No, I'm saying that maybe we don't wait for him to find us. Maybe we lead him here."

"And do what, then? Kill him?"

Chris didn't respond.

"Even if we did, wouldn't they just send another hired killer after us?"

"Maybe. Probably."

"You know how you're sounding?"

Chris looked at the pistol, then back to her. "Right now it's him or us, so how about if we make it him?"

Zoey flashed a nervous smile. "Sometimes I forget that you are a badass, Chris Bruen." She paused, a thoughtful look crossing her face. "You said you thought we couldn't go completely off the grid. What if we could?"

"What do you mean?"

"I know someone who's been living off the grid for years. From an electronic-surveillance perspective, he's a ghost. And I know how we could join him if we wanted to."

"Who is this person?"

"Damien Hull."

"Damien Hull! We convicted him under the ECPA when I was at Justice. He's been on the lam for—what?—three years?"

"Exactly."

"You really expect me to leave my life and career behind and go underground like a fugitive?"

"At least you'd *have* a life. And when things have settled down and the Chinese have stopped sending hit men to take us out, maybe we could come back."

Chris was silent for a while, stalking about the house and getting his head around their limited options. Finally, he said, "*If* we were to go off the grid, how would we go about it?"

"It takes time to reach Damien and for him to respond. Maybe a week, ten days."

"If we stop this guy who's coming for us, it might buy us that much time before the PLA could send someone else."

"I'll reach out to Damien, start the process," Zoey said.

"I reserve the right not to go."

"Damien won't like it if you back out."

"I can live with that," Chris said. "But if we draw that hit man out here to Stinson Beach, you need to leave," Chris said. "I'm the primary target. You don't have to be here."

"We've had this conversation before," Zoey said. "And you remember how it ended, right? I'm not leaving you to face this alone. We're better as a team."

"Are you sure about that?"

"I'm sure. Remember he killed a friend of mine. It's on me that I brought that flash drive to Geist's apartment. I have to help make this right the only way that I know how."

"This man is a professional, and we're not. This will probably not end well."

"All the more reason for me to stay. At least there will be two of us. And if I left you to face him alone, I don't think I could live with myself. So there's really nothing to talk about, is there?"

"I guess not," Chris said with a sigh. "Sometimes I forget that you're a badass too."

32

Chris walked down the long dirt driveway to the main road and then back into the town of Stinson Beach. The air was humid and moist, a harbinger of a coming storm. Lightning ripped the sky in the distance, and he could detect the ozone in the air, like cordite after a gunshot. He hoped that he could make it back to the cabin before the rain swept in.

In a community this small, people noticed visitors who were not tourists. That was okay, because Chris wanted to be seen and remembered. He passed a surf shop with a longboard leaning against a sign that bore the outline of a shark with a bar drawn through it: no sharks. He had once known an attorney who had kept a sticker with that same logo on his office computer. Since they were both working at one of the world's largest law firms, Chris had always considered it a bit of wishful thinking.

After passing an ice-cream shop and a gas station, Chris arrived at a place called Dallesandro's, which looked like a country store. An elderly man with a thick mane of white hair sat on a stool behind the register. He wore wire-rimmed glasses and a richly colored flannel shirt. He looked up from the crossword puzzle book that he was working and gave Chris a nod that seemed to say, *You're not a local.*

Chris stocked up on provisions for the cabin—soda, cold cuts, cheese, bread, and beer. While he and Zoey did need all of those things, the main point of the visit was to use his debit card for the purchase—the equivalent of a homing beacon for PLA hackers. The State Department as well . . . if they were interested in knowing where he'd gone. And if that wasn't enough, Chris had also put the SIM card back in his cell phone.

"Looks like a big storm coming," Chris said to the man behind the counter.

"We're used to 'em." As he rang up the last of the groceries, he added, "You look like you're settling in for a while."

"Yeah. My friend and I are staying up the road. The cabin off that dirt road just outside of town."

"Oh, you must be in the Jackson place. Is the girl there? The one with all the tattoos?"

"You mean Krissa?"

"Right, Krissa."

"No, she loaned us the place."

"Too bad."

"Sorry to disappoint you."

"My apologies, mister. I didn't mean it that way. It's just that Krissa knows that I like Westerns, but I don't know the new movies. She gives me recommendations. Last time she recommended *The Proposition*."

"That's a good one."

"I thought so too." The old man studied him for a moment, gauging whether he was the sort to put the question to. "You got any Westerns that you'd recommend? Don't bother with anything by Ford, Hawkes, or Peckinpah. I got the classics covered."

This was not the conversation Chris was expecting, but he gave it some thought. "Have you ever seen *Barbarosa*?"

"Who's in it?"

"Willie Nelson. And Gary Busey."

"Willie Nelson, huh? Can he act?"

"Well enough. Give it a try. It's Australian. Like *The Proposition*."

"Those Aussies do seem to get Westerns, don't they? Must be the landscape down there or something."

"Probably right," Chris said. "And if you like the really old Westerns, you might like *Hearts of the West*. It's about the making of the old Western serials in Gower Gulch in the nineteen twenties."

"And who's in that?"

"Andy Griffith and Jeff Bridges, when he was just a kid. Not the typical Andy Griffith role, but that's all I'm going to say about that."

The old man scribbled on a pad. "Sounds interesting. I think I'm going to like having you here. But don't tell Krissa that you gave me recommendations. Don't want her to think that what we have ain't special."

Chris nodded sagely. "She'll never know."

Raindrops began to patter on his jacket as he trudged slowly back up the dirt road to the cabin. The ground was already growing slick and muddy from the rain. Chris was still thinking about the classic Westerns. He was starting to feel like a character in one of those stories. There was a two-bit town. There was a lawman of sorts who was woefully outgunned and unprepared. And there was a bad man coming.

33

Tao's burner phone buzzed. The text message read simply, *"Your package is ready."* That was the signal from Ms. Wan that there was something waiting for him at the designated dead-drop site.

He drove to Washington Square Park in North Beach and sat down at the bench closest to the bustle and traffic of Columbus Avenue under a sky that looked like a science experiment, dark clouds roiling against sunny sky like two warring chemical compounds. Across the park climbed the white Gothic spires of Sts. Peter and Paul Churches, crowded on one side by a pale-blue Victorian that seemed to remind, *This isn't Europe; this is San Francisco.*

Tao had absorbed enough American popular culture to know that northern California was supposed to be a place where people were "mellow" and relaxed, but they certainly didn't seem that way to him. The locals stretched out on blankets, reading or listening to iPhones, on the green expanse of the park were among the few he'd seen in the Bay Area who weren't moving at high velocity. Even when they were at rest, these Americans seemed to vibrate with intensity and caffeine.

Tao resisted the urge to immediately reach for the package, spending a few minutes taking in his surroundings. He watched the tourists who filled the narrow sidewalks of North Beach, which were further narrowed by the café tables of the neighborhood's famous Italian restaurants. He surveyed the other park benches, the dog walkers, and the Frisbee throwers, looking for someone to make eye contact, someone who was there to observe him. There was no need to hurry.

He watched a pretty young American girl walk by in shorts, hauling a backpack. Her long hair was blond and shone in the sun. He smiled to himself, imagined the blood pulsing beneath that perfect, unblemished skin and what it would look like if he were covered in it. A part of him was repelled by these thoughts, but they crowded his mind with increasing persistence. He was changing, and it made him uncomfortable, but how could you despise something that revealed your true self?

Once he had convinced himself that the park scene was as normal as it appeared, he reached under the bench and found a manila envelope secured there with adhesive putty. He pried it free and slid the envelope into his copy of the *San Francisco Chronicle* and then placed the newspaper inside his satchel. After a few more minutes watching a group of young men playing some leaping game that involved a Frisbee, Tao rose and walked away.

He walked up Columbus for a couple of blocks, took a left, and sat down at a sidewalk table at Café Tosca, where he could study both passersby and those inside. With its red-and-black-checked floor tiles, weathered wooden bar, and yellowed, turn-of-the-previous-century framed portraits, the café seemed to celebrate its past, wearing its history—or what passed for history in the US—on its sleeve.

He enjoyed the rain-scented breeze on his face for a moment, then tore open the tab of the envelope. Inside, there was a short file on Zoey Doucet, information that might be useful in tracking the pair. Some of it would have been easy to obtain, such as the home address. Other information would have been more difficult to come by, such as her full work history and her most recent debit card statement, which was effectively a map of her movements for the past month.

Tao weighed the usefulness of the information contained in the file in tracking Bruen and Doucet. Doucet's past movements might not be that helpful. If she and Bruen had any sense, they would go someplace outside their ordinary sphere. But even someone trying to break from their patterns might need the help of a friend. And friends can be linked to the places that you've worked in the past. Zoey was still relatively new to her law firm job, so it was likely that her best friends would be associated with her recent job history.

He had already scoured his file on Bruen and thus far had not found any promising leads. Bruen seemed to be a bit of a loner and did not have a large network of friends, so there were not many obvious angles for tracking him down. Tao didn't judge Bruen for it. He lived that way himself.

Prior to the law firm job, Doucet worked at a music club called the Bottom of the Hill. She appeared to have worked there as a bartender intermittently over three years. The club was only a short drive away, so that seemed like a good place to start.

*   *   *

The Bottom of the Hill club was quiet as he pushed through the door in the late afternoon, a quiet that seemed all the more intense because it was clearly not the place's natural state. Dusty shafts of sunlight crisscrossed the dark room from a high window like support beams.

The walls were covered with photos of rock bands and scrawled band logos. Such a place would be considered a hotbed of political insurrection in his homeland. In China, a club that featured rock music seven nights a week could not exist, partly due to government censorship (Chinese rock, or *yáogǔn*, tended to be political) and partly due to apathy. With the exception of a brief, shining moment after Tiananmen Square, most Chinese young people were not particularly interested in rock and roll. They were far more interested in commerce and finding their place in the Chinese economic renaissance.

Bottles clinked behind the bar.

Tao walked through the gloomy pool room, approached the bar, and leaned down to find a young man wearing a black T-shirt and a two-day stubble.

"Excuse me," Tao said.

The man jumped, and bottles clanked. "Whoa. I didn't see you there."

"I didn't mean to startle you."

The bartender stood. He was tall, at least six foot three, and thin. He wasn't physically imposing, but it was a bar, and you never knew what might be tucked under the counter—anything from a baseball bat to a shotgun.

"What can I do for you?"

"I'm looking for someone who used to work here. Zoey Doucet. Do you know her?"

The man's eyes narrowed. "Who are you?"

"I have a package for her."

"What sort of package?"

"It's personal."

"If you're talking drugs, Zoey doesn't do them. So if that's what you're suggesting, it's a lie."

"Did I say that? Zoey will want to see me. You can call her and ask if you like."

It was a calculated gamble. If the bartender actually had Zoey's number, then he couldn't allow him to alert her that he was on her trail. On the other hand, if he didn't have Zoey's number, then it was a way of winning his confidence.

"What's your name?"

"Ken Ma. What's yours?"

"Justin." Justin stared at him for a long moment, then said, "Well, I don't have her cell number anyway, so I can't help you."

A pudgy young girl with a nose ring and red tights under a skirt stepped behind the bar, having overhead a snippet of the conversation.

"Are you looking for Zoey Doucet? She was just here. Krissa must know where she's at." She said this looking at Justin for confirmation, anxious to show that she was part of their clique, which clearly included the much-revered Zoey.

Justin scowled at her.

"Is Krissa here?" Tao asked, trying to make the question as bland as possible.

Justin started to speak, but the girl interrupted, anxious to help. "She's right upstairs. I can go get her."

"No, that won't be necessary," Tao said. "Thanks. I'll go myself."

"I'll go with you," Justin said, suspicious, but not suspicious enough to try to stop him.

Justin led Tao up the stairs to a small apartment above the club. The girl who must be Krissa was sprawled on a dingy couch, reading a paperback. She sat up when the two of them entered, looking a bit foggy after being immersed in her book.

"Who are you?" Krissa asked. She stood and seemed to snap into focus quickly.

"Ken Ma," Tao said. "A friend of Zoey's."

"She never mentioned you to me."

Krissa was lean and tattooed, and she had an alertness about her that made Tao think he shouldn't drop his guard. If the situation called for it, this was someone who might know what to do with a broken beer bottle.

"Well, I've never heard of you before either. I'm looking for Zoey."

"Why?"

"It's personal. I have something that I need to deliver to her."

"What is this personal thing that you need to deliver?"

"If I told you, it wouldn't be personal, would it?"

"I'm a good friend of Zoey, and I don't think she would mind."

"But I don't know that, do I?"

Krissa put her hands on her knees, ready to wrap up the conversation and get him out of there. "How about this? You give me your message, and I'll see if I can get it to her. You can seal it in an envelope if you like. I won't open it."

"That doesn't work for me."

"Then I guess we have nothing more to say."

Justin stared at Tao with what he probably hoped was a menacing glare. Tao considered escalating the situation right there in the room, but he recognized that would be far too messy. And the pudgy girl downstairs would also have to be dealt with, or she would call the police.

"Okay," Tao said. "But Zoey won't like it when she hears how uncooperative you've been."

"I'll live with that," Krissa said.

Tao descended the stairs and left the club. He took up a seat in his car, parked down the street, and watched the entrance to the club for an hour, waiting for Krissa to emerge. They would continue their conversation one-on-one, and he knew that she would be more forthcoming this time. He opened his bag and checked the power drill, making sure that the battery was charged. He would need plenty of battery life for what he had in mind.

After an hour of sitting in the warm car, Tao saw Krissa exit the bar. He picked up the bag with the power drill and climbed out of the car to follow her.

She walked for three blocks past several Potrero Hill bars and then disappeared into an old, brown-brick apartment building. A few minutes later, the curtains in a window were pulled open.

Now they could continue their conversation. His heart beating faster, Tao swung his bag over his shoulder and crossed the street.

On the sidewalk outside the apartment building, his burner phone pinged, and he stopped.

There was a text from Ms. Wan that read, *"Bruen used his debit card at Dallesandro's Market in Stinson Beach. Lots of groceries. They're clearly staying somewhere nearby."*

Tao debated whether to proceed upstairs and continue his conversation with Krissa or get in the car and drive to Stinson Beach. She seemed to know something about Zoey's location. Krissa seemed like a strong person, so it might take some time to get the information out of her.

He checked his map and saw that Stinson Beach was at least an hour's drive from where he was. In the time it took to finish with Krissa, Bruen and Doucet might be able to move on to a new hiding place. For all he knew, Krissa might have already called Zoey to tell her about the strange man who had been asking about her. And he already had a good lead on their whereabouts—Dallesandro's Market.

It was a close call, and he stood for a long moment on the sidewalk, weighing his options.

Tao decided that interrogating Krissa was probably not worth the time it would consume. He would drive directly to Stinson Beach.

Krissa would never know just how close she had come. He regretted the missed opportunity, but he was confident that he would soon have another chance to practice his craft.

34

The winding road out to Stinson Beach was treacherous in the hard rain, and Tao had to be careful not be lulled into drowsiness by the metronomic ticking of the windshield wipers. The narrow stretch of road in front of him blurred, then the wiper passed and it snapped back into focus. Blur and focus. Blur and focus. Like an eye exam. Perhaps the weather would ultimately work to his advantage. Bruen and Doucet would be more likely to stay put and hunker down in their hiding place.

The scenery was probably beautiful in different weather, but that was irrelevant. He had a job to do.

Tao tried listening to the radio to maintain his alertness—some sort of classic rock station—but eventually all of the stations faded to static as he got farther into the wild terrain.

When he reached the flats, the tension in his hands and back eased. He rolled slowly through the town of Stinson Beach, which was no more than a two-block stretch of stores. Dallesandro's was not hard to find.

He opened the door to the grocery, and a bell jingled. The shop appeared empty, but the Western-style music of a soundtrack swelled. He took a step or two into the store, and the old wooden floorboards creaked.

Then a gray-haired man popped up from behind the counter. "Hello there."

"Hello."

"Nasty out there, isn't it?"

"It sure is."

"Hardly anyone comes in on days like this, so I just sit down behind the counter here and watch a movie. Easier on the arches." The man pointed at a small television set on a stool with a VHS VCR resting on top. He clicked a remote and froze the movie. "What can I do for you?"

"I was looking for someone who's visiting here."

"Well, if someone's staying out here, they usually end up in my place sooner or later. We're the only grocery for about ten miles in either direction."

"His name is Chris Bruen."

"Don't recognize it."

"Tall man about six foot three. Dark hair. He's with a girl."

"Good for him."

"Her name is Zoey Doucet. She's a little bit younger."

"Once again, good for him."

"The girl has brown hair."

The old man shook his head. "Still not ringing any bells."

Tao's hand started to move toward the gun tucked in his belt under his navy-blue rain parka.

"Wait a second," the shopkeeper said. "I might have seen the man. They didn't come in as a couple. Dark hair? Kinda wild on top?"

"Yes, that's right."

"Well, I think I did see him then."

"When was he here?"

"Just yesterday."

"Do you know where he's staying?"

The old man hesitated. "Well, you know, some people come out here for a little privacy. I know that you're probably a friend and all, but I don't like to share personal information about my customers."

"I understand, but I really need to see them."

"I don't get many customers to begin with, so I don't need to be alienating anyone."

"They won't mind, believe me."

"I think it's best if you just give them a call. You have their phone number, right?"

"Actually, I don't," Tao said, his impatience welling. "See, he changed his cell number recently, and I haven't spoken to him since then."

"If you haven't spoken with him lately, how did you know he was here?"

"A friend told me."

"Couldn't that friend give you his new cell number?"

Tao looked back at the front door of the store. It was closed. There was no one on the sidewalk outside, and the rain was pouring in a sheet off the awning, providing a sense of privacy as if a curtain had been drawn across the doorway.

The shopkeeper caught the look and what it meant, and his eyes widened.

Tao glanced at the back of the store and saw that there was a door next to a restroom that must lead to the alley behind the shop. If he left through the front door, someone might spot him.

"I won't say anything," the man said.

"I know."

"Why?"

"You know why."

"No, I don't."

"You'd warn them."

"How do you know that? Maybe I don't give a damn what business you have with them."

"No, I can tell. You're a good person. You'd want to warn them."

"And you're not? A good person, I mean."

"No."

Tao drew his gun and put a bullet in the middle of the old man's forehead. He collapsed on the spot, eyes wide, and the look of surprise still there on his face.

Tao peered over the counter. Above the crumpled body, the television set was still frozen on a street scene from the Wild West, a gunslinger walking down a dusty town's main street, glowering from under a hat drawn low.

Tao exited by the rear door, careful not to leave prints on the knob. He pulled up the hood of his parka, the hard rain popping and spattering against it, and walked down an alleyway lined with Dumpsters.

He'd parked his rental car down the road, knowing that any unfamiliar cars on the short stretch of the main drag might be noticed. He sat and watched the front of the shop through the rain-streaked windshield.

There was a time when he would have felt an irresistible urge to flee after killing a person, put as much distance as possible between himself and the crime scene. Now, though, he felt a calm that came with the confidence that he was the deadliest living thing in this small rain-soaked town.

He was the apex predator.

35

Zoey saw the police car parked in front of Dallesandro's from far down the street. She thought about turning back right then, but she felt compelled to see. She put one foot in front of the other until she reached the crime scene tape strung from the posts in front of the grocery store and around the entrance.

It was hard to tell what was going on from the sidewalk as a couple of police officers crowded in, along with someone from the coroner's office. But she saw a brand-new Nike running shoe extended beyond the edge of the shop counter, along with an argyle sock and aged ankle, the skin stretched taut and dry like canvas over the bone.

A deputy came out of the shop and addressed the locals who were gathered on the sidewalk. "Please, they need room to do their work. I know you all knew Henry, but the best thing you can do now is go home. You're not going to learn anything here, and you can read about it in the *Beachcomber* tomorrow. Please."

Zoey stood with the crowd of locals for a few moments more and then turned and walked quickly back toward the house. As she climbed the winding dirt path, Zoey had the distinct sense that she was being followed. It took all of the discipline she could muster not to turn and scan behind her.

The dirt driveway was slippery with mud, and she nearly fell a couple of times as she trudged up the rutted path. She pulled up the hood of her sweatshirt against the rain. There was no point in showing her face now. He had either seen her or not. He was either coming or he wasn't.

She had made this walk the past two days, waiting for the killer to come calling. But this time it was hard to keep her terror under control because she knew he had arrived in Stinson Beach. This was the day when their plan would work, or they would die.

When Zoey reached the porch, she fumbled with the keys and got inside quickly, locking the door behind her. Her racing pulse began to slow a bit.

Zoey felt sick with the knowledge that the shopkeeper would not be dead if she and Chris had not brought the killer to Stinson Beach. When this was all over, she was going to have to reckon with that death, as well the death of Matt Geist. Death was following them wherever they went now, and that was not a figure of speech. This had to end, and she hoped Chris would be able to spring their trap soon.

*   *   *

Chris crouched in the bushes about ten yards back from the path up to the house. He had hated to send Zoey into town to draw the killer back here, but this was a two-person job, and Zoey did not want to be the one to pull the trigger. Chris figured that the man would follow Zoey rather than shoot her on the spot because he would want to make sure he found Chris, his primary target.

He heard wet sounds in the distance as someone advanced up the muddy path. Chris was relieved when he saw that it was Zoey, taking short steps to avoid slipping. Zoey glanced his way but didn't make a show of it. She didn't seem to see him hidden in the woods, though she knew he hid somewhere in that direction.

From his vantage point, Chris could see all the way back down the path to the main road. He saw no one.

Maybe the killer wasn't coming. Maybe he didn't have access to their credit card activity and had no idea they were in Stinson Beach. Perhaps Chris had given him too much credit.

Then Chris heard a rustling in the bushes below.

It might just be a squirrel, a cat, or some other animal looking for shelter from the storm. Then he heard the sound again, a little closer this time. If it was an animal, it was a large one. Adrenaline shot through him like a lightning strike.

Chris already had his gun at his side, but now he slipped the safety off and raised it in the direction from which the sounds were emanating. His hands were trembling, and it was hard to keep the gun steady. Hunters called it "buck fever."

The killer would recognize that this might be a trap, so of course he wasn't going to skip up the path to the house. The problem was that the man had instead chosen to sneak through the bushes, following a path that would lead him directly to Chris's hiding place. Chris was not going to have the clean shot he had hoped for.

Chris recognized that the element of surprise was the only thing he had going for him. Once the killer spotted him, it would come down to who was more proficient with their gun, and Chris was pretty sure that was a matchup he could not win against a professional hit man. Chris had fired a gun before, but he was no marksman.

The wet bed of ground cover steamed a bit after the rain, sending up a loamy scent. The branches around him ticked faintly, weighed down by the rain.

Chris stared with all of the focus he was capable of, trying to see as deeply into the trees as possible to spot the man as soon as he came into view. If Chris fired too soon, he would plant a bunch of slugs in the trees, and the killer would proceed to take him out in short order.

A branch rustled in the distance, about thirty yards down the hill from him. Chris made himself small, hunkering down into the underbrush without making a sound, and tried to steady his aim by resting his forearm on a log. He desperately hoped that the killer was alone and didn't have a partner who had already outflanked him and taken Zoey.

The branch rustled again, and a man came into view. It was the Chinese man who fired at them on Beale Street. And he had not seen Chris yet.

Chris took a breath, exhaled slowly, then squeezed the trigger and fired every bullet he had into the area where the man was standing. The gun sounded incredibly loud and kicked up in his grip. The shots tore and whistled through the leaves and branches.

When the chamber was empty and he had steadied from the recoil, Chris lowered the gun and looked at the place where the man had stood. The man wasn't visible, and Chris had no idea whether he had hit him.

Chris reloaded and then held perfectly still. The hit man might be lying in wait for him to advance to check for a body. But if Chris turned and headed back to the house now, the man could hunt him down from behind.

After a few interminable minutes, Chris realized he had to do something, and he decided that if he was going to be gunned down, he would rather that it not be in the back. He rose into a low crouch and began to advance through the underbrush.

Although he tried to move quietly, that proved impossible. To his ears, Chris sounded like a rampaging wildebeest as he made his way forward, cracking twigs and rustling bushes. The killer would definitely hear Chris coming—if he was alive.

Chris slowed as he neared the trees where the man had been. Then he stepped forward quickly into the spot, gun raised and swiveling.

No one there. Chris scanned the surrounding woods but found no figure in sight.

There was a spot at his feet where the ground seemed to be spattered with blood. Chris leaned down and touched the leaves, and his fingers were red when he brought them up. A bit farther down the hillside there was also a red smear on a tree trunk. If the killer was retreating down the hillside, then he must be badly wounded.

Chris advanced a few more steps, but the man was nowhere to be seen. He decided to turn back to make sure Zoey was safe.

36

By the time Tao saw Bruen crouching up ahead behind a fallen tree, it was already too late. Before he could get off a shot, he felt a punch and a sting in his left leg and right side. He had been hit and, even in the first numb moments when the gunshot feels no worse than a hard slap, he knew that he'd been badly injured.

Tao threw himself on the ground. He might pass out soon, and he needed to escape back down the hill as quickly as possible. Almost immediately he began feeling the effects of the blood loss, the sensation that his head was a balloon slowly filling with helium and drifting away from his body.

Going back the way he came through the brush would create plenty of noise, and he would be easy to follow. Tao gambled that Bruen would be frozen for a few critical moments, trying to decide whether Tao was dead or not, whether he should advance or retreat.

Tao ducked out of the woods onto the grass and staggered back down the hill as quickly as he could. Each time he put weight on it, his damaged left leg sent an electric spike of pain through his body, but he could not stop. If Bruen happened to step out to the path to look for him, he would have a clear shot. But Bruen did not emerge from the bushes, and Tao succeeded in putting some distance between him and the man he had hoped to kill.

Now he was far enough away that an amateur like Bruen would not be able to make the shot even if he saw him. Of course, if Tao collapsed before he could make it to the road, then he would make Bruen's job easy. He wondered if Bruen was the type who would turn him over to the police or shoot him on the spot. Tao certainly knew what he would do in that situation.

Tao made it down to the street that ran into town. His car was parked only a block away. He looked back up the hill and saw Bruen standing on the grass next to the dirt driveway, staring at him.

They spent a long moment sizing each other up from a distance, like two infantrymen across a muddy field of battle. Tao wondered if he had underestimated Bruen and his abilities. Bruen was probably thinking the converse, entertaining the mistaken notion that he could confront a professional killer and come out on top.

Tao gave a nod that he wasn't sure Bruen could see at that distance and then limped away. This was not over. Not even close.

He got in the car and drove away quickly. Although he needed to tend his wounds, he was still too close to the house. He wanted to make sure Bruen didn't appear behind him and start firing into the car while he was wrapping bandages.

The seat of the car was slick with blood as he drove slowly through the quiet town, past the yellow crime-scene tape strung in front of Dallesandro's grocery. The police cruiser remained parked out front and had been joined by an ambulance to remove the body. Tao slowed momentarily, like any ordinary rubbernecker, then rolled out of town and onto winding, forested Highway 1.

When he was a couple of miles outside of Stinson, Tao pulled off the road and onto a patch of gravel near a beach. He removed his shirt and tore it into long strips, leaving his undershirt on. He tied one strip around the bullet wound in his leg, which was leaking a mixture of blood and pinkish fluid. Fortunately, the bullet hadn't hit a major artery, but it remained lodged somewhere in his leg.

He then tied two strips of the shirt cloth together to make a binding for the bullet hole below the rib cage on his right side. The wound was large and it ached, but there was no way to tell if the bullet had damaged organs. At least that bullet had gone clean through.

He needed medical attention but could not show up in a hospital emergency room. Tao needed a place that would take him in and hide him, and that meant returning to Chinatown.

*   *   *

By the time Tao made it into the city and was driving down the steep incline of California Street, the streetlights had started to strobe and glow with an unnatural brightness. He felt like he was piloting a plane approaching a landing strip, wobbling on every axis like an aircraft in rough air. He had lost a great deal of blood, but he felt he could probably survive if he could just make it to Ms. Wan and her antique shop.

Tao left his car blocking an alley behind Chongqing Bazaar Antiques. He knew better than to enter through the front door looking like he did. If he were that indiscreet, Ms. Wan might very well kill him herself.

He went to the rear of the shop and leaned his forehead and a forearm against the iron door to steady himself, then pounded on it with his fist as forcefully as he could. Tao wasn't even sure what time it was. If the shop was closed and Ms. Wan had gone home, then he would probably bleed out where he stood in the grimy alleyway.

After what seemed like a long time but might not have been, the door began to open with a metallic groan, pushing him backward. Tao staggered back a step or two so that the door could open wide, and Ms. Wan appeared.

She looked him up and down with a look of unabashed disgust. "I take it the target is still alive?"

Tao nodded.

"Looks like you've made a mess of yourself. I suppose I'm going to have to help you. Come inside." Ms. Wan offered him her shoulder to lean on and led him into the building. "They're not going to like this."

"I will finish the job."

"Forgive me if I have my doubts at this point."

Ms. Wan sat him down in the leather desk chair in her office and immediately began making calls. Although he knew that what she was saying was very important, he found that he could only take in her conversation as a low, comforting hum. The hum filled his head, and he grew drowsy. He imagined himself in a darkened room watching an episode of *Game of Thrones* on television with his brother. He and Wenyan were both about ten years old, so the chronology wasn't correct, but somehow it all made perfect sense to Tao. Before he slipped away entirely, he thought that if this was the afterlife—watching *Game of Thrones* for eternity in a dark room with his brother—then it was not so bad.

Not bad at all.

* * *

Tao drifted upward into wakefulness to the glare of a bare bulb hanging from the ceiling in the sort of metal light fixture you would expect to find in a factory. The bulb threw shadows on the face of a tall man standing over him. In the harsh light, the lines of his face looked like crevasses, canyons viewed from an airplane.

Tao realized that he was no longer in Ms. Wan's antique shop. He was stretched out on a table covered with thin paper like the kind that was used to cover a toilet seat. He looked down at himself and saw that his chest was covered in blood, and the man was suturing the wound in his side. This did not look like a hospital or a doctor's office, though.

"Where am I?"

"Give him another one," said the man in Mandarin to someone other than Tao.

Ms. Wan came into view and pushed a fat white pill into his mouth. She placed a hand behind his head and raised it enough to pour a swallow of water into his mouth. He coughed as he swallowed the pill. His stomach muscles tensed with the cough, and he felt a nearly unbearable pain in his lower torso.

"Where am I?"

"You're in Chinatown."

"Am I in a hospital?"

"Does this look like a hospital to you? Don't worry. Your friend here has arranged everything. You're safe."

"Who are you?"

"That's not important. What's important is that you lie still and let me finish sewing you up. Those pills work fast, so you should be—"

Tao didn't hear the rest.

37

When Tao awoke again, he was on a bed in an apartment that was empty, save for a straight-backed wooden chair and a suspended IV bag dripping a clear fluid. It seemed that every time he awakened, he lay in a different place. It was very confusing.

He could see through the open door into the living room, which was entirely bare. Tao knew he was still in Chinatown, based upon his view of shop signs in Mandarin and English through the gap in the curtains. He must be in an apartment above the shops of Grant Avenue or one of Chinatown's other main thoroughfares. It was dark outside, and he wondered if twenty-four hours had passed since he had been wounded in Stinson Beach. Or it could have been forty-eight hours—seventy-two, for all he knew.

Whatever he had been given for the pain was wearing off, and his entire body throbbed. It felt like the pain was a knife and he was the whetstone; each time it came back a little sharper.

As he reconstructed the events that had brought him there, he realized just how close to death he had come. He had been lucky that Bruen wasn't a good enough shot to kill him on the spot on that wooded hillside in Stinson Beach. Lucky to make it all the way back to Chinatown without bleeding out. Luckier still to have received the services of Ms. Wan's back-alley doctor.

It was an embarrassment to have been outsmarted by an amateur, an affront to Tao's professional pride. But he also took the fact he was still alive as a sign that he was meant to finish the job.

He heard footsteps approaching on hardwood, echoing in the bare rooms. A man appeared in the bedroom doorway. He was Chinese, in his midthirties, wearing tobacco-brown slacks, a cream-colored pullover, and an expensive-looking leather jacket.

"You don't look so good," the man said.

Tao tried and failed to pull himself up in bed. "Who are you?"

"I'm a person who knows when things happen here in Chinatown."

"What do you want with me?"

"I represent a local benevolent organization. We provide community services, small business loans, that sort of thing."

"You mean a tong."

"That word carries so many negative connotations. It's a remnant of another time."

While he might object to the use of the term, Tao doubted that the tongs had evolved beyond their well-known control of prostitution, gambling, and drugs in Chinatown. "What brings you here?"

"Ms. Wan told us why you're here in the US."

"That was supposed to be confidential."

"Ms. Wan understands that we are not people that you withhold information from. You're going to have to leave."

"Why?"

"Because we can't be seen to be harboring someone who is opposing the US government. We have enough trouble with local law enforcement. We don't need to bring the feds down on us."

"You're not harboring me. I assume that you didn't arrange for this apartment."

"No, we didn't. But this is our turf, and we are accountable for what happens here. To suggest that something like this could happen under our noses without our knowledge is, frankly, a little insulting."

"No offense was intended."

The man picked up Tao's pants, which were hung over the back of the chair next to the bed. He fished out the wallet and examined his ID and passport.

"I assume that these are fake."

Tao shrugged in acknowledgment.

"My boss asked me to find out who you are. I'm going to need to have an answer for that question when I return."

"I'm not going to give you my real name."

The man approached the bed and examined Tao's wounds. "Those look painful. You really want me to do what comes next?"

Tao knew what was coming next, and he hoped to avoid it. "I can tell you this. If you want to know who I am and what I do, take a look at the 'White Wolves Professionals' page on the Silk Road website. I work under the name Red Sun. Hopefully that'll be enough for your boss."

"Maybe. We'll see. But you're still going to have to go."

Tao attempted to move, then groaned at the sharp pain it caused. "I'm not in any shape to leave yet."

"I think that probably depends on how motivated you are."

"If you know why I'm here, then you must know who's backing me. Don't you feel some loyalty to your homeland?"

"We respect the tradition, but we're Americans now. This is our homeland. And, most importantly, we have to live with American law enforcement. Gambling and prostitution, even drugs, is one thing. Condoning a hit sanctioned by another government on US soil is something else entirely. We can't tolerate that kind of trouble."

Tao winced as he tried again to straighten himself up in bed. "I'm not sure you understand."

"Please, enlighten me."

"I take my orders from representatives of the People's Liberation Army. You should be more concerned about them than the FBI."

The man laughed, though his expression didn't change. "Are you actually threatening me?"

"I'm explaining the dynamics of the situation."

The man said nothing for a moment, perhaps trying to decide how much clout Tao might actually have within the PLA. "Your case would be more convincing if you identified yourself. We have no way of knowing that you are what you say."

"You know that Ms. Wan vouched for me."

"Ms. Wan is an interesting person. She plays so many roles that sometimes I think even she forgets where her best interests lie."

"I'm not asking you for anything, just to let me heal and be on my way. If you plan to stand in the way of that, just know that you are interfering with the PLA's plans. If I were you, I wouldn't want to do that."

"Most people here in Chinatown know better than to threaten me."

"Maybe that's because the people backing me are not from around here—and I know what they're capable of. I just want to make sure that you know that too."

"Whoever you are, you'll do well to watch your mouth." The man moved closer to Tao. "Do you understand?"

Tao offered only the merest nod.

At that the man took a step back from the bed. "I'll speak with my colleagues."

"Aren't you a decision maker?" asked Tao. "They call tong bosses dragon heads, correct? Aren't you the dragon head?"

The man winced at the distasteful term. "I'm not the boss, but I speak for him."

"What you'd better do is speak *to* him."

But the man had already walked out of the apartment, slamming the door behind him.

38

When Chris opened the door to the cabin, wet and muddy with the gun dangling at his side, the room was dark, and it took him a moment to notice her. Zoey was standing to one side of the door, gripping a large kitchen knife. She had been poised to leap at whoever came through the door, and her eyes showed what it had taken to ratchet up her nerve to that point.

When she saw that it was Chris, she let the knife clatter to the floor. She ran and threw her arms around him.

"I heard gunshots," she said, her voice choked with emotion. "I thought you were dead."

"There were a few moments there when I wasn't so sure myself," he said.

"Were you hit?"

"No."

Zoey looked over Chris's shoulder and out the open front door. "Is he coming?"

"No."

"Is he dead?"

A cold, wet gust of wind muscled through the doorway. "No, but I think he's pretty badly injured."

They locked down all the doors and windows, then sat down in front of the fire to regroup. The heat of the fireplace and the stress reaction from the shootout produced a powerful tiredness, and he wanted to close his eyes. Zoey seemed to also be collapsing after the adrenaline surge of waiting to see who walked through that door.

"We can't stay here anymore, can we?" Zoey asked.

"No. Even if he's already dead from the gunshot wounds, he could have passed along our location to the people who hired him before he came up here. And they knew the general area to begin with. Someone could be coming to finish the job already."

Chris went to the window and stared out into the gathering darkness. The rain was coming down harder now.

"It's getting dark," Zoey said. "Do we leave now?"

"Let's wait a couple of hours, give our man a chance to bleed to death or make it out of Stinson Beach. Then we drive back to the city."

"You think that's necessary?"

"If he's still alive, he's armed, and I don't want him taking a last shot at us as we pass through town. There's only one road out of here, so it would be easy to lie in wait."

"I got a call," Zoey said, her face tense and pale. "From Krissa. He was at the club asking for us."

"Hmm," said Chris. "Is *that* how he found us here?"

"No. Krissa says that she didn't tell him, and I believe her. I told Krissa that she and her friends at the club needed to make themselves scarce for a while in case he came back."

"We won't be safe until we know that guy's dead," Chris said. He stopped there, not wanting to complete the thought.

"And even then we're not safe, are we?"

Chris chose not to respond to that.

Zoey brought him a mug of black coffee, and he warmed his hands on it. They fell quiet for a while, taking in what had happened. He caught her studying him.

"I think there's a part of you that actually likes all this," she said.

"This?"

"You know. *This.* Hunting bad guys, the bad guys hunting us."

"Are you kidding?"

"No. Don't bother denying it. I can tell. There's something wrong with you, isn't there?"

"And there's *not* something wrong with you?"

"I think we've already established that there is plenty wrong with me. But I'm just afraid you're going to keep doing this sort of things until something really bad happens. Until it kills you." After a pause, she added, "Or me."

"I never meant to put you in harm's way. And I think you know I don't have the skill set to be an action hero."

"So why do you do it?"

Chris stared into his coffee. "I could say it's my job, but that wouldn't be good enough for you, would it?"

Zoey shook her head.

"I guess I spent quite a few years after Tana died in a kind of hibernation. I showed up at the office and did my work, but it wasn't much of a life. It's like I can't even remember anything that happened during those years."

"You still miss her a lot, don't you?"

"Sure I do. Always. But it's not out of proportion anymore. It doesn't crowd everything else out the way it used to."

"So now doing stuff like this makes you feel more alive. Is that it? Because that's kind of messed up."

Chris shrugged. "I guess it makes me feel like I'm using all my parts."

She moved to his side and sat next to him. "I get it. I do. But there have to be other things to get you through."

"There are," Chris said, glancing at her. "More so all the time."

They gazed at the fireplace for a while as the fingers of flame clenched and unclenched around the logs. The rain began again outside, settling over the roof with a whoosh like a breaking wave.

Chris went to the front window and parted the curtains to look out at the sheets of rain coming down across the hillside.

"Any word from Damien Hull yet?"

"No, no response. It usually takes about two weeks to make contact with him. Like I said, he's deep underground."

"If I had to guess, I'd say that might be long enough for that hit man to try again. But hopefully not long enough for the PLA to send in a replacement."

"What are you getting at?" Zoey asked.

"If we just have to survive for two weeks before we can disappear, then I don't think I want to spend it waiting for that killer to regroup and take another shot at us. We got lucky this time, and he got a little sloppy. I'd much prefer to get on the move and go after *him*. Wouldn't you?"

Zoey responded with a raised eyebrow. "Exactly how do you propose we do that? Call the police?"

"It's worth a try," Chris said. "But they weren't very helpful before, and we don't have much more to offer them as evidence now." He shrugged. "I'll make the call anyway."

"Okay, but what *were* you thinking, then?"

"Think about it this way," said Chris. "Where would a Chinese national be most likely to find shelter and assistance? And unlikely to draw attention to himself?"

"Chinatown," Zoey said.

Chris nodded. "Chinatown."

39

The streets of Chinatown were wet from the rain, and the sky was mottled with clouds as Chris and Zoey walked down Grant Avenue in midafternoon. The sun had come out, but Chinatown remained largely in the shadows of the old buildings that crowded the narrow streets.

"What are we looking for?" Zoey asked.

"I don't know," Chris said. "Chinatown's not that big a place. If that hit man is hiding here, he's probably somewhere within a five- to ten-block radius."

Zoey studied the apartments above the shops. Drying laundry had reappeared on some of the iron fire escapes overhead. "Then he could be watching us right now."

"True."

"And he's probably a good shot with a high-powered rifle."

"Yes."

"So maybe we should have worked a little bit more on our strategy before we got here."

"Don't worry. I think he's too injured for that right now."

"And if he isn't?"

"Then he'll probably take me out with the first shot, and you'll have a chance to run."

"Thank you. Very comforting."

Chris and Zoey walked the length of Grant Avenue, which clung stubbornly to its perch on the slope of Nob Hill. They arrived at the intersection of Broadway and Columbus Avenue, which marked the boundary of the North Beach neighborhood, ersatz Italy abutting ersatz China in Epcot-like proximity. Then they turned back and wandered the side streets of Chinatown, where there were fewer shops selling antiques and tourist trinkets and more businesses actually dedicated to serving the local community.

The side street they'd chosen inclined upward at a steep angle, which slowed their pace to a crawl.

"I think we need a Sherpa," Zoey said, gasping a bit from the climb. "Let's take a break."

As they stood on the sidewalk catching a breath, a Chinese man in his midthirties with long sideburns wearing a Drive-By Truckers T-shirt passed by them, moving quickly downhill with loping strides. About fifteen seconds later, Chris and Zoey looked at one another with the same realization.

"I know that guy," Zoey said.

"I know him too."

"Hey, Jefferson!" Zoey shouted.

Jefferson turned and extended his arms in greeting and surprise.

"You know Jefferson Fong?" Zoey asked as they waited for him to climb back up to them on the steep sidewalk.

"He's sort of a hacker, isn't he?" Chris asked Zoey. "Or at least he attends DefCon. He came up to me after a presentation I gave there, and we talked. He said he runs a comic-book shop."

"I used to run into him on an IRC board where a lot of local hackers hang out. Nice guy. Never did any harm as far as I could tell. I think he's more of an enthusiast."

"That was my impression too. But we could use a friend who knows Chinatown."

When Jefferson reached them, he smiled broadly. "Chris Bruen and Zoey Doucet. Together! Like Batman and Robin." He had an incongruous, soft Southern inflection to his voice. Chris recalled that Jefferson had grown up in south Alabama.

"We prefer Green Hornet and Kato," Zoey said. "He's Kato."

"What brings you to Chinatown?"

"We'd actually like to discuss that with you," Chris said.

"That's cool. Why don't you walk with me to my shop? It's just a block from here, and I need to open up."

They caught up a bit as they walked down the hill, until they reached a tiny comic-book shop called Fifth Dynasty Comix. Jefferson pulled a key chain from his pocket and opened up the store. Instead of a bell jangling as they entered, they heard a recorded sound effect from a '70s kung fu flick. *Thwap. Whap. Whap.* The crunch of bone. A cry of triumph that sounded something like *Ayah wakow!*

Jefferson took up his spot behind the cash register and rested his elbows on the glass case. "So how can I help you?"

Chris stood in front of the counter, but Zoey wandered the aisles of plastic-wrapped comics, occasionally running her fingers over them lightly and reverently, as if she could absorb their superpowers by osmosis.

"How long have you been here in Chinatown?"

"Going on eight years now."

"We're looking for someone who is probably hiding out in Chinatown somewhere. We thought you might be able to help."

"Is this a hacker that you're after?"

Chris shook his head. "No, it's related to our work, but this person is not a hacker. He's something different. More dangerous."

"What do you have to go on?"

"He's injured with a gunshot wound, and he probably sought medical attention here."

"Wouldn't he go to Chinese Hospital?"

"No, he couldn't show up in the ER."

"You have *The Amazing Spider-Man* Number 129!" Zoey said, bending down to bring her face close to a glass case. "The first appearance of the Punisher!"

Jefferson beamed. "Mah preciousss," he said, channeling a Southern-fried Sméagol.

Chris tried to nod appreciatively before getting the conversation back on track. "If you were going to find someone hiding out in Chinatown, what would you do?"

Jefferson pulled his elbows off the counter. "Well, I hesitate to recommend this."

Chris and Zoey stared at him, waiting for the rest.

"You know who knows everything that happens here in Chinatown? The tongs. There isn't a pie they don't have their fingers in."

"Do you know them?"

"I know who I kick back to," Jefferson said. "But I don't think it's a good idea for you to approach him. You don't want these people to know your name."

"Maybe we have a common interest in this case," Chris said.

"They don't have common interests with anybody. They don't share information or anything else. They just take."

"How do we meet them?" Zoey asked.

40

Chris, Zoey, and Jefferson climbed the steps of one of the more modern office buildings in Chinatown and stood before a door bearing a placard that read "Hang Seng Chinatown Benevolent Society."

"You don't have to do this," Chris said for the third or fourth time.

"I know. It's okay. Like I said, I'm just making an introduction."

"They might not like it."

"True, but we have a long-term relationship. They've been bleeding me for years. For once I might as well get some service in return."

Chris could see the tension in Jefferson's eyes, despite his blithe attitude.

Jefferson knocked on the door and said in Mandarin, "I'm here to see Mr. Lai. I've brought someone who would like to meet him."

The door opened, and a man with a scar across his windpipe replied in staccato Mandarin, "Who said you could come here? And who are they?" The man's cold eyes appraised Chris and Zoey.

"I think Mr. Lai will want to hear what they have to say."

"I hope you know what you're doing. Mr. Lai maintains an open-door policy to the community. But if you knock on his door, he just might knock on yours."

"I realize that," Jefferson said.

"He's over at the Golden Door. There's a fund-raiser tonight for the new community clinic."

"Thank you."

Jefferson led them two blocks down the street to the Golden Door Restaurant, which was on the second floor, with big windows overlooking the streaming traffic of Columbus Avenue. The restaurant was closed at this hour, but the front door was open, and they climbed a flight of steps to a massive dining room festooned with red-and-gold lanterns.

Workers were busy buffing the floors, setting tables, and hanging decorations for what must have been a very important community event. Amid the hive of activity, Chris detected an island of calm, and it surrounded a table in the rear corner where one man sat. Even before Jefferson led them to him, Chris knew that this was the tong boss.

Jefferson approached a young man in a cream-colored sweater and conferred with him for a moment. Another gatekeeper. The man shook his head a few times, but then he waved them on with an "it's your funeral" shrug.

They were led over to a table at the rear of the dining room, where Mr. Lai sat behind platters of Chinese delicacies on a lazy Susan. The man looked to be in his early fifties, with the blandly pleasant demeanor of a businessman. He was talking on his cell phone while simultaneously dissecting a dumpling with a chopstick. In an impressive display of multitasking, he also managed to take in Chris's trio as they approached.

When they were standing before him across the table, he said, "I think you've got what you need, don't you? Call me when it's done."

The boss clicked off his phone, put down his chopsticks, and gazed at them curiously.

The young man in the cream sweater supplied the introduction, speaking in Mandarin. "Boss, this is Jefferson Fong, who runs Fifth Dynasty Comix on Ross Alley. We've known him for many years now. He seems to have a favor to ask."

"Hello, Jefferson. I'm glad you know that you can come to me. That's what you pay your dues for." Then in English he said to the group, "Sorry, but I should have asked if there's anyone here who doesn't speak Mandarin."

Zoey waved a hand.

"My apologies. Then we'll stick to English," he said without missing a beat in unaccented English. "I'm Henry Lai." He waved a manicured hand at the platters of food before him. "This is one of my favorite parts of this job. I get to help select the menu for the annual health-clinic fund-raiser banquet. The privilege of being a benefactor."

"Nice spread," Chris said.

"And you are?"

Jefferson stepped forward. "This is Chris Bruen, an attorney here in San Francisco. And this is his colleague Zoey Doucet."

"What firm are you with?"

"Reynolds, Fincher & McComb."

"I know them. Good firm." Lai lifted a platter before him that was filled with a horrifying array of chicken beaks and claws, all lightly battered and fried, with sauces on the side. "Would you like to sample? This is a very rare specialty in our culture. You won't find this on the menu at P.F. Chang's."

Chris didn't want to offend Lai before asking a favor, so he leaned in to examine the small plates, trying to determine whether one looked less stomach churning than the rest.

Before he could pick one, Lai withdrew the platter with a chuckle. "Just yanking your chain. Even I don't eat this stuff. Everyone just likes to see it on the menu so that they can feel authentic. What can I do for you?"

Lai smiled a lot, Chris noticed, but the mirth never seemed to reach his eyes.

"We're looking for someone, and we think he may be in Chinatown."

"We get a lot of visitors here. Why should I care about this one?"

"Because he's a hit man who's been brought over from China to do a job here."

"And who's the target? Wait, I think I know the answer to that one."

"I'm the target," Chris said. He nodded to Zoey. "And probably her too."

Lai didn't reveal the slightest trace of alarm. Instead, he gave them another cold smile. "And what did you do to merit such attention?"

"Let's just say that I deeply offended the Chinese government and the PLA, interfered with one of their operations."

"What operation was it that you interfered with?"

"I'd rather not say."

Lai was not used to being told no; it surely angered him, but he wasn't going to show it.

"This is all very interesting, but what makes you think that I know anything about this man?"

"He's been shot," Zoey interjected. "And he probably sought medical attention somewhere in Chinatown. From someone who doesn't take Blue Cross."

"I don't know everything that goes on here. But just for the sake of argument, let's say that I do. Why would I tell you where he was?"

"Because there will be blowback from the feds if you harbor this man. Just let us know where he is, and we'll take it from there."

"Are you working with the State Department or law enforcement? Because this sounds like a matter for them."

"Neither," Chris said. "We're on our own."

"If what you say is true, then maybe I don't want someone like that associated with our community—or with me. But forgive me if I don't see you two being a match for someone like that. No offense."

"We mentioned he was seeking medical attention, right?" Zoey said.

Jefferson squirmed at the remark.

Lai looked down to sample a green bean with chopsticks. "I'll look into it. I don't like things happening in this part of town without my knowledge. And while I love my homeland, my loyalty is to this country. It's been very good to me."

"Clearly," Zoey said.

Lai raised an eyebrow, weighing whether he should take offense at the impertinence. Instead, he merely shrugged in acknowledgment. "Do you have a card?"

Chris produced one of his business cards.

"Good," Lai said, fixing him with another smile-that-was-not-a-smile. "Now I know where to find you, don't I? I'll look into it."

41

Later that day, Mr. Lai's associate in the cream-colored sweater left a message on Chris's office voice mail, requesting a meeting at Jefferson's comic shop.

When Chris arrived, the man was already on the sidewalk in front of the shop, sucking on an e-cigarette with a disgusted look. "The man you're looking for is at 485 Grant Avenue, Apartment 12," he said without any prologue. "We don't want the body to be found in Chinatown."

"We're not going to kill him," Chris said. "We're going to have him arrested."

"Yeah, right. In case you don't know, he doesn't look like the type to go quietly."

"What do you know about him?"

"I know that he goes by the name of Red Sun and advertises himself as a professional hit man on Silk Road. I thought anyone advertising there as a hitter would be a fake, but apparently not."

"Why are you telling me that?"

"Because I don't like the guy."

"Why aren't you handling this yourselves?"

"This has all the makings of an international shitstorm. It's not our fight, and this conversation never happened."

* * *

Chris and Zoey approached the apartment building at 485 Grant Avenue.

"I knew I was right about that connection between the PLA and Red Sun," Zoey said. "The security team at Zapper can suck it."

"Yes, you said that."

They walked quietly up the steps. Chris drew his gun and tested the doorknob.

"Shouldn't we just call the police? He'll be armed," Zoey said.

"So are we," Chris said. "Besides, I want to know that he's really here before we call them. We have enough credibility issues already." Chris didn't feel nearly as fearless as he sounded, but he didn't want Zoey to know that.

The door was unlocked. Chris drew in a breath but couldn't seem to release it. Chris pushed the door open, and it swung back on its hinges, revealing a sun-dappled and nearly empty apartment. On the other side of a bare living room, the door was opened on a bedroom that contained a bed, a chair, an empty IV bag on a cart, and a window in which thin curtains billowed.

They checked the bathroom and all of the closets until they were certain that he was gone. Chris approached the bed and examined the sheets, which bore several bloodstains that looked fresh.

"He's still bleeding," Chris said. "He probably didn't want to leave here when he did."

"Do you think the tong told him that we were coming?" Zoey asked.

"No, but he must have guessed."

Zoey examined the pillow and found a strand of dark hair. "Do you have a plastic bag? We might need a DNA sample later."

Chris produced one of the baggies he used to protect hard drives and retrieved the hair sample.

"We've had two opportunities to surprise this guy and both times he's slipped away," Chris said. "We may not get another chance like this."

* * *

After the visit from the Chinatown gangster, Tao knew that he couldn't stay in his makeshift recovery room much longer. The only reason he was alive was that killing him was above the pay grade of the middle-management thug who had visited him.

Tao removed the IV from his wrist and sat up painfully in the bed. He placed his feet gingerly on the floor. He wasn't sure how many days he had been in bed, but it had been long enough to turn the muscles in his legs to jelly. He sat down quickly in the apartment's one chair and spent fifteen minutes trying to get his clothes on without ripping out any stitches. Once that painful task was completed, he moved like a ninety-year-old down the steps of the apartment building.

When Tao made it to his rental car without being stopped, he knew that no one had been watching the building. He drove out of the narrow streets of Chinatown and into the crowded shopping district of Union Square.

He needed a couple more days to recuperate before he would be capable of taking any action. Clearly, he should not stay in any hotel that was within the borders of Chinatown. He needed a place where he was unlikely to be remembered or noticed, so he chose San Francisco's largest hotel (according to his Zapper search), the Hilton San Francisco Union Square. It was only a few blocks from Grant

Avenue and Chinatown, but it was far beyond the jurisdiction of the tongs.

Near the hotel, Tao found a pharmacy, where he purchased a few rolls of gauze, some antibiotic ointment, and pain relievers. Carrying only the plastic bag with his purchases, he trudged slowly through the cavernous hotel lobby adorned with massive sand-colored columns and crystal chandeliers. Tao watched for anyone who might be taking notice of him, but the lobby was full of businessmen and tourist families, who all seemed wholly engrossed in their tourist brochures and cell phones.

"Can someone get your bags, sir?" The clerk noticed that he did not have a suitcase.

"No, thank you, I'm fine," Tao said.

"Enjoy your stay."

*   *   *

For the next two days, Tao rose only to greet the room service waiter and go to the bathroom. He wasn't sure if two days would be enough, but it would have to do. He needed to complete his assignment, and it was possible that Bruen could be on the other side of the world by now.

Tao doubted it, though. Bruen seemed every bit as determined as Tao to resolve their situation.

As he recuperated, Tao watched a *Real Housewives of Atlanta* marathon on television, filled with horror and amazement. By the time the last big-haired, overdressed housewife had been slapped, any remaining doubts Tao had about the decadence of American culture had been dispelled.

On the morning of the third day, Tao rose, stiff but mobile. As the hot water streamed over him in the shower, he examined where the bullets had been extracted, the fresh scars puckered and pink.

This job was not going as smoothly as the others, but there was still time for Tao to set things right. He wondered whether Bruen was lucky or skilled. There was nothing in Bruen's résumé to suggest skill or training, so Tao had to assume that he had simply gotten the benefit of some lucky breaks.

Tao wondered whether his new orientation to his work had unbalanced him, thrown off his equilibrium somehow. Ever since the Naruse hit in Tokyo, he had enjoyed his work more than ever before. But that didn't mean he was better at it. Quite the contrary. The world was full of passionate amateurs who produced unreadable books, unlistenable music, and a host of other botched projects. A true professional had passion for their work, but they also had the dispassionate judgment to recognize when they were blowing it.

He knew that it was time to stop indulging his baser instincts and finish the hit on Bruen without mess, without collateral damage, without senseless bloodshed.

But what was the point of work if you couldn't enjoy it?

42

Chris and Zoey decided to see how far they could get with the information from the Chinese mobster. Now they knew what Zoey had suspected for some time—that the hit man offered his services through the Silk Road website under the name Red Sun.

Problem was, it wasn't safe to return to the law firm and use their own computer forensic lab. Moreover, they had to assume that the PLA hackers had access to the Reynolds Fincher servers, much in the way they'd hacked Zoey's electronics to get to Geist. Because of this, Chris had called in a favor and gotten access to the facilities of Hologram Security, a security consulting firm that he often collaborated with. Chris and Zoey had the lab to themselves through the dead hours of the night until Hologram's team started arriving at 7:00 a.m.

Zoey was at the monitor, with Chris sitting next to her.

"There he is," she said as she pulled up Red Sun's page on Silk Road. "Every time I see this it freaks me out. It makes ordering a hit look about as easy as ordering a pizza."

"Can you crack this, find some way to track him from here?"

Zoey gave a frustrated shrug. "If Silk Road were easy to crack, then the FBI would have done it a long time ago." Her hands flew over the keyboard. "I'm going to see if I can get behind Silk Road's firewall, find an email message to Red Sun, and decipher it."

"But because this is the Deep Web, Silk Road has to be accessed through TOR," Chris said. "Every node the email's routed through is separately encrypted."

Zoey nodded. "Right. Peeling back all of those layers and getting to the original sender is nearly impossible. But we have to try, right?"

"If we don't find him, he's probably going to find us," Chris said.

"That's not helping," Zoey said. "I prefer to think about what will happen when we hear from Damien. I don't know how that dude pulls his disappearing trick, but if he takes us in, I don't think even the PLA could find us."

"I hope you're right," Chris said. "How about the bitcoin payments that Red Sun receives for his services?"

"Exactly," Zoey said. "Bitcoin transactions aren't inherently anonymous, so that's the angle to pursue."

"Is there anything I can do to help?"

"You can get me two large coffees from Peet's with nonfat milk and two Splendas. And a breakfast burrito."

"I'd say get it yourself, but we need to keep you at the monitors, don't we?"

"Exactly, lab wench."

"You know I hate it when you call me lab wench." Chris was happy to play along if it lightened Zoey's mood.

"I think we've established that my hacking skills are superior to yours."

"Marginally perhaps." This was not the first time they'd had this conversation.

"Okay, so that means that I take the lead on the forensic work and you, my lovely assistant, are the lab wench."

"I'm going to take this as motivation to sharpen up my skills. Then maybe you'll be the lab wench."

"I love seeing someone trying to better themselves. But until that time—lab wench."

Chris left the lab in order to escape further taunting. Using a computer in the consulting firm's reception area and an anonymized IP address, Chris accessed his law firm email account to see how impatient his clients were getting with his sudden unexplained absence.

Among the contents of his clogged inbox, Chris noticed a message from Richard Grogan, which read, "How's it going, Chris? I noticed that you haven't been in the office lately. Hope all is well."

He must be even more paranoid about me leaving the firm than I realized.

Concerned that Richard might start undermining him with his clients if he didn't offer an explanation, Chris sighed and typed out a response.

CHRIS: Working on a big project for Zapper that's been taking me out of the office.

Chris shouldn't have been as surprised as he was when he received an immediate response at 5:00 a.m. Richard probably slept with his smartphone.

RICHARD: Glad to hear it. Related to the China trip?
CHRIS: You could say that.
RICHARD: You working with Zoey? You two seem very close.
CHRIS: Yeah, she's invaluable.

Chris hoped it wasn't yet common knowledge around the office that he and Zoey were a couple. He knew he couldn't keep it private for much longer, though.

RICHARD: Just remember that you two shouldn't be on an island at the firm. You have colleagues who are more than willing to support you. In the end, Zoey, capable as I'm sure she is, is just an ex-hacker who was working as a bartender less than a year ago.

CHRIS: That's a pretty dismissive way of putting it. Zoey and I are partners, and I couldn't do what I do without her.

RICHARD: I understand. But just remember that in the end she's an employee. She's not actually your partner—I am. Your partners at the firm recognize and value your contribution. Especially me.

CHRIS: It's nice to be appreciated. But doesn't true appreciation usually take the form of dollars?

Chris smiled. It was just too easy to push Richard's buttons.

RICHARD: I've been thinking about what you said. You just sit tight and we'll figure something out. In the meantime, don't make any rash decisions.

CHRIS: Believe me, Richard, I have other things to attend to right now.

RICHARD: Good. I want to sit down with you the next time you're in the office. Call me.

When Chris returned to the forensic lab with coffee and breakfast, Zoey was deep into her work, her hands flying over the keyboard as she glanced back and forth among her three large monitor screens.

"How's it going?"

"It's not. As you would expect from someone who's offering murder for hire over the Internet, Red Sun set up his bitcoin transactions so they are anonymous. He probably used the TOR browser for each step in the process. Then he used Mt. Rox to anonymously create a bitcoin wallet online. When payment for a hit arrives, he can just withdraw it to the anonymous Mt. Rox account." Mt. Rox was a leading bitcoin exchange website.

"So what we're looking at is a dead end."

"Nearly. What we can see is the payments going into the Mt. Rox account. The dates and amounts of those transfers might give us some clues as to the hits that Red Sun has performed in the past."

"What sort of amounts are we talking about?"

"Well, here's a thirty-five-thousand-dollar payment that was transferred to the account three weeks ago. That's probably you."

"I'd have hoped I'd command a higher price."

"Don't get down about yourself," Zoey said. "If Red Sun fails, I'm sure they'll pay the next guy even more to take you out."

"Thank you for that." Chris ran a hand through his hair. "What about the other payments?"

"Well, there's a twenty-five-thousand-dollar transfer about two weeks earlier. Then another for forty thousand dollars last year. But that tells us nothing. If we can't access the emails, how do we track him down?"

"We're going to need to take a different tack," Chris said.

"A different tack. Sounds good. Anything more specific?"

"I've got a card that I can play. I've considered using it before, but I know it's a source I can't tap very often, and I have to pick the right time."

"Considering that there's a professional hit man after you, I'd say this is the time to use any lifelines that you have."

"I agree. It's time to see the Wizard."

43

Even though Paul Saperstein had distanced himself from Chris in order to avoid the political fallout from the events in Shenzhen, Chris suspected that he felt guilty about it. Saperstein was not a bad guy; it was just that he was constrained by his role as the CEO of one of the world's largest corporations. It was a lot like being the president of a country. You had to be aware at all times of how your actions were perceived by various constituencies—shareholders, stock analysts, employees, your government, and even other governments.

Sitting in the computer forensic lab of Hologram Consulting, and routing through an anonymized IP address with a secure email account, Chris typed out a message to Saperstein.

CHRIS: I have a favor to ask.

Less than five minutes later, the response came back.

SAPERSTEIN: What can I do for you?
CHRIS: I have a problem. A tough one. There's been fallout from my trip to China. I'm being pursued, and I need protection. The kind of protection that you could provide.

A long pause stretched. Finally, the computer pinged with a response.

SAPERSTEIN: You're lucky this connection is secure, but I'll need a phone number to continue the conversation.

Chris provided the number of his burner phone. About a minute later, the phone rang. Saperstein did not want their conversation preserved as an email thread.

"Chris, I can't take you in. I shouldn't even be talking to you."

Chris had anticipated the response. "Then I have one request. For old times' sake."

"What is it?"

"I'd like some time with BD."

After a moment, Saperstein said, "It would have to be a one-time thing. And if you ever mention this, we'll deny it happened."

"Understood," Chris said.

"I want to see you come out of this, man. I really do."

"I appreciate that."

"Lewin would probably tell me not to do it."

"You're probably right."

After a moment of radio silence, Saperstein said, "Okay. I'll make the arrangements. I hope it helps."

"Thanks, Paul."

"Don't thank me. I think I owe you this much."

*   *   *

Chris drove through the main gate of Zapper's corporate headquarters in Menlo Park, just as he had that painfully early morning when he had first learned of the intrusion and the theft of the company's algorithms. This time he wouldn't be visiting the executive offices or seeing Paul Saperstein or even Dez Teal. Chris understood that this was supposed to be an under-the-radar visit. He was expected to get what he needed and leave.

He drove along a tree-lined drive and parked in front of a five-story redbrick building on the outskirts of the corporate campus. There were no signs on the building, just "Building Three" over the arched entrance.

Chris gave his name at the front desk to an attractive middle-aged woman. He suspected that only Zapper's most trusted employees worked in this building, the ones who could distinguish the true and false parts of the company's creation myth. She squinted at his driver's license, then said, "He's expecting you."

The receptionist escorted him to an elevator, and he was taken three floors down into a subbasement. When the elevator doors opened, the place had the pristine, glass-and-chrome look of a laboratory.

The woman swiped her badge on three separate pads as they passed checkpoints. At the last checkpoint, she also had to submit to a retinal scan. The secure doors opened with a pneumatic gasp. Chris knew of this place, but he had never been granted access before.

Surprisingly, the room was largely empty. There were a few printers and long wooden tables, which reminded Chris of a library. There was very little clutter in the room, just a few neat stacks of printouts on the table.

On the other side of the wooden tables a man sat with his back to Chris, hunched over eight monitor screens arranged in a nearly closed circle around him. Data scrolled across several of the screens in front of the intensely concentrating man like projections of his febrile thoughts. And maybe they were.

As Chris approached, the man swung around in his chair. He had probably been watching Chris's reflection in the monitors.

"Chris Bruen. I know who you are."

The man was skinny, nearly emaciated, with bony wrists protruding from a white dress shirt buttoned at the collar. He was wearing jeans and radioactive orange New Balance sneakers. He had lank blond hair that fell over his forehead, skin the color of putty, long lashes, and nearly invisible blond eyebrows. Chris was reminded of some sort of creature that had adapted its coloration to a life lived out of the sun.

"Can I call you BD?"

"Everyone else does."

Chris had heard the stories about Bram Dyson ever since he began representing Zapper eight years ago. But that wasn't what the BD really stood for. To those in Zapper's executive suites who knew he existed, BD was short for Big Data. As the company's senior data analyst, Bram was responsible for directing the development of Zapper's search algorithms and finding new ways of culling the company's vast sea of personal data.

"I guess you know that I've been authorized to conduct some searches using your data."

"You have friends in high places," BD said. "A lot of our top executives have never been in this room."

Chris nodded. If BD didn't already know that Saperstein had authorized his access, Chris wasn't going to tell him. "I was expecting more hardware."

"What do you think this is, IBM in 1985? It's all in the cloud," BD said. "But we have access to all the good stuff."

"Zapper's search histories alone must represent a staggering amount of data."

BD grinned. "Yeah, and that's only the beginning. We're linked into NSA data, telecom data, banking data, HMO claims data. The word 'big' doesn't even begin to describe our data. We're borderline omniscient."

"Is that legal?"

"Not my concern. I just work here. Would you mind if I test a couple of assumptions I've made about you?"

"Assumptions?"

"You're a Democrat, right?"

"How did you know that? Do you have access to voter registration records?"

"Nothing that crude. There was an eighty-nine percent probability that you were a Democrat based upon the charities that you donate to, the friends you have on Facebook, your taste in music, and, of course, your San Francisco zip code."

"You could say that about just anyone in San Francisco and you'd probably be right. You're starting to sound like one of those strip mall psychics."

BD nodded eagerly. "Okay, fair enough. Then how about this? There's a ninety-two percent probability that you entered into a serious relationship within the past six weeks. Or an existing relationship became much more serious."

"You've been talking to Dez Teal or someone else who knows me."

BD was starting to enjoy himself. "I didn't do that, nor would I. I have no interest in you as a person, just as a collection of data points."

"Okay, I'll play. How did you know that?"

"Mainly through a substantial uptick in your weekly grocery store purchases, along with an increase in Internet and water usage. Women do take long showers, don't they?"

Chris stared impassively at BD, hoping that this exercise in personal-data mining was concluded. BD was a rare and annoying creature—a know-it-all who actually did know it all.

"You enjoy your work, don't you?" Chris said.

"Enormously," BD replied. "The one frustration is that we can't fully use what we know. It makes people a bit queasy."

"How so?"

Chris had advised enough clients on Big Data analysis to know the answer to that question, but he asked it anyway to humor BD. Hopefully, allowing BD to expound on his favorite topic would buy Chris a little extra cooperation.

"I'll give you two examples. A big box retailer knows that if a customer purchases orange juice and throat lozenges then they probably have a cold, so they send an email offering a discount on Kleenex. No problem, right?"

"I might be a little—discomfited—by that. But, no, not a real problem."

"Okay, how about when that same retailer sees that a seventeen-year-old female customer has purchased scent-free lotions, an extra large purse, some zinc and magnesium supplements, and a pink rug? What does that tell you?"

"Zinc and magnesium supplements tell me that she's pregnant," Chris said. "The pink rug tells me that it's a girl." He considered for a moment and then added, "The big purse will double as a diaper bag."

"Very good," BD said. "For you, that's a reasonable guess. But for us, based upon those factors and other probabilities established over a vast volume of data, it's much more than a guess. We *know*. And, based on the timing of the purchases, we also know what trimester she's in and her delivery date, give or take a week or two."

"So then the question is what do you do with that knowledge."

"That's right. If we send a targeted ad for diapers to that household, and her parents don't know yet that she's pregnant, that could make for a very angry call to our customer relations department. Outcome—unhappy customer."

"So what's your next move?"

"We send that household a book of coupons, and one of them happens to offer a discount on diapers, along with discounts on power tools, motor oil, and cornflakes. She thinks getting the diaper coupon is a lucky coincidence and uses it after she's had that awkward conversation with her parents. She and her parents never realize just how much we know about her. Outcome—happy customer."

"Happy, clueless customer."

"That's the way we like them."

"And you've broken no laws, have you?"

"Well, you're the privacy lawyer, but that's what I hear."

"Privacy laws tend to be about ensuring that a company doesn't share the personal information of its customers with third parties," Chris said. "The laws don't place any limits on how much you might be able to learn from that data, or what you might do with that knowledge."

"That's the line that we have to walk, isn't it?" BD said. "Going back to our example, even if the parents know their daughter is pregnant, that doesn't mean they won't be creeped out to learn that we know it too."

"The ick factor. I felt that way myself a minute ago."

"Yes, the ick factor. And just be glad that I didn't tell you the rest of what I know about you."

"Please don't. And so if one of your customers buys nylon rope, duct tape, a kitchen knife, and extra-large trash bags then they are—"

"Most likely a homicidal psychopath. We'll send them a discount coupon for ski masks," BD said. "There will come a time when law enforcement starts taking pointers from us—once they get past some constitutional issues."

"So can we proceed to my query?"

"By all means."

BD turned around to face his monitors. "What are your data points?"

Chris sat down next to BD and watched his long, pale fingers move over the keyboard. "I'm looking for a man from China who entered the country about two weeks ago. Probably flew in through

SFO. He's been in the San Francisco Bay Area during most of that time. He was in Stinson Beach last Friday."

"Have you ever been in close proximity to him?"

"Twice that I know of. He tried to kill me in an alley off Beale Street in San Francisco on the night of April 20."

"What time was it?"

"About 6:00 p.m."

"Did you have your cell phone with you at that time?"

"Yes, I always carry it."

"When was the next time you were close to him?"

Chris provided the coordinates for that rainy hillside outside Stinson Beach.

"And, again, you had your cell phone?"

"Yes."

"Anything else that comes to mind?"

"Not really. I've gotten a couple of glimpses of him, but his physical appearance isn't all that striking."

"No, I mean, was he driving a rental car?"

"Probably, but I never saw it."

BD was no longer looking at Chris. He was asking the questions over his shoulder as he worked on the monitors. BD opened a bag of sunflower seeds and began to avidly dice them in his front teeth. Screens popped open, maps appeared and numbers scrolled, the outputs too fast for Chris to follow.

"Well, that's not helpful," BD muttered to himself at one point.

About ten minutes later, BD began striking the keys of his keyboard emphatically like a concert pianist performing a final coda. He reared back and struck the Enter key with a raised index finger, eliciting a definitive pop.

"There you are," he said. "Gotcha."

BD sat staring at the screen, basking in self-satisfaction.

"Well?" Chris asked. "What did you find?"

Only then did BD seem to remember that he wasn't alone. He popped some sunflower seeds in his mouth, happy to make Chris wait and extend the moment.

When he was finished chewing, BD said, "The key was triangulation of cell phone signals. By tracking when your cell phone pinged the nearest cell tower on those occasions when you were close to him, I was able to identify the burner phone that he's using and track its location. His phone was pinging the same tower as yours. After that, it was really fairly—"

"Where is he?" Chris said.

"Room 819 of the Union Square Hilton. He's under the name Paul Fang. Would you like his cell number?"

As Chris prepared to leave, he looked back and saw BD as a pale stick figure busily moving against the black background of the monitors. BD probably felt he was at the center of the world, because every movement out there seemed to twang the cords of his web of data and probabilities. But there was a difference between being connected to the world and living in it.

44

Chris walked down the long, gray-carpeted hallway of the Union Square Hilton, slowing before the door to Room 819. According to BD, this was where Red Sun was staying.

He gripped the gun in his jacket pocket tightly because he knew that he could encounter the contract killer at any moment—returning from the vending machines, leaving the room. Chris had insisted that Zoey wait for him in the lobby because they only had one gun, and he didn't want her taking a stray bullet. For once he had been able to persuade her.

Chris and Zoey had considered calling in the San Francisco police to open up Room 819 but decided that it was better to wait until they had confirmed Red Sun's presence. Although Richard Berkheiser at the State Department had recommended that they file a report with the SFPD after Red Sun's initial attempt on Chris's life, they had not done so. They knew that they had very little for the police to go on then, and they really didn't have much more now. It would have even been difficult to convincingly explain how they arrived at the conclusion that the killer was in this room.

It was midafternoon, and there were a couple of cleaning carts in the hallway stacked high with rolls of toilet paper and towels. Finally, a maid opened up Room 819, and Chris heard the sound of a vacuum cleaner running inside. About five minutes later, the vacuum stopped, and the maid emerged and disappeared into another room to chat with one of her friends.

Chris strode up the hallway and ducked past the cleaning cart and through the open door of Room 819, his hand still on his gun. His anxiety spiked, and he began to breathe through his mouth. There was no telling when the killer might return.

As expected, Red Sun was not inside. The bed had been used and was unmade, but there were no other signs of occupancy. Chris checked the closets and the bathroom for a suitcase or toiletries, but there was nothing. As minutes passed, his efforts became more frantic. The risk increased exponentially the longer he stayed in the room, but he still hoped to find something that would help them, such as evidence of a link between Red Sun and the PLA.

As he was leaning over to open the drawer of a nightstand, he heard a loud thump behind him. Chris spun around with his gun raised.

He found himself pointing his Glock in the face of a young Mexican girl in a maid's uniform.

"Please, no!" Her face contorted, and she looked like she was trying to scream, cry, and plead at the same time.

As Chris lowered the gun with a trembling hand, he could only imagine what his own face must look like.

*   *   *

In the hotel lobby, Zoey ordered a coffee at Starbucks. Even though she was a disciple of Peet's Major Dickason's dark roast, it would have to do. The tables inside the coffee shop were all full, so she walked back into the lobby to find a seat and wait. As she searched for a seat, she heard a man's voice behind her with an accent she couldn't place.

"Hello, Zoey."

She turned to see the Chinese man whom she had last seen emptying his gun into her car in the alleyway south of Market. Red Sun. Zoey instantly envisioned this man doing to her what he had done to her friend Geist. For a moment she was paralyzed by a wave of panic and adrenaline.

Her eyes darted over his shoulder. She desperately hoped that Chris and the SFPD officers would step through the elevator doors. She saw no one who could help her.

Red Sun pulled open his jacket to reveal the gun tucked into his pants. "Walk with me now, or people are going to die. You'll be the first, but you won't be the last."

Zoey threw herself down in a nearby chair. "I feel sick," she said, clutching at her chest.

Red Sun grimaced. "Do you see that little girl over there?" he said in a whisper. He nodded at a girl about six years old, who was reading a picture book and twisting a strand of blond hair in the seat next to them, so tiny that she nearly disappeared into the oversized chair. Her mother was standing next to her talking on her cell phone.

Zoey nodded painfully, maintaining the act. Some people nearby were beginning to notice that something was happening, but no one had decided to intervene yet.

"If you don't get up right now—and I mean *right now*—they're both going to die. I'm not going to wait for Bruen to come back downstairs."

Zoey stopped feigning a heart attack and stood up.

"Good decision," Red Sun said as he took her by the arm and led her out of the lobby and onto the teeming sidewalks of Union Square.

45

Chris looked for Zoey in the Starbucks, but she wasn't there. He felt the sickening flash of recognition that comes when something horribly irreversible has happened. Sure, Zoey could be in the restroom, she could be buying a newspaper, but he knew that she wasn't. Moving quickly, he made a circle of the lobby, scanning every couch and alcove.

Zoey was gone.

Chris asked several of the hotel guests in the lobby if they'd seen Zoey, but no one had. He tried dialing the number of Zoey's burner phone, but it went directly to voice mail, which was unlike her. Chris and Zoey had purchased burner phones so that they could stay in touch without giving PLA hackers the ability to track their geolocation.

Chris waited in the lobby for two more hours, trying Zoey's cell phone repeatedly. After the initial call that had gone to voice mail, the rest of the calls returned a message that her phone was not in service. Another bad sign. Although he couldn't prove it to anyone, Chris grew increasingly certain that Red Sun had taken Zoey. He made an inventory of everything he knew about the assassin, anything that might give him an indication of where they might be headed.

Chris searched the faces of the tourists filing in and out of the hotel for a glimpse of Zoey or Red Sun. He couldn't help but dwell on what the man was capable of. Zoey had told him what Geist's body had looked like after Red Sun had tortured him.

That was not the work of a professional. That was the work of a psychotic.

* * *

As Red Sun marched her through the crowds of Union Square, Zoey searched for a policeman or an armed security guard she could call out to. She did not want to get an innocent bystander killed, but if she saw someone with a weapon and a clear shot, she was willing to risk her own life to stop her abductor.

It was a short walk to the parking garage beneath the green oasis of Union Square, a park ringed by the tall buildings of Macy's, Saks, and hotels like The Westin St. Francis. They took an elevator down four floors into the dark and dingy parking garage. The only other occupant of the elevator was a young man in his early twenties who looked like a college student. In a display of standard elevator etiquette, no one made eye contact. Zoey was particularly scrupulous about avoiding the young man's gaze because she realized that if Red Sun thought she was signaling him in any way, he would be dead before the elevator doors opened.

The elevator pinged. Red Sun glanced at the man and apparently concluded that his obliviousness was not an act. He led Zoey to his rental car, a white Ford Focus.

Once she had regained some of her composure after the shock of seeing Red Sun in the lobby, she began to study him. He seemed like a nondescript guy, in his tan windbreaker and khakis, with a round, bland face. But there was something different about him, and it wasn't just the fact that he was holding her at gunpoint.

It was the way he looked at her. All women are students of the way men look at them. Men try to be that perceptive, but they usually aren't that sensitive and, in any event, men are easier to read. They are genetically hardwired to be visually stimulated, to be fetishists.

Zoey knew when a man was looking at her breasts or her ass or her legs or, for the kinkier sorts, her feet. She also knew when a man was trying so very hard not to look at her in that way. But the way Red Sun looked at her was different, and she perceived it right away. His eyes roved over her body with an avidity that had a sexual charge to it, but it was not sexual. Maybe she was imagining it, but she thought he was looking at her like she were a toy he wanted to disassemble to see how it worked.

Red Sun clicked the key fob and popped open the trunk of the car with a beep that reverberated in the cavernous, concrete parking garage.

"Give me your cell phone," he said.

She handed it over, and Red Sun removed the SIM card, wiped it down for fingerprints, and then smashed it on the pavement, shattering the screen. Then he patted her down quickly.

After glancing around to confirm no one was observing, he lifted the lid of the trunk and said, "Get inside."

Once more Zoey scanned her surroundings for someone who might help.

"Do it now or I'll shoot you right here," he said.

Zoey climbed inside the trunk. When she was halfway in, Red Sun shoved her forward, and she smacked her forehead on the underside of a car stereo speaker. The trunk shut with a whump, and she was in darkness.

46

When the trunk slammed shut, Zoey was overcome for a few moments by the blind, animal panic of claustrophobia. She screamed and kicked at the inside of the trunk. Her thoughts raced.

I'm going to die here.

I can't die here.

I'M GOING TO DIE HERE.

This is not how I die.

Zoey was not someone who had given a lot of thought to her death, but she felt an overpowering sense that the fate that seemed to be awaiting her was wrong, a mistake. A Chinese hit man was something out of a movie or a video game. Such things did not belong in her life and did not deserve to play the key role in its final act. It was like an implausible twist ending in a book. It hadn't been set up properly. There was no foreshadowing, nothing in her past that would have made it seem just, or at least ironic. That was the difference between art and life. It didn't have to make sense. It didn't have to satisfy anyone's expectations, much less her own.

The ignition turned over, and the car began to move, backing out of the parking space. Zoey tried to steady herself after the exertion of kicking against the inside of the trunk.

The car turned in slow arcs as it climbed through the levels of the parking garage. She realized that this was a critical juncture. The car had to move slowly, and they were probably near people who were walking through the garage to or from their cars.

Zoey began screaming, hoping that one of the shoppers outside might hear and call the police.

"Help! I'm being kidnapped! I'm in the trunk!"

She realized that the trunk was muffling much of the sound, along with the rumble of the engine. She needed to do something more to be heard.

Zoey examined her surroundings, which were dimly lit by the red of the brake lights and the faint illumination that filtered in through the seams of the trunk lid. Everything grew more discernible as her eyes adjusted. Wasn't there supposed to be a release inside a car trunk to permit someone inside to pop the lid? She thought she had heard that somewhere.

Zoey ran her hands around the sides of the trunk until she found what appeared to be a button. She pressed the button, but nothing happened. She pressed it again. Same result. She pressed it a dozen, two dozen times, but it was broken. Red Sun had known that he was going to stash her in the trunk. He had probably disabled the release.

This is not how I die.

THIS IS NOT HOW I DIE.

Zoey stared at the brake light and realized how easy it would be to punch it out. She adjusted her body around in the trunk so that she could kick out the red plastic brake light cover. After a few hard kicks, it popped off.

The car was still slowly circling upward through the garage.

How many levels have we passed through? We were four floors down, and he's probably passed through at least two, maybe three. The car will be out of the garage soon, which will make it much harder to attract someone's attention.

Zoey shifted herself around again in the trunk until her face was in front of the broken brake light. She could see that it was brighter outside now. It was actual sunlight, not fluorescents. The car was in the top level of the garage.

She placed her lips right up against the hole she had made and screamed, *"Help! I'm in the trunk! I'm being kidnapped!"*

Apparently, this was loud enough for Red Sun to hear, because the car came to an abrupt stop—so hard that it hurled Zoey to the back of the trunk.

The trunk popped open, and she saw Red Sun holding a crowbar. She saw him pull back, his face contorting, just before the blow landed.

*   *   *

When Zoey came to, she couldn't see through one eye, which was encrusted in blood. She tried to raise her hands to touch her face, but they were bound together with a zip tie. She wanted to scream, but a rag had been shoved in her mouth.

The brake light cover was back on and, from the dark shadow across the plastic, it appeared to have been secured with duct tape. She wanted to kick it out again but her feet were also tied together.

Even with the zip tie, she was able to raise her hands and gingerly touch her face. She wanted to know if she had lost an eye and was relieved to find that it was just blood from a cut on her forehead. She blinked and rubbed at her eye until she regained her full vision.

There was a steady humming sound. The car was on a freeway now and seemed to be moving at full speed. She tried to extricate herself from the zip tie on her hands, but it was no use.

Zoey stopped struggling and lay there listening to the sounds outside to see if she could tell where they were. She might have been able to guess the route if she hadn't been unconscious from the blow.

Because she didn't know how long she had been out, there was no telling how far they were from Union Square. All she could hear was the hiss of tires.

Then Zoey remembered. She reached down and found that the HealthBot device was still strapped to her ankle. Samples of the new device had been given to several members of the firm's staff when the device's maker, FrostByte, celebrated its IPO. It monitored her walking mileage, heart rate, temperature, and *geolocation*—and stored that health data on a cloud server. That meant someone somewhere had access to that data and could trace her whereabouts.

But how could she reach out to that someone?

Zoey recalled a bit of Morse code—like many hackers, she was a student of cryptography. Morse code was one of the simplest codes imaginable, but that was exactly why it still had its uses.

She pressed the on-off switch on the HealthBot once, then paused, then switched it on and off three more times. In Morse code, she hoped that each on-off might be viewed as a dot. Four dots equals the letter *h*.

A space between letters was represented by a space three times as long as a dot, so she paused for three beats, then switched the device on and off again. One dot stood for the letter *e*.

Next came the letter *l*—dot-dash-dot-dot. On-off. Two beats. On-off. On-off.

Finally, a three-beat space between letters, then the dot-dash-dash-dot to signify the letter *p*.

H-e-l-p.

She recognized that the chance that someone would notice her signals was slimmer than the chance of someone finding a message in a bottle tossed in the sea by an island castaway. FrostByte's cloud server probably stored terabytes of data, and most of it was never actively reviewed.

But it was something. She had to do something.

47

Without Zoey, the firm's forensic lab seemed achingly quiet and empty to Chris. This time he saw no point in hiding or wasting time trying to gain access to someone else's forensic lab. If Red Sun wanted to come for him here, let him come.

Chris tried to reach Paul Saperstein so that he could obtain BD's help in tracking Zoey and Red Sun. He phoned and emailed but was told firmly but politely that Saperstein was not available, no matter how serious the matter.

Next Chris dialed up Charlie McGuane, one of his former colleagues from the Department of Justice's Computer Crime and Intellectual Property Section, to see if he could help track the location of Zoey's burner phone. McGuane's secretary said that he was in a meeting, but Chris said to tell him it was urgent, and he took the call.

"Hey, buddy, I assume that you're calling to pay me back for helping you out a while back. Since it's taken you so long, I figure you've been shopping for something special. Maybe a bottle of Pappy Van Winkle. That was a hint, by the way." A few months before, McGuane had pulled some phone records for Chris that helped him in a prior case involving a hunt for a team of hackers plotting cyberterrorism.

"Not today, Charlie, but soon. And Pappy is overrated. Just because it's hard to find, doesn't mean it's the best."

"Now you're just being provocative."

"I need a cell phone tracked. A burner."

"You know the DOJ is not your personal investigative unit. You don't get to play in our sandbox. Not anymore."

"It's an emergency. An abduction."

"You try the police?"

"It just happened, and I don't think I could convince them to move on this fast enough."

"Are you okay?"

"Not really, but I don't have time to talk about it. I just need this now. The phone's probably been disabled, but I have to know for certain."

There was silence on the line, then Charlie said, "Okay, give me the number, and I'll see what I can do. I'm going to put you on hold, okay?"

"Thanks." Chris knew that Charlie's first instinct was to make him squirm a bit before granting a favor, so he clearly recognized the tone in Chris's voice. On a typical day, Charlie would have taken some time to goad him about his move to the private sector.

As he waited on hold, Chris noticed the traces of Zoey's presence scattered around the lab. Her magazines, her bulky headphones, a sports water bottle, and a lanyard with the membership card for the fitness club she never used.

A few minutes later Charlie returned. "Sorry, buddy, but I got nothing. Or not very much. That phone is out of service; somebody must have removed the SIM card. The last time that phone pinged a cell tower was at 3:25 p.m. today, and it was somewhere in Union Square."

"Okay. That's what I figured. Thanks anyway." Red Sun had probably taken the phone off Zoey and removed the SIM card as soon as he grabbed her.

"Does the person who was taken have any other devices? These days everything you own seems to be broadcasting something to someone. What do they call it? The Internet of Things. Whatever happened to devices that just did their damn jobs and shut up?"

"No, no, I don't think she had anything else on her."

Then Chris was struck by what he had just seen—Zoey's seldom-used fitness club card. Zoey hated going to the gym—and that was why she had started wearing a HealthBot device around her ankle. It wasn't visible, so he wasn't sure if she was still wearing it or not. By the same token, it was also the sort of thing that might slip by Red Sun when he frisked Zoey. If she was wearing the HealthBot, it would be storing her geolocation data on a cloud server.

"Chris, you still there?" Charlie asked.

"Yeah, I'm here, but something just occurred to me. I have to go, but thanks for the assist."

"I'm all about customer service," Charlie said. "Take care of yourself."

Chris wasn't sure if he would be able to obtain Zoey's geolocation data from FrostByte, but he knew exactly where to direct the inquiry. First, Chris examined the privacy policy posted on FrostByte's website. Then he dialed up Paul Saberhagen, FrostByte's privacy officer. He and Saberhagen had been on a panel together at an International Association of Privacy Professionals conference in DC, where they had discussed big data. Ten years ago privacy officers had been a rarity, but now nearly every Fortune 500 company had one, and the IAPP was their club.

Saberhagen was a goateed, bespectacled man with a professorial demeanor. Over drinks after their session, Chris had learned that his hobby was river kayaking. Saberhagen seemed like a nice enough guy, but he struck Chris as cautious by nature, like most good compliance professionals, and that could pose a challenge.

"Chris Bruen! To what do I owe the pleasure?"

"I have a favor to ask. A big favor."

"Really." Chris could already hear the reticence in his voice. "What sort of favor?"

"Your HealthBot device records geolocation data, doesn't it?"

"That's right."

"And it's stored in the cloud, right?"

"Also correct. We use the geolocation data to determine which ads to deliver to users. We have deals with fitness clubs, vitamin shops, athletic-wear places, that sort of thing."

"I believe that Zoey Doucet, the head of my forensic lab, has been abducted. And I believe she may be wearing a HealthBot."

"Jesus. What happened?"

"It's a very long story, and I'm not at liberty to tell it. Attorney-client privilege."

"Fair enough. So you're looking to track her?"

"That's right."

"Of course I want to help, but let me think this through. As you know, we can't violate the terms of our privacy policy." When a company like FrostByte describes how it uses and discloses personal information in a website privacy policy, then it is legally obligated to abide by those terms. And if a company breaches the promises in its privacy policy, then it may be subject to an enforcement action by the Federal Trade Commission or a state attorney general for engaging in unfair or deceptive business practices. A privacy officer who authorized disclosures in violation of the privacy policy probably wouldn't remain a privacy officer for long, so Saberhagen's wariness was understandable.

Chris was ready for Saberhagen's response. "I understand completely. You have to answer to your board and management—and your principles. If a privacy officer doesn't play by the rules, who will? That's why I took a look at your privacy policy before I called. There's a provision that says you can use personal information if necessary to protect the safety of your users."

Saberhagen was silent for a moment. He was probably pulling up and reviewing the policy himself.

"Hmm. Yes, that's right. That was intended to permit us to cooperate with law enforcement, but it could be read more broadly than that."

"There's no question that this is a safety issue." Chris found it hard to say the next sentence. "In fact, I'm not even sure if she's still alive."

Chris could almost hear that statement sinking in.

"Of course I can help," Saberhagen said. "So her name is Zoey Doucet. Is that Zoey with a *y*?"

"Yes. Zoey with a *y*. *D-o-u-c-e-t.*"

"Let me call you back."

Chris paced around the forensic lab, willing the phone to ring, and about ten minutes later it did.

"Well, I found something interesting," Saberhagen said. "It appears that she may be using the device to send a signal."

"How so?"

"Someone is turning the device on and off over and over again in what seems to be a timed pattern."

"And what is the pattern? Read it to me like numbers. Let's call a simple on and off a one. A two-beat pause is a two. A three-beat pause is a three."

Saberhagen studied the patterns. "It seems to be a phrase that's repeated over and over. The phrase is, one-one-one-one-three . . . one-three-one-two-one-one-three . . . one-two-two-one."

"It's Morse code." It had been a while since Chris had worked with Morse code, so it took a minute for him to work it out. "And the message is 'Help.' Clever girl. That's her. She was alive when that signal was sent. Is the message still being transmitted?"

"The message was sent from 4:05 to 5:30 p.m. today. Then the message stops, but the geolocation data is still transmitting." Another pause. "Based on the coordinates, she's still in San Francisco, and the address should be 22 Clay Street, at the corner of Clay and Powell."

"Chinatown," Chris said.

48

Zoey was still punching in the signal using the HealthBot's on-off switch when the car came to a stop. She wasn't sure how long they had been driving, but they had left the freeway about a half hour before, and she heard the sirens and car horns of a city street. The pneumatic brakes of a bus hissed somewhere close by.

She tried to twist herself around in the trunk so that she could kick out the taillight again, but with her feet zip-tied together it was futile. She knew the lid of the trunk was going to open soon, and it was very possible that she would be murdered on the spot while still trussed.

If he doesn't just kill me right away, then he'll probably want me to walk to somewhere he can hide my body. Easier for him if I walk than if he has to drag me.

Zoey hadn't given up, but something like a calm had begun to settle over her. At first she found it hard to accept the reality of the situation—that her life might end this way. She blamed herself for being reckless enough to end up in this nightmarish situation. But as time passed ever so slowly in the trunk of the car, she stopped blaming herself. Zoey figured that if she had drawn someone as evil as Red Sun to her, it was probably because she was doing something that was good. She was proud of the work she had begun with Chris. And she would really have liked to see how the relationship with him developed. But if this was all of the time she was allotted, then okay.

She heard footsteps on concrete, and then the trunk sprang open. They were inside a garage with fluorescent lighting fixtures glowing over Red Sun's shoulder. To her darkness-adjusted eyes, the garage seemed brighter than the sun, and she squinted and blinked until she could see him clearly.

Red Sun had a box cutter and used it to cut the ties binding her feet. He didn't look her in the eyes, grabbing her legs and pulling them out of the trunk like he was hoisting a rolled carpet.

As her pulse raced, Zoey found it difficult to breathe through her nose with the gag filling her mouth. She tried to calm herself, slow her breathing, to avoid passing out from asphyxiation.

He hauled her to her feet, and for the first time she was able to see where she was. It was some sort of warehouse, but it was not like any place she had ever seen before. The space was filled with a riot of multicolored silk and bared fangs. It took her a moment to realize what she was looking at. This was the place where dragon floats used in the Chinese New Year's parade were stored.

As he was lifting Zoey's legs out of the trunk, Red Sun touched the HealthBot strapped to her ankle. He spat some sort of curse in Mandarin as he pushed Zoey down roughly on the floor, the back of her head striking concrete. Red Sun removed the HealthBot with a ripping of Velcro and examined it for a moment, then removed her gag.

"What is this?" he asked. His English was flat and uninflected.

She gasped and coughed for a few moments, filling her lungs, then finally said, "Just a pedometer. It measures how far I walk."

"What else does it do? It has a location signal, doesn't it?"

Zoey shrugged.

"Don't lie to me!" he shouted. "If you don't tell me what you know right now, I'm going to end you right here. Right here. Your choice."

Zoey figured that Red Sun probably already knew the answer to his question. Answering truthfully would only buy her a bit more time. "Yes, there's a geolocation signal."

He slammed down his satchel, angry for having missed the device. He paced around for a minute as Zoey looked up at him from the floor. Then he seemed to reach some decision, walking away across the warehouse with the HealthBot.

When he returned, Zoey said, "You don't have to do this, you know."

"No, I don't. My contract is for Bruen, not you."

"But you want to do this, don't you?"

"Yes."

"How did you find this place?"

"A friend told me about it. The dragon's lair."

"What are you going to do?"

"The same thing that I did to your friend Geist." He placed a hand on a heavily weighted satchel that he had slung over his shoulder. "I brought my tools. You don't know how close you came that day."

The sight of Geist bound in the chair, along with the smell of the blood, came back to Zoey in a sensory flood. Once more she tried to tamp down the panic, stay logical, but each time it was harder. The fear was like a rising tide, glossy and malignant, swelling against the floodgates. Soon, she knew, it would overwhelm her, and she'd let loose the scream that was building inside.

"There must be some part of you that isn't like this," she said. "Do you have kids? A wife? A sister? A brother?"

She thought she detected a change in Red Sun's features. Zoey figured that it was in her interest to keep him talking. She'd heard that was what someone should do if they were taken. Make the abductor recognize your humanity; make it harder for him to turn you into some mannequin in a fetishistic fantasy.

Sensing that she might be getting through to him on some level, Zoey continued: "You can't change what you've done in the past, but you can change this."

"You should stop. I know what you're doing, and it's not helping. If you don't, I'm going to start here." He tapped the center of her forehead with his index finger. "Instead of here." He tapped her knee.

Zoey forced a smile, but she could imagine how tense it must have looked. "I'm not sure which of those I'd actually prefer."

"You'll know when the time comes."

Red Sun was leading Zoey across the floor to the rear of the warehouse, past endless rows of beaded, jeweled dragon floats that glared at them like sentinels of the netherworld.

Somewhere in the building a door creaked. Red Sun extended a hand to bring her to a stop as he listened for other sounds of movement. He retrieved the gag from his pocket and shoved it back in Zoey's mouth. Red Sun clutched Zoey by the arm and pulled her away behind a nearby shelf, upon which an enormous scarlet-and-emerald dragon crouched.

They waited to see who would show themselves. Zoey tested the stiffness in her knees, gauging her ability to hurl herself at Red Sun when the time came, disrupt his aim. If she moved too soon, Red Sun would simply shoot her, and nothing would be accomplished.

She heard a footstep an aisle or two away. Red Sun heard it too, and he drew his gun and held it ready in front of him. There was a faint rustling in the silk skin of a dragon about ten yards in front of them, like the thing was drawing shallow breath. It was catching the movement of whoever was approaching.

Zoey tensed and got ready.

49

Chris knew that the fastest route to Chinatown from his office in Embarcadero Center was via BART. As tempting as it was to jump in his car and step on the gas, he knew that with Financial District traffic it would take longer that way. Chris had already called the police and given them the address where Zoey was being held, but if he could get there first he wasn't going to wait.

He found it difficult to stand still on the jammed train, and if any of the evening commuters that surrounded him bothered to notice, they probably would have thought he looked like a suicide bomber about to flip the switch. Chris couldn't afford to draw too much attention to himself, though. If he was stopped by BART police, they would find the gun in his computer bag. Even with a permit, he would be detained for questioning.

While he waited for the train to reach the Powell Street station, he dialed Jefferson Fong on his cell phone.

"Jefferson, I need your help."

"Sure, man. What's up?"

"What do you know about 22 Clay Street, at the corner of Clay and Powell? I checked it out on Zapper Earth, and it looks like some kind of warehouse."

Jefferson thought about it for a moment. "Yeah, right. There is a warehouse there. It's actually kind of interesting."

"Interesting how?"

"I was in there once. That's where they store the dragons for the Chinese New Year's parade. They keep them close by because they're so fragile and hard to move. What do you want with that place?"

"I'm meeting someone there."

"Is everything okay?"

"Anything else you can tell me about the place?"

"Not really, no."

"Is there a connection to the tongs?"

"Just about every place in Chinatown has some connection to the tongs. Nothing special that I'm aware of."

Chris hung up as the doors opened on the Powell Street station, and he began running—up the long escalator, through the shoppers of Union Square, up the hill to the ornate gate at the Grant Avenue entrance to Chinatown. Maybe it was just his agitated state, but in the early dark under a bright full moon the garish neon of Chinatown looked malevolent. The electric greens were putrescent, and the glowing reds were bloody.

When he reached the intersection of Grant and California, Chris's eyes were drawn upward to the brick clock tower of Old Saint Mary's Cathedral. The inscription under the clock's face read, "Son, observe the time and fly from evil." When the cathedral was built, there had been a brothel across the street, but the quote from the Book of Sirach still seemed to be speaking directly to Chris that night.

A few side streets later he stood before the two-story-tall warehouse at 22 Clay Street. The building was made of old brown bricks that must have been red once. It appeared that at one point in its long history the structure had been charred by fire. It was situated between a martial arts studio and a branch of the Bank of Canton.

Chris approached the iron door out front and saw it was ajar. He leaned in close but heard no sounds coming from inside.

Chris reached into his bag and produced the small, rectangular device that was tracking the HealthBot's geolocation signal. The display looked much like the Maps app on a smartphone, with a pulsing red dot to represent Chris's location, and a pulsing green dot that was the HealthBot. Now that he was so close, the display no longer showed a map of city streets, just a red directional arrow pointing him to the device. Pointing him to Zoey.

Zoey seemed to be moving slowly and erratically. Perhaps she was injured.

Chris pushed through the door and into a gloomy, cavernous space lit only by a couple of fluorescent security lights. When his eyes adjusted, he was startled to see a dozen dragons from the Chinese New Year's parade glowering at him from the shelves of the warehouse. Jefferson had not been kidding. It was a strange sight.

He held the tracking device close to his chest so that its bright display wouldn't give him away. The arrow directed him forward toward the rear of the warehouse. Drawing closer to Zoey's location, he still heard no voices or footfalls. It was absolutely quiet.

Chris turned down an aisle, the tracker's red arrow directing him to a corridor of multihued silk, beads finely layered to resemble reptilian scales. With each step, the arrow grew larger to indicate that he was drawing very close.

Chris drew a deep breath through his clenched jaw and then peered around the corner of one aisle and down another. Then he saw what he had been pursuing: a brown tabby sitting in the middle of the warehouse aisle, intently chewing on a paw, trying to remove an unwelcome encumbrance.

Strapped to the cat's paw was Zoey's HealthBot.

Chris spun around, but it was too late. The iron shelf next to him tipped, and silk and papier-mâché dragons cascaded down upon him. Just before he was buried, he got a glimpse of Red Sun standing nearby with a gun in one hand and his forearm around Zoey's throat, using her as a shield. Zoey had a gag in her mouth, her hands were bound, her forehead was bloody, and her eyes were wide and screaming.

She pushed herself backward against Red Sun, throwing him off balance so that his first shot was wild. One of the dragon heads struck Chris, and he nearly fell to his knees. When he righted himself, all that he could see was crimson. He was immersed in a skein of silk as big as a parachute. Chris tore and pulled at the material, but he couldn't seem to get clear.

A gunshot sounded, and Chris felt heat and pain in his left shoulder, spinning him back and down. Before he could even process what was happening, he was on his knees, still seeing only a field of red. Chris wanted to fire back blindly at the place where he thought Red Sun was standing, but he couldn't risk hitting Zoey.

His thinking was cloudy from the shock of the gunshot wound, but he continued to swim through the red silk, now laterally, trying to avoid further gunshots while freeing himself to find Red Sun and Zoey.

More gunshots. Several in rapid succession.

Panic gripped him like a seizure. When sensation returned, Chris realized much to his surprise that he was still alive.

Could Red Sun have fired that many shots and still somehow managed to miss me?

Chris lunged forward and finally got his head free of the slippery fabric.

Stretched out before him was Red Sun, motionless, the front of his shirt a bloody mess.

Zoey was standing next to the body, but her eyes were still on the source of the gunfire. Chris turned to follow her stricken gaze.

And there stood Jefferson Fong—owner of Fifth Dynasty Comix, amateur hacker, Southern-fried Chinese geek—holding a very large pistol, with a steely expression that left no doubt he knew how to use it.

* * *

The first thing he did was stand up, go to Zoey, and hug her. As satisfying as that was, it came with a price, as he felt a stabbing pain from the bullet in his shoulder.

"You okay?" he asked, examining the gash on her forehead.

She was trying to maintain her typical cool, but he could tell what an effort it was.

"Yeah. It's not as bad as it looks. You're the one with a bullet wound. Are you okay?"

Someone who didn't know her so well might not be able to see it, but Chris spotted every tremble and quiver on Zoey's face, the wild eyes. He knew she was not okay.

"I will be," Chris said. "Did he hurt you?"

"No. He was getting to it, but no."

Chris held up Zoey's bound wrists and considered what tool he could use to cut the zip ties. Jefferson helpfully stepped forward and snipped them with a long and very sharp knife.

"Who *are* you, anyway?" Chris said to Jefferson.

"FBI Special Agent Henry Hua. I've been assigned undercover to Chinatown's triad gangs for several years now. Lately, the focus has been on their connections to cybercrime. The comic shop is a front."

"So when we met that day on the street in Chinatown—"

"It wasn't an accident."

Agent Hua tore a piece of silk from a fallen dragon and used the fabric to pick up Red Sun's gun, which had landed several yards away from the killer's body. Hua tucked the gun into his waistband and then kneeled down. First, he checked for other weapons, and then he checked his wrist for a pulse.

"He's still alive," Hua said. "I'm going to call for an ambulance, but he's bleeding out."

Red Sun's eyelids fluttered. "I can hear you."

Hua turned to him and said, "Like I give a shit? You're dying. Deal with it."

Chris went down on one knee to assess Red Sun's injuries. It was hard to tell without removing his shirt, but it looked like he had been hit at least three times in the chest. It looked bad.

"There's an ambulance on the way." Chris had an urge to keep murmuring reassuring things, because that was what compassionate human beings did in that sort of situation, but he reconsidered in light of whom he was talking to.

Ever since he had killed Li Owyang and Bingwen Ma in that apartment in Shenzhen, Chris had been questioning himself and whether there was something inside him that enjoyed doing that kind of damage. When Chris looked into the eyes of the dying killer, he finally knew that in no way were they alike. Maybe they both had dark impulses roiling inside them, but the difference was that Chris struggled with his, beat them back, and suffered anguish after giving in to them. He would never really know whether he could have avoided pulling the trigger and killing the two hackers, but the fact that he would never let himself off the hook for those deaths was the critical difference between him and Red Sun. Anyone who applied a power drill to another human being was clearly not in the throes of any moral qualms.

"I'd like to call my brother," Red Sun said, his breathing labored.

"Where's your brother?" Chris asked.

"In a prison in Shanghai."

Chris thought about it for a moment. "How do we know it's not some signal?"

"You don't," Red Sun said. He looked down at his bloody chest. "I just want to speak to my brother. I did this for him."

"Tell me your real name, and I'll dial the number for you."

"Tao Zhang."

Chris looked at Hua and Zoey, and they both nodded, agreeing that it was worth the risk. Just learning which number Red Sun wanted to dial to impart his final words could be very useful.

"Okay," Chris said. "What's the number?"

The killer's head rolled back, and he gazed at the ceiling. He was fading fast.

Chris said it loudly this time. "Can you hear me? What's the number?"

50

Tao knew that he was dying, and it didn't feel as terrible as he'd feared it might. It even felt . . . fitting.

When a normal person, like the journalist he'd murdered, died violently, it seemed abnormal. Unexpected. For someone like Tao, who had the blood of so many on his hands, it was merely a matter of when and by whom, and even the answers to those questions weren't all that interesting.

No, death didn't perplex him. Instead, he wondered at what he'd become.

In the beginning, taking assignments as a hit man had seemed a fair exchange for his brother's freedom. He had been willing to enter into that transaction, but only now, as he bled out on the warehouse floor, did he realize the extent of the collateral that he had put at risk.

He had done wicked things, but he had considered those deeds a weight that, while heavy, could be borne. But evil wasn't really something that you did; it was something that you were. Perhaps if he had stayed rutted in the routines of an ordinary life, he would never have discovered the thing inside him. He might have been able to maintain the illusion that he was a good man.

But he was long past that point now.

Bruen spoke loudly, seemingly repeating himself. "Can you hear me? What's the number?"

Tao recited by heart the number to the prison's main office. "Ask for Li Chen. Tell them his brother is dying and wants to speak to him."

Bruen dialed the number, then set the phone next to him on the ground, wincing at the pain from the bullet wound in his shoulder. "You have to leave it on speaker," Bruen said. "We need to know you're not calling in another killer."

Tao nodded. "Hello?" he asked in Mandarin.

"Who is this?"

Tao explained.

"Li Chen does not have a brother."

Tao was confident that every member of the prison's staff knew who among the inmates were substitute criminals. Using his brother's assumed identity should not confuse anyone.

"Please just put him on the phone. Please. I think you know who I am."

"Whoever you are, Li Chen is gone. He was released a week ago."

Tao couldn't believe that he had heard correctly. "That can't be."

"Actually, it can. I gave him back his belongings myself. I called him a taxi. I'm positive."

Tao told Bruen, "I need another call. My brother wasn't there."

Bruen bent painfully, picked up the phone, and keyed in the digits as Tao told him Wenyan's cell number, then left it next to Tao's head.

Tao listened to the phone ring and ring, and then Wenyan's voice.

"Hello? Who is this?"

"It's Tao."

"Brother! Where have you been?"

"What are you doing out of prison?"

"I was paroled. I thought the hearing was just a formality, but it was for real. One of my friends inside told me that the government is embarrassed by the practice of substitute criminals and is trying to get them off the books."

"Did anyone say anything to you about me when they released you?"

"No. What do you mean? Why would they?"

"I did some things that I thought would help secure your release, but it looks like I didn't need to after all."

"What things?" Wenyan paused. "What did you do, Tao?"

"It's not important now."

"Who were you dealing with?"

"I thought I knew, but I guess I was wrong."

The sickening realization came to him that perhaps he had not been contracted by the PLA through Silk Road. Someone else had played him, hiding behind the anonymity of the website's onion routing. He had always felt like a pawn, but now he didn't even know whose hand had been moving him across the board.

"You don't sound well. Are you under the weather?"

"A bit. Nothing to concern yourself with. Where are you right now?"

"I'm walking along the Bund. It's a beautiful day. But you know that, right?"

"I'm not in Shanghai today. I'm traveling. So tell me what you're looking at."

"Since I got out of prison, I just can't get enough of the sky and open spaces."

"Tell me."

"I just sat down on a bench beside the Huangpu, and I'm watching the river run."

"What color is it today?"

"It's green, almost jade. A smoky jade."

Wenyan carried on describing the scene, and it sounded so lovely that he felt transported to the seat next to his brother on that bench beside the Huangpu. He could almost feel the breeze off the river stirring his hair. Wenyan's voice became steadily fainter, like the fade-out at the end of a record. There was a breeze, and the sun was bright, impossibly bright.

Then it became brighter still.

*   *   *

Chris leaned down and checked for a pulse with two fingers to Tao's neck. The movement sent another spasm of pain through his shoulder.

"He's gone."

Zoey massaged her wrists where they had been bound. "You two speak Mandarin. What did he say?"

"He spoke to his brother," Chris said. "Mostly small talk."

"Do you think he sent a signal? Is someone else coming here to finish the job?"

"No, I don't think so," Chris said.

Zoey was drawing fast, shallow breaths and gripping the nearest iron shelf with white knuckles. Chris recognized a panic attack when he saw one.

"Take deep breaths," he said, inhaling deeply by way of example.

Zoey took a gasping breath, following Chris's lead.

"Do you have any medication for this?"

After another gasp and a nervous glance at the FBI agent, Zoey replied, "Not with me."

They continued the breathing exercises while Jefferson looked on. Gradually, Zoey's breathing and heart rate returned to normal. As she sat on the concrete floor and regrouped, an ambulance siren began to bay in the distance.

"So what are you doing here? Looking out for us?" Chris asked. "How did the FBI get involved?"

"It started when you went to the State Department. We've been watching you ever since you left their offices on Market Street."

"So the government never really cut us loose."

"No, of course the FBI recognized what was happening, but the State Department was not going to take action against the PRC government on this in any official, public way. And we didn't want you two going around suggesting that you had the backing of the State Department or that they believed your story."

"So you preferred to treat us like we were nut jobs," Zoey said.

"Yeah, basically."

"So where were you when he came hunting for us in Stinson Beach?" Chris asked.

"That got a little off the leash," Jefferson said. "Our guy should have been closer to the situation. But that wasn't me; it was another agent."

"That man who ran the grocery store was killed," Chris said.

"We would have prevented it if we could," Jefferson said. "At least I was here when I needed to be."

"I'll give you that," Chris said. He extended a hand to brace himself against a shelf, feeling light-headed from the blood loss.

The door to the warehouse banged open as the police rushed in, followed by a team of paramedics. After quickly establishing that Tao Zhang was dead, the paramedics made Chris lie down on a gurney and wheeled him away.

Chris stared upward past the looming paramedics at the rusted tin ceiling of the warehouse. A host of Chinese dragons paraded past overhead, grinning at him with toothy, open-mouthed smiles and glaring popeyes.

One paramedic stayed behind with Zoey, who was clearly still in shock.

"I'm going with him," she said, pushing past and running after the gurney.

When she caught up with them, one of the paramedics said, "Sorry, there's no more room in the ambulance." He was heavily tattooed, wore a two-day stubble with his sweat-stained green scrubs, and looked like he was comfortable giving orders.

Zoey slapped a hand on the inside of the rear door to keep it open and, without an invitation, climbed inside, sitting down on the floor beside the gurney. The paramedic glared at Zoey, and she glared back. It was a standoff worthy of Sergio Leone.

"I'm bleeding here, guys," Chris offered through clenched teeth. Then to the paramedic, "And she's not going to back down. You don't know her."

"Believe it," she said.

"Let's go," the paramedic shouted to the driver.

51

Two days later Chris was already out of the hospital and back at work in the law firm's computer forensic lab. There was a bulge under his shirt where the gunshot wound was bandaged. He had been lucky. The bullet had gone cleanly through his left shoulder, tearing some muscle but not doing any major damage.

Chris had spent the morning catching up on emails and phone calls from clients but found that he wasn't quite ready to launch himself into a new project. He couldn't stop thinking about what had happened in the Chinatown warehouse and something that didn't make sense.

"You've been quiet this morning," Zoey said, peering over her array of monitors. "You're still thinking about it, aren't you?"

"Yeah. Lying in that hospital bed, I just kept turning it over in my head."

"It's only natural. I can't stop thinking about it either. We both came pretty close."

"It's not just that," Chris said, taking a sip of coffee.

"Well, what is it then?"

"I didn't tell you everything that Zhang said to his brother. It's been bothering me."

"So tell me."

"Well, with that first call to the Chinese prison, Zhang asked for his brother by the name Li Chen. But he referred to him as Wenyan when they were speaking directly."

"Maybe Wenyan was a nickname, a term of affection."

"No, Wenyan is a proper name. I believe that was his brother's correct name."

"So what do you think that means?"

"I think Wenyan may have been serving a prison sentence under another name for another person."

"That sounds a little farfetched."

"I know, but there is a practice in China known as substitute criminals, where wealthy families pay someone to serve a prison sentence for one of their own."

"And you think Wenyan Zhang was a substitute criminal?"

"I couldn't believe it either, but as I thought about the rest of what Zhang said, it seemed to fit."

"What else did he say?"

"Well, he was really surprised his brother was out of prison."

"That's understandable."

"But it was more than surprise; he was shocked. Zhang said that he did some things to help secure his brother's release. I think what he meant by that was he took the assignment to kill me as part of some arrangement to obtain favorable treatment for his brother."

"So you think he was taking hit man assignments to save his brother? I'm sorry, but that guy was twisted beyond all comprehension. I can't see him having any human feelings."

"Believe me, I'm not defending him," Chris said. "I'm just trying to understand. It would explain why he was so shocked when he learned of his brother's release. He thought that the people who had hired him were using his brother as leverage, and they wouldn't just give up that leverage."

Zoey nodded, beginning to get on board. "But maybe he was mistaken about who had hired him."

"Exactly. Zhang's brother asked him who he was dealing with to secure his release, and Zhang said that he thought he knew, but he was wrong. What does that tell you?"

"Someone had hired him to do this contract hit, but they did it through an intermediary—or through the Internet—so that he thought he knew who was hiring him, but he wasn't sure."

Chris nodded. "And we know that he offered his services through Silk Road, which is designed for anonymity on both sides of the transaction."

"So who *did* hire Zhang to kill you?"

"Well, despite all evidence to the contrary, it might not have been the PLA or agents of the PRC."

"So who was it then?"

"I don't know, but I think we can no longer assume that the motive was revenge for the deaths of Li Owyang and Bingwen Ma."

"But doesn't the hiring of a Chinese hit man suggest they're related?"

"Yes, but not necessarily. It could be someone who knew about what happened in China and wanted to throw suspicion on the Chinese government—and away from themselves."

"So we're back to square one. Knowing that it's someone who wants you dead doesn't really narrow the field all that much, particularly when you consider all the hackers you put behind bars when you were at the DOJ."

"True, but we're not really at square one. First, we know that whoever hired Zhang knew about my trip to China and what happened there. Second, we know a few things about Zhang and how he pursued us. I have to believe that there are clues there somewhere. We just have to go back over everything we know, looking at it from this new perspective. We were so sold on the PLA as the culprits that we made every fact fit that theory."

"So we go back over everything, huh?"

"Right."

"I'm not even sure what that means. What am I actually supposed to do?"

"Just let that Zoey brain of yours meditate on it."

"Clearly you have a lot more confidence in the Zoey brain than I do."

*   *   *

Attorneys are big on work plans, lists, and methodical research to solve a problem, but those analytical tools didn't help much with this sort of puzzle. Chris didn't know the answer or how to approach it, but he had the unmistakable sense that it was just beyond his comprehension. If he was right that Zhang's brother had been a substitute criminal and that Zhang had been hired by an anonymous person trying to create the illusion that he was with the PLA, then he knew he was close to a breakthrough. It was like a cryptography problem where you had to step back and let the numbers and symbols speak to you, reveal their pattern.

Chris tried writing down a chronology of events on the whiteboard that encircled the four walls of the forensic lab, starting with his arrival in Shanghai and ending with the shootout in the Chinatown warehouse. As he paced around the lab following the narrative, Chris traced and retraced his steps across China and back to the US, looking for some anomaly—and it didn't take long to find one.

"Zoey, look at this," Chris said, pointing to the whiteboard.

"Zhang went to the Bottom of the Hill after we were there. How did he know to do that?"

"Could he have followed us?"

"If he had been following us, he wouldn't have waited until Stinson Beach to take a shot."

"Maybe he had access to my law firm employment file. We suspected that the PLA could have hacked the firm's system."

Chris started to interject.

Zoey immediately caught his meaning. "But, right, we're not dealing with the PLA anymore. We have no reason to think that Zhang would have access to those sorts of technical resources. I mean, hacking Reynolds Fincher might not be that challenging for the PLA's army of superhackers, but it's not like anyone can do it."

"So let's say for the sake of argument that someone here at the firm, someone who could gain access to your employment file, was working with Zhang."

"Are you thinking someone at Reynolds Fincher wanted to have you killed?"

Chris's thoughts raced, combing through hallway conversations and office gossip, sifting for the connection.

Until he found something.

It wasn't exactly a smoking gun, but it was a data element that did not fit, something that required an explanation he very much wanted to hear.

Zoey was now standing next to him. "What is it? You have something, don't you?"

"You're right. There is someone at Reynolds Fincher who would like me out of the way. Maybe that's not all that surprising. But what is surprising is that they actually paid to have it done. And I think I know who did it."

52

Richard Grogan appeared in the doorway of Chris's office, looking dapper in a charcoal-gray suit and a violet tie. He was smiling subtly. Grogan seemed to do most things subtly.

"Chris. I got your message," Grogan said. "I assume you want to pick up that conversation we were having earlier."

"Sort of."

"Good. Because I've been giving it a lot of thought."

"Sit."

Grogan sat in one of the chairs across from Chris's glass and granite desk. Chris knew roughly how he wanted this conversation to proceed, but the whole thing was a long shot. Grogan was so careful, so polished, that if he was to fall into a trap, it would have to be a very carefully constructed one.

"Those billing credits are very important to you, aren't they?" Chris said.

"Well, I could say it's all about the work and serving the clients, but that wouldn't be entirely true, would it? It's how we keep score."

"And is keeping score really that important?"

"You know it is. Money is how we all keep score. And those credits represent several million in my paycheck every year."

"But what if you have enough money?"

"You never have enough. Because if it's not about putting food on the table and a roof over your head—and it's not at this point—then it's about respect, winning. And who ever gets enough of those two things?"

"Not everyone is like that."

"Everyone I know is like that. At least everyone who's played the game well enough to be a partner here at Reynolds Fincher. What's really going on here? You going to join the kids in Berkeley protesting multinational corporations? If you've practiced law as long as we have and don't suffer from a little self-loathing, you probably just haven't been doing it right."

Chris smiled. "Just trying to understand you a little better."

"Understand yourself, buddy. Because we're playing the same game."

"Maybe," Chris said. "I'd like to talk with you about Zoey for a minute."

"Okay. I hope we're getting to the point of this conversation."

"We're getting there. When you mentioned her earlier, you knew that she had worked as a bartender at that club the Bottom of the Hill."

"Right."

"How did you know that?"

Grogan smiled and shrugged. "So is *this* what you want to talk about? I really have no idea. I probably overheard a conversation in the hallway, or maybe you told me at some point. What does it matter?"

"It matters because you have the ability to access staff employment records. I checked the system audit logs, so I know you looked at Zoey's file. I think you told the hired killer Tao Zhang that Zoey and I might go there to hide when he was hunting us."

Grogan shook his head and chuckled incredulously. It was a nice move, but it didn't quite play.

"Wait a second. You're going to have to repeat that. Because I thought you just accused me of helping a hired killer track you down."

"I'm saying more than that. I'm saying that you hired him."

Grogan's look of surprise quickly gave way to a grim calm. "I hope you know what you're doing," he said slowly, as if speaking to an opposing counsel who was in the middle of making a fatal miscalculation. "Because you've just made the kind of unsupported accusation that can get you run out of this law firm."

"Oh, I have support. We were able to trace the bitcoin transaction paying Zhang for his services. We linked it back to you."

Chris kept his expression still and his eyes focused on Grogan as he said this. He didn't want any tell or twitch to give away the fact that he was bluffing.

It was barely perceptible, but something in Grogan seemed to collapse a bit.

"What are you talking about? Bitcoin transactions can't be traced. They're anonymous."

"You never were very tech savvy, were you, Richard? Sure, it's difficult to trace a bitcoin transfer, but did you forget who you were dealing with? This is what Zoey and I do for a living. The bitcoin exchange Mt. Rox is in bankruptcy, and the feds have been able to access transaction records."

"My God, you are serious, aren't you?" Grogan said. "I'm going to use this to have your partnership revoked. Hell, you might even lose your license. Forget about taking my tech clients to another firm. When I get done with you, there won't be anything left."

"Didn't you hear me? I just told you that I have proof that you paid Tao Zhang to kill me."

"You have nothing." Grogan stood and pushed away the chair. "You're recording this, aren't you? You want me to make some kind of admission."

Chris patted the front of his shirt. "I'm not wearing a wire. Feel free to check if you like."

Grogan held up a finger as if to put a placeholder in the conversation. "I think I'll do that."

He stepped around the desk and patted Chris down. When he was finished, he said, "We're not done yet. Stay here."

Grogan disappeared into the hallway, returning a few minutes later with a bug sweeper that he had borrowed from the forensic lab. He switched the device on and began swiping it around the office as it crackled and surged with feedback. He waved the device around Chris several times, seemingly unable to believe Chris hadn't bugged himself for the discussion.

"That's not necessary," Chris said.

"Uh-huh."

When Grogan was satisfied the office was clean, he sat in the chair again. "If you want to play this out, just take these accusations to Don Rubinowski and see what happens."

"I intend to do that right after I take them to the police. But I just have one question for you. Why? Why did you do it?"

Grogan stared at him for a long moment that stretched and then stretched some more. He looked over his shoulder to confirm the door to the office was shut. And then he said softly, "You think I didn't know what you were planning? I'm not going to let you walk out of this firm with millions of dollars in billings that belong to me."

"And it was worth so much to you that you'd actually kill for it?"

"I worked hard to get to where I am, and I'm not going to lose it now, not at this point in my career."

This was helpful, but it was not an admission. Chris realized he needed to goad him to go further.

"Did you really think that if I died those clients would stay here? Stay with *you*?"

Grogan's face flushed. "Of course I did. Are you out of your mind?" He rose. "We're done here."

"You're right about one thing," Chris said. "We're definitely done."

Chris swiveled his desk chair around to face his computer, pressed a key, and the monitor filled with faces peering into the office as if through a window.

"Smile for the webcam, Richard. And meet FBI Special Agent Hal Trask and his team."

During the next few seconds, Grogan's face seemed to display a lightning-round version of the seven stages of grief.

"I want to call my attorney," he finally said.

"I'm sure you do," Chris said.

"Will you please step a little closer to the monitor, Mr. Grogan?" It was the voice of Special Agent Trask through the computer's tinny speaker. "I need to read you your Miranda rights, and I want to make sure that you hear every word."

53

The sun was coming up over the Bay Bridge, its light inching across the floor of Chris's apartment. Glad that he'd never bought curtains to cover the upper pane of glass, he watched the sunlight approach, nonchalant as a cat, as he softly played one of Bach's Goldberg Variations on the upright piano in the corner.

Today he'd chosen BWV 988: Variation 4 a 1—one of the simpler, midtempo variations, only a half minute or so long. Chris knew his playing sounded raggedy—his right hand remained much stronger than his left—but as he kept working through the simple variation, he thought he could hear a bit of what the composer had intended, and that was enough.

Like all of Bach's variations, this one was rigorous and mathematical, but if that were all there was to it, then it wouldn't have been worth playing. There was also a kind of contained joy in the piece that was all the more joyous because it didn't proclaim itself. Chris thought it was the sound of rightness in the world.

That sense of rightness was a little harder to come by in the world at large. As with most APT1 hacks, it proved impossible to trace the intellectual property stolen in the Zapper intrusion. Chris and Zoey were ultimately able to track the algorithms to a drop site used by

APT1 hackers, but from there it was anyone's guess. Paul Saperstein was constitutionally paranoid about staying ahead of the tech industry competition, and that paranoia now seemed more justified than ever before.

In the wake of the Chinese intrusion, Zapper continued to be the world's leading search engine, but the theft was likely to bring a challenge to its dominance. Hoodu, China's leading Internet search engine, was poised to enter the US market in six months, and it was probably armed with Zapper's most vital corporate asset—the algorithms. If Hoodu succeeded in capturing a sizable portion of US Internet search traffic, the economic and national security ramifications would be far-reaching. Just as the NSA induced US Internet search engines to cooperate in its surveillance programs, the PLA would almost certainly induce Hoodu to cooperate in its economic espionage efforts. China's plundering of US intellectual property wasn't about to stop anytime soon.

According to press accounts, the president and the State Department were preparing to announce a much tougher stance with Beijing over China's systematic theft of the intellectual property of US corporations. In his announcement, the president would evidently be citing new classified reports directly linking the People's Liberation Army to the APT1 hacks. It had only been a matter of time, Chris knew. If the administration hadn't planned to use the evidence Chris had obtained in Shenzhen, then Paul Saperstein and Zapper would have.

Like Saperstein, Chris and Zoey were living with uncertainty. Although the PLA hadn't actually assigned Red Sun to kill them, there was no guarantee that some form of retribution wasn't on the way. Chris hoped that the coming negotiations between the State Department and Beijing on IP theft would offer some degree of protection for them.

Chris hoped the upcoming talks would accomplish something else as well. Through Saperstein, he had urged the State Department to work for the release of Guiren Song and Quan Shao, the two dissidents who had helped him escape from China. Saperstein had said that the White House had put the issue at the center of the negotiations with China, so there was at least hope the pair might be freed or traded to the US in some sort of exchange of clandestine operatives.

As the FBI assembled the murder-for-hire case against Richard Grogan, it learned that Grogan, while not entirely tech savvy, knew how to acquire criminal resources online. Through Silk Road, Grogan had anonymously contracted with hackers who were able to track the credit card purchases of Chris and Zoey. He had also engaged the services of a Ms. Ah-lam Wan, who had acted as his agent in Chinatown and was likely to be charged as an accomplice. Grogan had led everyone he hired to believe that they were dealing with someone affiliated with the PLA. By spying on Zoey's email communications and other activity on the law firm's system, Grogan learned of Zoey's suspicion that there was a connection between the contract killer Red Sun and the PLA. So when he anonymously hired Red Sun to kill Chris, he knew Zoey would make sure that everyone reached the conclusion that the PLA was behind the hit.

Grogan was also being charged with the murder of the journalist Matt Geist. In the course of spying on Zoey at the firm, Grogan discovered that Zoey had made a copy of the emails from Owyang's laptop. He figured that if Red Sun was really hired by the PLA, then it would want to prevent the public disclosure of the evidence linking it to APT1. Grogan had instructed Red Sun to do what was necessary to retrieve the flash drive and prevent the disclosure, including murder Geist, simply to bolster the credibility of his ruse.

As Chris prepared to play the Bach piece again, from the corner of his eye he caught Zoey tiptoeing down the stairs from the bedroom of the loft in bare feet, underwear, and T-shirt. He smiled and began to play. She didn't say anything, just poured a cup of coffee, curled up on the couch near the piano, and listened.

Finally, Chris stopped, letting his fingers rest on a chord.

"You are getting shockingly good at that," Zoey said.

"It's how I fool people into thinking I can really play. It's only a half minute long, it's not all that hard, and I practice it like crazy."

"Well, trick or not, it's lovely."

Zoey had given up the lease on her apartment on Eleventh Street a week ago and moved in with him. So far, so very good. He knew that things wouldn't always be so effortless, but he already had the sense that even when they weren't, it would probably be worth it.

"You know, I've noticed something about my playing since you moved in."

"Oh? Have I inspired you?"

"I've stopped humming."

"Oh, really. You hum?" She said it as if it hadn't been annoying the hell out of her.

"I think I picked it up from listening to Glenn Gould recordings. Gould hummed while he played. It drove the recording engineers nuts, but he couldn't seem to help it."

"Actually, I did notice it. I wasn't going to say anything."

"It was annoying, wasn't it?"

"Not really. Okay, maybe a little. It just seemed like—you. So why'd you stop?"

"Well, I can see now that it's one of those quirks that you get from living alone too long. I had listened to those recordings so many times, and it was always just me playing to myself and so, why not hum along? But now that there's someone around to listen to it, it just doesn't seem—necessary—anymore."

Zoey pulled a comforter up over her and grinned. "Look at you. You're getting all normal on me, aren't you?"

"I suppose I am."

"Don't worry, you still have a long way to go. And I really don't think you're ever going to get there. At least I hope not."

Chris went to the kitchen and poured another cup of coffee.

"So what are you doing up so early?" Zoey asked from the other room.

"I've been making plans."

"What sort of plans?"

Chris came in and joined her on the couch. "I've decided to leave Reynolds Fincher and start a new law firm." He took a sip and raised his eyebrows. "You in?"

ACKNOWLEDGMENTS

Because this was my first book written to a deadline, there are fewer people to thank than usual. I pretty much had to put my head down and get it done. Nevertheless, the following people all played invaluable roles in making *Intrusion* a better book. I'm lucky to have an editor, Alison Dasho, who knows just about everything there is to know about mysteries, thrillers, and crime fiction, and also happens to be a joy to work with. Thank you to my copyeditor, Marcus Trower; proofreader, Michelle Hope-Anderson; cover designer, Marc Cohen; and the entire team at Thomas & Mercer, including the fabulous Jacque Ben-Zekry, Tiffany Pokorny, and Kjersti Egerdahl. If there's a more efficient, fun, collaborative, authorcentric way to produce a book, then I'm sure the innovators at T&M will be the ones to devise it.

My agent, David Hale Smith, at Inkwell Management, is the best person that a mystery/thriller writer can have in their corner. Ed Stackler has improved each of my books with his head for thriller plotting and the electronic equivalent of a sharp red pencil. Ed played a key role in getting this book into shape. Jay Hershey, my longtime friend and a talented editor, helped point my first draft in the right direction.

Shane McGee, chief privacy officer at Fireye, provided some invaluable from-the-trenches cybersecurity details. On a related note, Shane was formerly general counsel at Mandiant, which was acquired by Fireye. In February 2013 Mandiant published a report linking the APT1 hacking incidents to the People's Liberation Army. The investigation described in Chapter 3 draws liberally from that Mandiant report.

Thanks to the authors who generously took the time to read and blurb *The Adversary*—David Liss, Graham Brown, Rebecca Cantrell, and my fellow T&M author Andrew Peterson.

And as always, thank you to my wife, Kathy, whose infallible BS detector is the true secret weapon in my writing process. Without her patience in allowing me to balance my legal career and my writing, none of my books would have been written.

ABOUT THE AUTHOR

Reece Hirsch is the author of three thrillers that draw upon his background as a privacy and data security attorney. His first book, *The Insider*, was a finalist for the 2011 International Thriller Writers Award for Best First Novel. Hirsch is a partner in the San Francisco office of an international law firm and co-chair of its privacy and cyber-security practice. He is also a member of the board of directors of 826 National (www.826National.org). He lives in the Bay Area with his wife and a small, unruly dog. His website is www.reecehirsch.com.

Made in the USA
Lexington, KY
04 September 2015